The Bird Sisters

**Center Point
Large Print**

**This Large Print Book carries the
Seal of Approval of N.A.V.H.**

the
Bird Sisters

Rebecca Rasmussen

CENTER POINT LARGE PRINT
THORNDIKE, MAINE

This Center Point Large Print edition is
published in the year 2011 by arrangement with
Crown Publishers,
an imprint of The Crown Publishing Group,
a division of Random House, Inc.

The text of this Large Print edition is unabridged.
In other aspects, this book may vary
from the original edition.
Printed in the United States of America.
Set in 16-point Times New Roman type.

ISBN: 978-1-61173-088-3

Library of Congress Cataloging-in-Publication Data

The Bird sisters / Rebecca Rasmussen.
p. cm.
Includes bibliographical references and index.
ISBN 978-1-61173-088-3 (library binding : alk. paper)
1. Sisters—Fiction. 2. Single women—Fiction.
3. Reminiscing in old age—Fiction. 4. Large type books. I. Title.
PS3618.A78B57 2011
813'.6—dc22
2011001917

For Kathryn

These are the days when Birds come back—
A very few—a Bird or two—
To take a backward look.

—EMILY DICKINSON

1

U sed to be when a bird flew into a window, Milly and Twiss got a visit. Milly would put a kettle on and set out whatever culinary adventure she'd gone on that day. For morning arrivals, she offered her famous vanilla drop biscuits and raspberry jam. Twiss would get the medicine bag from the hall closet and sterilize the tools she needed, depending on the seriousness of the injury. A wounded limb was one thing. A wounded crop was another.

People used to come from as far away as Reedsburg and Wilton. Milly would sit with them while Twiss patched up the *poor old robin* or the *sweet little meadowlark*. Over the years, the number of visitors had dwindled. Now that the grocery store sold ready-bake biscuits and jelly in all the colors of the rainbow, people didn't bother as much about birds.

On a particularly low morning, while the two sisters were having tea and going over their chore lists, Milly pulled back the curtains when she heard an engine straining on one of the nearby hillsides. When all she saw was the empty gravel drive, the hawkweed poking up along the edges, she let go of them.

"We should be glad," she said. "Maybe the birds are getting smarter."

Twiss brought the breakfast dishes to the sink. They were down to toast and butter now, sometimes a hard-boiled egg from the night before. "How can you stand to be so positive?"

"We're old," Milly said. "What else can we do?"

But even she missed the sound of strangers in the house, the way the pine floors creaked under new weight. Had it really been a month since a person other than Twiss had spoken to her? Time had a funny way of moving when you didn't want it to and standing still when you did. Milly didn't bother to wind the cuckoo clock above the sink anymore; there was something sadistic about the way it popped out of its miniature door so cheerfully every quarter hour. But the visitors! Though she and Twiss had devoted their lives to saving birds, not wishing for them to be injured, the last few years Milly had perked up whenever a car turned into their driveway instead of continuing up the road. Most of the time, the people would be looking for directions back to town. They'd spread out their laminated touring maps with expressions of shame because "just in case," the words they'd used to justify buying the maps in the first place, meant they were lost, and there were no noble ways to say that. The men would look up at the sky, trying one last time to discern east from west, and the women would look down at the ground because their husbands had failed to understand a simple map. Milly would put the couples at ease by admitting that she missed a turn every once in a while, even though there wasn't one to miss. She'd point to the blank space between the hills and the river.

This is where you are.

When the sound of the engine grew louder, unlike all of the others during the last month, Milly pulled back the curtains again. This time, a green minivan was barreling down the driveway, kicking up dust that did not quickly settle.

"I knew this one was for us," she said.

"Better get ready," Twiss said, leaving her cup of tea and going for the medicine bag in the hall closet. "People who drive minivans usually know where they are."

And the driver of the green minivan did, although the country wasn't where she was supposed to be at eight thirty in the morning. On her way to drop her children off at the elementary school in town, the woman had run over a goldfinch, and her daughter had cried enough to make her do something about it. The minivan's tires, rutted monstrosities that belonged on a tractor, had severed one of the goldfinch's wings and crushed the other one. The goldfinch was also missing his left eye, which the little girl said she'd looked for on the road but couldn't find among the crumble of loose blacktop.

"Poor thing," Twiss said, which meant the goldfinch wouldn't live. Twiss had spent her life saving birds; all she had to do was glance at one to know if it would recover or not. And all Milly had to do was glance at Twiss, who'd never been especially skilled at hiding what she saw.

Twiss kissed the goldfinch's tawny beak.

"Yes, you are a poor thing," Milly said, kissing it too.

Twiss took the goldfinch, the medicine bag, and the little girl to the bathroom off the kitchen. After she laid out her instruments on a towel, Twiss would pick up Dr. Greene's old stethoscope. If she heard even a faint heartbeat, she'd patch up what she could and splint whatever she couldn't with strips of balsa wood from the old model airplane in the attic. She'd offer the goldfinch a teaspoon of millet and peanut butter and hold him up to the window so he could see the sky. Once a bird had lost his ability to fly, not much else could be done in the way of mending him. Losing a wing was a little like losing a leg and the freedom of movement, of spirit, it granted you; most people could live without the former but not the latter.

Milly steered the mother, a woman with the frame of a thin person but the flesh of one who'd had too many children and worries to keep her figure, to the kitchen. Instead of taking the seat

Milly offered her, the mother paced across the linoleum, pausing to examine the surroundings now and then. She paid particular attention to Milly's collection of ceramic salt-and-pepper shakers lined up like avian soldiers, orange beak to orange beak, hummingbirds to owls, on the shelf above the stove, and to the damask wallpaper Milly and Twiss had helped their mother put up when they were girls, which had bubbled at the outset because they'd applied the glue too liberally. Over the years, the wallpaper had peeled back little by little so that now it clung to the wall desperately when it clung at all.

The mother seemed the most interested in the milk-glass lamp in the far corner of the kitchen and the *WC* stenciled in blue paint on the bathroom door. Like many other visitors before her, she seemed surprised to find the house equipped with indoor plumbing and modern electricity. Milly expected the mother to say what everyone from her generation said: *We used to have that exact shade in our kitchen!* What they didn't say but what Milly had gleaned from their collective tone, and the decorating magazines in the general store, was that they'd replaced the opaque milk-glass fixtures with track lighting the moment they could afford it. And the moment they could afford track lighting, they could afford to be sentimental.

Oh? Milly would say, wondering why anyone

would want the equivalent of a runway on his or her ceiling. But the mother didn't say anything about track lighting.

"I kept telling her a bird's nothing to cry about," she said about her daughter. "When you've had your heart broken, you'll run over a person and you won't even notice."

The mother finally took the seat Milly had offered her, which pleased Milly since she was used to people sitting down and telling her things, seeking from her a kind of emotional support only strangers could offer while Twiss patched up the birds in the bathroom; that kind of listening made Milly feel useful when most of the time now she felt useless.

The rest of the woman's children, three gangly boys, were standing on the front porch daring one another to jump off the steps into the mud puddle that had formed beside Milly's freshly watered flower beds.

"Would you like a biscuit and jam?" Milly said, mentally hauling out the mixing bowl and the sack of flour from the pantry. There had to be a jar of jam left in the cellar that mold didn't inhabit. Another stick of butter, too.

"I have to stay away from things I enjoy," the mother said, pulling her T-shirt over the part of her stomach that had become exposed in the process of sitting down. "This book I'm reading says if you want to be as thin as a stalk of celery, then that's what you should be eating. I'm not sure I want to look like celery, but I know I don't want to look like a biscuit."

Her wristwatch began to beep, softly at first, then louder and louder. She smacked it against her leg, which changed the cadence of the beeping but didn't stop it. Before she could turn it off, her middle boy came in and took a yellow pill out of her purse.

"Seizures," the mother said, after he swallowed the pill and went back to the porch. "He's had them since he was a baby. The other ones have food allergies. I can't make anything without one of them puffing up. *Rice puffs* make them puff up."

"That must be difficult," Milly said.

"It is when you have a husband like mine."

When Milly didn't say anything, the mother added, "He sells carpeting. The kind that's been doused with toxic chemicals."

Milly glanced at the green linoleum, the slick of wax beneath the table.

"Depending on what part of the country he's in, I wish for a disaster that corresponds to that region. If he's in California, I think about earthquakes. In Florida, it's hurricanes. In Colorado, it's avalanches. Great cascading, obliterating avalanches."

The mother put her hand on her hip. "You wouldn't know it to look at me, but I used to be a runner. I set a national record once."

"You don't run anymore?" Milly said.

"I don't do a lot of things anymore," the mother said.

Usually, visitors would eat a biscuit and talk about the price of gasoline or the corn coming up in the fields along the river. *It isn't as sweet as it used to be,* they'd say, when what they meant was *I'm almost used to being unhappy.*

"I know exactly what you mean," Milly said, looking out the window at the patch of earth where the garden used to be. "I used to grow everything—tomatoes, squash, zucchini, peppers, lovely little potatoes. Fingerlings, I think they were called."

Before the mother had a chance to say anything, the little girl ran into the room.

"WetriedtosavethebirdieMama!"

"Slow down," the mother said. "I can't understand you."

"We tried to save the birdie, Mama, but it died."

The mother sighed deeply, as if she'd expected this outcome from the very beginning. Rather than causing her sadness, the events of the morning seemed merely to have exhausted her. "Remember what I said about heaven, Molly?"

"But it can't fly," the girl said.

Milly placed her hand on the girl's curls. Their softness and the scattering of freckles at the girl's neckline, the sudden camaraderie she felt with the mother, opened up something inside her that hadn't been opened in a long time. She was lured to the feeling the way other people were lured to trespass on property that was not their own.

"I'm not sure about heaven," Milly said to the mother while she stroked the girl's hair. "I used to believe heaven was a place in the clouds and God was a nice old man who sat on top of the highest, fluffiest one. Then one day our priest, Father Rice, announced that God either didn't exist or He didn't care. It wasn't what he said— that was the same as learning Santa Claus wasn't real. It's what happened after that made me believe he may have been right."

The little girl's mouth dropped open, and a high-pitched mewling, not altogether different from the sound calves made when they were separated from their mothers, came streaming across her lips. Then came the glassy eyes and the sniffling.

"Santa died too?" she said.

The mother lifted the girl onto her hip as if Milly had become dangerous.

After that, everything happened so quickly that an apology, let alone a gesture of apology, was impossible for Milly to achieve.

The mother called to her other children to stop jumping and get into the car. Before she buckled the four of them in and drove off, she looked at Milly with an equal mix of fierceness and pity. "You just made my day ten times harder," she said.

And then, "Only a person without children would say something like that."

Twiss came into the kitchen a few minutes later carrying the goldfinch, which she'd wrapped in one of their mother's embroidered handkerchiefs. Whenever birds died in their care, they buried them in the gladiola bed out back.

"Where did everyone go?" Twiss said.

"The children were late for school," Milly said, picking up her tea and then setting it down again on the kitchen table.

She was still trying to understand what had happened. It must have been all that talk about natural disasters, a disastrous marriage. In reaction to the woman, and the toxic fumes she imagined rising from the floors in the woman's house, the pessimist had broken out of its shackles. Heaven? The topic was too tempting.

What she couldn't stop thinking about was the way the mother had looked at her and how that look, more than her words, had exposed the fact that Milly had never had children, a fact that usually didn't bother her, because she had the birds to fall back on when she invited people into their home. Most visitors were too busy worrying about karmic retributions (were there any?) for running over a bird on their way to work to notice that she'd never experienced the pain of childbirth, the pleasure of loving someone more than she loved herself.

The luxury, Milly thought when Twiss set the goldfinch on the table. She stroked his neck the same way she'd stroked the girl's, although instead of curls, she felt broken bones. "That woman didn't think a goldfinch merited a kink in her schedule," she said to Twiss.

"Then we can only hope someone runs over her one day," Twiss said.

"Is death always your solution?"

"At least my dead people go to heaven," Twiss said.

Milly sat down at the table with the empty teacups, the napkins she'd folded the moment she saw the car coming up the driveway. "I don't know what got into me."

"Three-quarters of a century's a long time to live like a saint."

"I'm not a saint," Milly said.

Twiss patted her shoulder. "Not anymore."

While the two sisters finished their pieces of toast, the goldfinch sat on the table between them, shrouded in the last of their mother's handkerchiefs. The bottom dresser drawer in her bedroom was now officially empty, and neither sister knew whether to be happy or unhappy about it, although each had known for some time that their bird-saving days were coming to a close. They hadn't been able to save the last four birds brought to them—a wren, a bluebird, a cardinal, and a lovely little mourning dove they'd both adored.

"Do you want to do it, or do you want me to this time?" Milly said, wondering if she had the energy or the strength of heart to dig another hole. She used to perform elaborate ceremonies for the fallen birds—she'd say prayers, sing songs, and recite poems about avian cousins that had not yet fallen, although the cruelty of the latter homage had recently occurred to her and the poetry had stopped.

"I'll do it," Twiss said. "Do you want me to dig a hole for you, too?"

"We're too old for that to be funny," Milly said.

"Are we?" Twiss said, rolling up the sleeves of her beige coveralls.

She'd gotten up from the table and was leaning against the door that led to the dining room. When they were girls, the two would stand against the molding to record their heights. The pencil marks began when Milly was six and Twiss was four, etching their way upward like rungs of a ladder. Halfway up the molding, Twiss had figured out how to make herself taller than Milly. She'd put coasters in the heels of her shoes.

"Look at that!" she'd crow. "I grew two whole inches overnight!"

The marks stopped at sixteen and fourteen, even though Milly and Twiss had continued to grow, sometimes legitimately, sometimes not.

"Look how tall I used to be," Twiss said.

"You were never that tall," Milly said, standing up to emphasize her point. She smoothed the front of her green housedress. After all these years, and the coming and going of the women's liberation movement, she still wouldn't wear slacks.

Twiss stood on her tiptoes. "I might have been."

Milly washed the breakfast dishes and Twiss dried them. Together, as they did when they were girls, they carried their mother's bridal tea set to the sideboard in the dining room. The poor light made the embossed finials look less regal than they did in the kitchen.

Twiss traced the rim of a teacup. "Remember what she used to say?"

Milly thought of the old lilac bush beside the barn, the little square window sealed shut behind it. "I remember."

The two sisters lingered in front of the sideboard, as if waiting for their mother to appear and caution them, before they took up their lists and went about their chores.

Bone china is like your heart. If it breaks, it can't be fixed.

• • •

Since her hip replacement Milly kept mostly to the house. Whenever she sensed Twiss watching her—especially on the days she used a stepladder to dust the top of the bookshelves and the hutch —she'd make a joke to ease her sister's concern.

"I'll be fine," she'd say, knocking on her hip. "I've got more titanium than a rocket."

"But you don't have a launcher."

"Who says?"

"Gravity."

Twiss liked to have the last word and, because this seemed a small concession, Milly allowed her to. She'd direct her attention to an empty corner of the room, as though she needed privacy to consider her sister's remarks, when really she'd be thinking about the feel of the duster in her hand, the snow-white feathers.

"I'll be in the barn then," Twiss would say, and leave her to her thoughts.

This morning, as she dusted the bookshelves, the rows that mingled culinary delights with field identification and bird anatomy, Milly stopped when she came to *The Curious Book of Birds*. Out of instinct or perhaps habit (Milly knew the words by heart), she took the book off the shelf to read the inscription on the worn title page:

For Milly,
Because.

"Horseshit!" Twiss had called the book after she'd fished it out of the mailbox years ago, but Milly had been inclined to keep it.

"For the illustrations," she'd said. "Not for the history."

But history was exactly what Milly was interested in this morning: the time before she loved birds, when the wing beat of a humming-bird seemed as ordinary as the rustle of leaves, the sound of rain falling on a gravel road. Before Cousin Bettie came to visit for the summer, when Milly was sixteen and Twiss was fourteen, birds were background noise: something you heard but didn't listen to. By the next summer, Milly could tell you which bird the *pip-pip-pip* and the *pup-up-up* belonged to, and she could tell you why.

When Milly opened the bird book, its spine cracked the way hers did when she bent over too quickly. Like her face, the pages had yellowed around the edges. They smelled sweet and sour and tingled the tips of her fingers when she touched them. The cover had buckled outward over the summers and inward over the winters, which had made peaks and valleys out of it, difficult topography. Milly turned to chapter one: a story about a woodpecker doomed by her disobedience never to quench her thirst in lakes or rivers, brooks or fountains. As punishment for her refusal to help build the water basins of

23

the world, the Lord decided the woodpecker would spend her days pecking at dusty wood. Her voice would be heard only when a storm was approaching and her thirst would be quenched only when it arrived, and so the woodpecker spent her life forever looking at the sky, waiting for the first drops to fall.

Milly looked out the window at the blue above and Twiss below; she was sitting on the porch pulling on the same muck boots she used to pull on when she was a girl and the fields were wet, though today the fields were dry. All summer they'd waited for rain and all summer it hadn't come. For months the fans had been stirring up dust, which clung to tabletops and lamp shades and made the house feel weighty even though the specks were weightless. Milly thought about what the house used to look like (strikingly similar to its current state), then she thought about what it could have looked like if their lives had gone one way instead of the other. The book, which had arrived more than half a century ago wrapped in blue paper, was a gift, though on a day like today it was difficult to see it that way.

When Milly heard the chime of church bells, she looked down at the book curiously, as if the sound had come from it instead of from the country chapel up on Lilly Road. The chapel had been closed after a tornado tore off the roof and dropped it back down into the river, but it was still used for weddings occasionally—mostly couples from Minneapolis or Chicago who were charmed by the overgrowth of honeysuckle and romanced by ruins. No one from Spring Green had been married there since she was a girl. A young woman. Young.

When the sound of the bells faded and then disappeared altogether, Milly was left with the image of her childhood love climbing onto the John Deere, blades of freshly cut grass stuck to the back of his neck, lines of sweat streaking his work shirt like rain.

"Asa," she said, willing him to spring forth from the pages.

Her will was met with the facts of history, which she blamed the mother for dredging up this morning. *Only a person without children. A person without children . . .*

The truth was that the past and the present, hope and actuality, had been rubbing up against each other, and against Milly, before the arrival of the minivan. Instead of time continuing forward as it typically did, lately time had begun leaping about as it pleased, unsettling all that had been settled years ago. When Milly stood in the backyard, for instance, some days she saw a stump where the oak tree used to be. Other days she saw the oak tree itself, even though they'd paid a man from Wilton to cut it down twenty years ago now.

This morning, Milly watched gold light work its way across the parlor floor and was transported to the last pew of the Lilly chapel, where dust motes swirled in the air and the air smelled of incense and damp feet. *Death,* she thought, even though she felt all right.

On one side of her was Twiss, on the other her mother.

Milly closed her eyes, hoping that when she opened them she'd be back in the living room again with the more singular smell of age, which she shared with the books and the upholstery, to affront her senses. She didn't know if she could bear to see herself young again. Full of possibilities. Happy as the corn was sweet.

Despite her hoping (or to spite it?), when Milly opened her eyes, she found that she was still sitting between Twiss and her mother in Lilly chapel, which she used to do every Sunday until she was sixteen—that is, until Cousin Bettie came to visit for the summer and took her place in the pew. When Milly looked at her legs, she saw patches of silky hair where waves of loose skin used to be. Peeking out from the patches was the old kidney bean scar on her left knee, except that it wasn't faded anymore; instead of white, the scar was red.

2

"How would you like to be stuck with some-one like Adam?" Twiss said to her, frowning at the depiction of the Garden of Eden in the stained-glass window above their pew. "I'd have eaten that apple too. Just to get away from him."

Father Rice was standing behind the pulpit, staring at Jesus's right arm, which he claimed had come unhinged from the cross the same way President Truman had from the heart of the country. It was a warm spring morning in early May, the kind that led to afternoon picnics, plates of baked chicken and wax beans. The crocuses had given way to the tulips, which surrounded the chapel like a yellow collar. The Sewing Society had donated the bulbs even though all of the members (except Milly's mother) went to the church in town, where silver dollars came out of people's pockets instead of lint.

"Why do you think they're all yellow?" her mother said about the tulips. "It's no coincidence scientists just discovered the color puts people in a state."

Even though her mother disliked the other members of the Sewing Society, she insisted on going to all their functions. When Milly asked her why, her mother said, "I can't have them thinking they're better than me. I'm the one who's been to Europe!"

"I thought you went to France," Twiss said.

"That's part of Europe," Milly said.

"Why is it called the Sewing Society if you never sew?" Twiss said.

"Shhh," their mother said.

On this particular spring morning, just as he did every Sunday after the Apostles' Creed and before the Sanctus, Father Rice walked up and down the row of pews accepting contributions: a box of medicinal soap flakes, a jar of preserves that had sat too long in someone's cellar, an egg from a nearby coop. By the time he got to the last pew, the basket brimmed with tarnished silverware, stained tablecloths, and secondhand clothing that had turned into third- and fourth-hand rags. Father Rice always gave thanks, but he gave special thanks when people donated something useful. That's why, when their own father had spent the last of the week's money again, and all that sat in the pantry was a lonely tin of molasses, Milly and Twiss decided to fish for their donation. Despite the shame it caused their mother, when it was their turn, Twiss placed a string of smallmouth bass into the basket.

"I prayed for their souls," Milly said.

"Fish don't have souls," Twiss said.

"Sure they do," Father Rice said, licking his lips. "When you cook them with cornstarch, they melt in your mouth."

Their mother wagged her index finger at Twiss. She stared at her the way she stared at their front door whenever they came home. Though she'd had fourteen years to become accustomed to Twiss's wide brown eyes and cropped black hair, the line of freckles that fanned out across her nose, she always seemed slightly surprised by Twiss, like she didn't believe Twiss truly belonged to her, or should.

Twiss tugged at the hem of her dress. "Why can't I be playing golf?"

"Because this family can only afford one person who doesn't care about his soul," their mother said.

"He prays for holes in one," Twiss said.

"That's the only thing your father prays for."

If in marriages disagreements were like roots, their mother and father's were like the roots of the oak tree in the backyard that had grown into the house instead of away from it, cracking the foundation and setting the floors aslant. When Milly and Twiss placed a marble on one side of the front parlor, it would roll to the other.

"Maybe he's buying you a birthday present right now," Milly said.

"I refuse to have another birthday," their mother said.

"Because you're old?" Twiss said.

"Because I'm tired," their mother said.

Father Rice set the collection basket next to the pulpit and signaled Mrs. Bettle, who wasn't technically a Mrs. since she lived with a parrot instead of a man, to play the organ. *Bang* went her fingers on the keys. *Thunk* went her feet on the pedals. Then came the singing, which was even less lovely than her playing.

Holy, holy, holy Lord
God of power and might
Heaven and earth are full of your glory
Hosanna in the highest.
Hosanna in the highest.

"You can be sure the Society's still congratulating themselves about getting rid of the Beetle," their mother said, adjusting her hat so it sat on the side of her head. She tried her very best to be fashionable. In the general store, she'd study the ladies' magazines to see what the latest styles were. Always, she lacked the proper materials to achieve accomplished mimicry; she'd have to make a dress out of cotton when the pattern called for silk. Gray thread when it called for red. But however patched together she looked, their mother possessed a certain kind of power, a way of posturing that didn't allow people to feel sorry for her.

30

"Who donates a person?" she said. "Now they've got a music student from the divinity school up in Wausau. They say the boy sings like an angel."

When the Sanctus was over, Father Rice raised his hand to quiet everyone. This was the part of mass where he usually asked everyone to bow their heads and kneel, but today he asked everyone to keep their heads level and stay in their seats.

"Wood rails aren't very gracious hosts," he said. "I don't know why I didn't think about that before. So many of you have arthritis. Rheumatism."

"Won't the Lord mind?" someone said.

"What kind of Lord would He be if He did?" Father Rice said.

"The Lord."

Father Rice unzipped his black robe, revealing a blazer and pants the color of cream instead of his usual red union suit. He discarded his slippers for a pair of shiny penny loafers, with even shinier pennies placed at the toes. All the years he'd been a priest, Father Rice had delivered mass in those dingy slippers, which everyone could smell despite the incense burning.

"How many years have we waited for a new steeple?" Father Rice said. He stepped out from behind the pulpit with a suitcase in one hand and a straw hat in the other. "How many years have we waited for the Lord to repair what He destroyed with lightning?"

"Twenty years?" someone called out.

"Forty-five years!" Father Rice said. He picked up his suitcase and walked down the center aisle to the holy-water font, where he set his Bible and watched it sink to the bottom.

"I think it's safe to say He's not coming."

"What are we supposed to do?" someone called.

"Take what's owed to you," Father Rice said. "I, for one, have always wanted to drink a margarita and sleep with a Mexican woman."

A *thunk* from Mrs. Bettle. A wail from the organ.

Twiss leaned forward. Milly leaned back.

"Cover your ears, girls," their mother said.

An old country woman in an even older country dress pushed her way past the people in her pew to the center aisle. "What if I refuse to live in a godless world?"

"Then I'm afraid you'll have to shoot yourself, my dear," Father Rice said in the kindest possible voice. "Either God doesn't exist or He's too busy to do it Himself."

The woman fainted, and all of the parishioners began to scramble around her, except Milly and Twiss, who minded their mother and stayed put in the last pew while she went forth to offer the woman a piece of chocolate because she believed it could cure any ailment.

At the door, Father Rice looked back at the people whose morality he'd instructed for most of his life and theirs. He put the straw hat on, which he tipped in Milly and Twiss's direction. "Thanks for the fish," he said and stepped out into the sunlight.

"I'd sell my soul to the devil," Twiss said to Milly on the walk home from church. "Just to see the look on that woman's face again."

"You already sold it for a licorice rope," Milly said.

"Oh yeah," Twiss said.

Their mother had gone on to the Sewing Society's annual luncheon to explain that not only had Father Rice abandoned them for Mexico, he'd also taken the Society's donation —money to build a Sunday school classroom— with him to the tropics.

Twiss had picked a tulip and was plucking the petals off one by one. *There is a God. There isn't a God. There is a God.* They were halfway down the country road, alone except for the hum of crickets and the croak of a lone tree frog. According to the petals, there wasn't a God.

The two veered off Lilly Road into the wheat fields. Though no clouds were overhead, the air smelled of rain, earth. When they reached Mill Creek, they waded through it since the soles of their shoes were muddy and the water wasn't.

By the middle of the summer, the water would turn deep brown and become home to snakes and leeches, squiggly blue worms that would make Milly think of the map of the Amazon in the atlas. For now, though, the water was clear and swift moving. The gray stones at the bottom weren't even covered with algae yet.

"Margaritas must cost a lot of money," Twiss said, letting the hem of her dress get wet. "Do you think he's really going to Mexico?"

"There's only one place he can go," Milly said, holding hers up.

"You mean hell?" Twiss took off one of her shoes and sent it floating down the creek. "I think about saying stuff like that all the time. I bet you do too."

"I bet you get the belt if you lose that shoe."

"*He* wouldn't belt me," Twiss said.

"But *she* would."

A moment later Twiss was standing on the bank of the creek with her shoes neatly placed on her feet. Water dripped from her dress onto the ground.

"I never saw her give you the belt."

"That's because I've never given her a reason," Milly said.

The two of them lingered on the bank of the creek, watching the water bugs balance on the surface and the first of the season's dragonflies hover over it, before they walked the rest of the way home to prepare for their mother's birthday. She'd asked them to treat the day like any other, but they knew she'd be disappointed if she came home from the luncheon and didn't find a card on the kitchen table and a freshly iced cake on the counter.

"Your mother's people put gold in their soup," their father would say to explain the difference between what she said she wanted and what she expected.

"At least we don't water ours down like your people," their mother would say back. She and her sister, who lived in Minnesota, had given up their inheritances and married for love. "And look where that got us," she'd say. "On either side of the Mississippi without so much as a paddle!"

"There should be another word for love," Twiss said to Milly while Milly measured out flour at the counter. Twiss had already changed out of her dress and back into her coveralls.

"Like what?" Milly said.

"For him it should be 'golf.' What's the opposite of golf?"

"I don't think it has an opposite," Milly said.

"Anything French, I guess," Twiss said.

Since they were little their mother had taught them French alongside their English lessons. When Twiss thought their mother wasn't listening, she'd put a clothespin on her nose.

"Merde, merde, merde!" she'd say. "I'm *Frauwnch as Frauwnch* can be!"

Their mother, who was always listening, would pour a handful of soap flakes into Twiss's mouth and make her say *je suis désolée* until the flakes dissolved.

"What would your word be?" Twiss said.

Something to do with baking. Whenever Milly could scrape together enough flour, sugar, and butter, she'd bake a dessert. Often, her parents would stop what they were doing and wander into the kitchen, where Twiss would already be sitting with a napkin tucked into the collar of her shirt. Something about sugar made their family sweeter.

" 'Sugar,' " Milly said to Twiss, measuring out two cups' worth.

She mixed the batter and poured it into a cake pan. After she put the pan in the oven, she gave Twiss the bowl to lick and took the spoon for herself. While the cake cooked they sat on the porch steps. Twiss stuck her whole head in the bowl and was attracting everything from brown-bellied beetles to cicadas. Even the grasshoppers lunged at her.

" 'Wisconsin,' " Twiss said. "That's my word."

"The word or the state?" Milly said.

"Both," Twiss said.

Twiss knew every dip and rise on their land, every anthill and every snake hole. She knew what kind of grass grew where. You could blindfold her and she'd be able to tell you what kind of bark belonged to what kind of tree. Pines were her favorite; she liked how they looked so different from the other trees in the woods, yet relied on the same underground springs to stay alive. Instead of a cotton-filled pillow like the rest of the family slept on, Twiss slept on a pillow stuffed with pine needles. She envied the birds that lived in the actual trees.

Twiss mashed her toes into the flower bed beside the porch. When her feet turned black, she stuck one of them in Milly's face. "Look, I have river fungus!"

"The river doesn't have fungus," Milly said.

"Why do you think the water's brown?"

"Sediment," Milly said.

Twiss stopped mashing her toes in the earth when Rollie, the groundskeeper of the golf course, started up the driveway on the red Farmall, the tractor he used to mow the course.

"Father!" Rollie yelled, when he got close enough for them to hear. "Accident!"

Bad news provoked responses in Twiss more quickly than in Milly, who stayed on the porch, knowing she should run after Twiss but standing still instead, the way she did when storm clouds gathered on the horizon. The thing about clouds was that you never knew what would come out of them. You could end up in the cellar for rain or in the house for a tornado.

"Run!" Twiss said, and Milly let herself go.

But not entirely. Before she followed Twiss to the tractor, she took the cake out of the oven and turned the oven off. As she ran out of the house, across the porch, and down the driveway, her white apron flapped like a flag in the wind.

After Rollie explained their father was in the hospital, but was going to be all right, Milly and Twiss slumped onto the wells of the front wheels while Rollie drove the Farmall down Lilly Road, up County C, and around Back Bend, a stretch of land beside the river where families poorer than them lived in shacks made out of cardboard. People said Back Benders ate worms the way regular people ate spaghetti.

A little girl with long black hair and pretty white skin waved to Milly, and Milly waved back. Without thinking, she unclasped the oval locket she was wearing and tossed it in the girl's direction. The girl ran after the flash of silver and caught the locket before it fell to the ground. The girl made it all the way to her front door before Milly realized that food would have been the more useful thing to have thrown.

Milly also realized she'd given away something that could be replaced and something that couldn't. The locket contained a photograph of Milly's mother and father before they were married, a week after they'd been introduced on the golf course in Butterfield, the town where both of them had grown up. The day they met, Milly's father carried her mother's golf clubs the length of the course before he had the courage to ask her out. He carried them the length of it back before her mother had the courage to say yes.

Her mother had just turned sixteen, her father seventeen.

In the photograph, they were on their first date: a Friday night at the county fair. Midway through the evening, an old man convinced them to stop and have their photograph taken. "What's a nickel in the face of love?" he said.

The old man positioned them in front of a paper moon, a sky filled with cardboard stars. He didn't tell them to smile because it wasn't the style at the time; hard-faced expressions were. Milly's mother and father had just eaten watermelon slices at the stand across the way, and one of the seeds was stuck to her father's collar. Her mother leaned forward to pluck it off. Either because he was quite skilled or quite unskilled, the old man snapped the photograph after her mother had retrieved it, when they were looking at each other, laughing as if a watermelon seed were the funniest thing in the world.

Milly wondered what her story would be.

There was a boy at school named Asa, whom she'd brushed shoulders with in the hallway between math and art before the quarter ended and summer recess began. Instead of embarrassment, Milly had felt a surge of inexplicable panic when, at first, he'd continued along without noticing. Plenty of boys had written notes to her or stuck their gum to her locker or pretended to drop pencils in an attempt to look up the skirts of her dresses, but Asa was different from all of them. He was quiet and shy, like her. Tall. Thin. He knew how to rope a calf and he also knew the square root of four hundred eighty-four.

"I bumped you," Milly said, and Asa turned.

"I don't mind," he said, smiling crookedly for the briefest moment before his cheeks grew pink and his wheat-colored bangs fell across his eyes and he looked down at the floor.

"I don't mind either," Milly said, smiling and looking down too.

She didn't know what their encounter meant, if anything, but the feeling of it—like swinging higher and higher, up, up, and up—stayed with her that day, the next, and the next, which was how Milly's mother had described meeting Milly's father.

Rollie drove the tractor over the river and the County C bridge. He drove past the ice-cream stand and the underground house with grass for a roof, the Clydesdale farm, cornfields, and the petting zoo. When they arrived at the hospital, Twiss uprooted everyone in her path until she found their father. The nurses chased after her with bottles of peroxide and rolls of gauze. They thought the dirt on her feet was dried blood, but they couldn't make sense of the cake batter plastered to her face and hair. "Vomit?" they called after her as if that was her name.

Milly found her mother in the waiting room and the two followed the trail of footprints until they found Twiss curled up next to their father in a windowless room. He was stroking her sticky hair, telling her the story of how he came to reside in a hospital bed.

"I'd just helped Alyce Sweeney shave off two strokes on the moguls between the seventeenth and eighteenth," he said to Twiss with the kind of wide smile you wouldn't expect from someone who'd gone off a bridge. "Just so you have a sense of the mood I was in."

"I thought she was away at that fancy women's college," their mother said.

"Bryn Mawr," their father said. "She's just gotten back from a semester in France. When her ball landed in the woods and we had to go searching for it, she said, '*C'est la vie.*'"

"Oh," their mother said, a little sadly.

"You never give lessons on Sundays," Milly said.

"After Alyce and I finished playing, I was on my way home," their father said.

He said he was so pleased with his teaching

41

that when he saw the ice-cream stand he decided to stop off for sundaes. He picked butterscotch for their mother, strawberry for Milly and Twiss, and chocolate for himself. He never got the flavors right. Milly and Twiss liked butterscotch and their mother liked chocolate. Their father didn't even like ice cream.

"What happened next?" Twiss said.

Their father said he was halfway across the County C bridge when he couldn't help but look at the sundaes on the passenger seat, at the whipped cream and chopped nuts, the gleaming maraschino cherries. Before he realized what was happening, the car went plunging off the bridge and into the river. The last thing he saw before he hit the water and everything went black was the sundaes flying in formation out the window.

All he knew was that the current carried him a mile down the river, past the new docks and the old boat launch, all the way to the bait shop, before a fisherman pulled him out of the water. He bruised his hip and his shoulder, and sprained the pinky finger on his right hand, but was otherwise unharmed, or so all of them thought at the time.

"They would have melted before you got home," their mother said.

"We could have drunk them like frappés," Twiss said.

"When have you had a frappé?" their mother asked.

Twiss moved closer to their father. "At the course restaurant."

Milly stood an equal distance from each parent. "They're French, aren't they?"

"Since when are you a diplomat?" their mother said to Milly.

"Diplomats do quite well, Margaret," their father said. "If Milly keeps this up, you'll have all the china in China."

"And you'll have all the debts in Wisconsin," their mother said.

She opened her purse to look for loose change. She hadn't eaten since breakfast, when she'd spooned up the last few bites of Twiss's oatmeal before church. She'd refused the ham sandwiches offered at the Sewing Society luncheon because she didn't want to give the other members the satisfaction of watching her eat something she couldn't afford.

"You must be starving," she said to Milly.

When she emptied the contents of her purse onto the foot of the hospital bed, a comb, a case of powder, and a pincushion shaped like an apple came tumbling out. She picked up the pincushion by its green felt stem and turned it in her hands as if she were examining it for edibility. "You wouldn't happen to have any money left over from those sundaes?" she said to their father, who held his hands up to show they were empty.

"It's at the bottom of the river, Maisie."

The result was never positive when their father addressed their mother by her nickname. Something old was buried beneath the familiarity that ended up making both of them sad. Their mother put her purse back together. She looked at their father the way she looked at the pantry when there was nothing in it.

"Of course it is, Joe."

Even though they didn't have money to buy anything, Milly walked down to the cafeteria with her mother. The kitchen had been closed an hour; the buffet was empty and the lights had been dimmed. In the far corner, a janitor was mopping the floor with a bucket of astringent, which smelled like the formaldehyde Mr. Stewart used to preserve sheep's brains in the laboratory at school. Milly had earned an F on dissection day because she wouldn't slice into the folds of gray matter with a scalpel. Mr. Stewart wrote in a letter to her parents to explain the poor mark on her report card:

Your elder daughter believes she can save what's already dead. I admire her as much as I pity her; not so long ago, I felt precisely the same way.

Milly's mother sat at one of the long wooden tables. She put her head down, even though the surface of the table was wet. Her hair had come out of the neatly pinned bun she usually kept it in, and the backside of her best dress, the light green one she'd picked out of the charity bin at the Catholic church two towns over to show the Sewing Society ladies she wasn't a charity case, was stained with her monthly blood.

"I'll never make it to France again, will I?" she said.

Milly thought about the partially baked cake sitting on the counter, the construction paper card she and Twiss had started but never finished:

Happy . . .

Milly untied her apron and wrapped it around her mother's waist to cover the stain. She tucked a loose strand of hair back into her mother's bun and secured it with one of the bobby pins from her own, letting her hand linger longer than was necessary.

"One day," she told her mother, "you'll sip Château Margaux on the Seine."

3

Before Twiss took the goldfinch up to the barn, she put on her muck boots and walked the perimeter of their property: a half-mile loop that had seemed large when she was young and large again now that she was old. She followed the tractor ruts, weaving around anthills and snake holes, breathing the first real air of the day. Twiss had never been able to stand being in the house longer than eating or sleeping required. When the end came, she hoped she'd be struck by lightning or whirled up into a tornado. Dying inside was to her a misery that couldn't be borne; she'd made Milly agree to wheel her onto the porch if she couldn't manage it herself.

A windstorm had passed through the night before, breaking off oak branches and leaving impressions of the debris in the sandy soil. Still, no rain. Not a drop had fallen all summer, a cyclical happening according to the 2006 *Farmers' Almanac*, a fact that eased everyone but the land, which had begun to bristle under the stress. The air contained all of the water the land needed to flourish, but wouldn't let go of its claim either to the sky or earth; it hung between the two like a curtain. Twiss cupped at the air, half expecting to feel something solid in her hand. Though it was early, she could feel the heat coming. The *Gazette* had predicted temperatures in the triple digits—LOCAL WARMING! the front page said.

"Promise me you won't play today," Milly had said before the mother arrived with the goldfinch, which now sat in Twiss's front pocket, yellow as a tape measure.

Although the goldfinch had done nothing but linger in the middle of the road for too long, and she knew he deserved a resting place as fine as that of any other bird they'd been unable to save, Twiss didn't go after the trowel just yet. She'd heard what the mother had said to Milly —*Only a person without children would say something like that*—as if she'd known exactly how to sting Milly in a way that wouldn't allow Milly to sting back. If it had been Twiss and having children had been important to her, she'd have slapped the woman's face.

Shame on you, the outline of her hand would have said.

"Play what?" Twiss had said to Milly.

"You know what," Milly had said.

Twiss walked around the pond, pretending to look for golf balls in the reeds when she was really looking for Snapper, a forty-year-old turtle that lived in the pond. When she found him, she tapped on his shell with a willow stick. The last time, he almost lopped off her toes just like his mother had almost lopped them off when Twiss was a girl.

In his effort to attack her, Snapper tipped over and couldn't right himself. Even with this disability, he snapped at her in a wild, entitled way. Though Twiss had the opportunity to win their ongoing war, she used the stick to hoist him back onto his limbs.

"You owe me a bucket of Dunlops," she said to Snapper, whom she was certain could understand her but chose to ignore her. Twiss had always been jealous of the snapping turtles that lived in the pond. When their plans were thwarted, they made new ones. When the new ones were thwarted, they swallowed a few golf balls and went about the rest of their day as if nothing out of the ordinary had occurred. "Stop eating up my game," she said.

The game, which Twiss played on most days, took place in the barn and consisted of a bucket of balls and Persy, her father's old No. 1 driver. She'd line up the balls at the threshold and aim for the pasture. Most of the time, she'd hit the roof of the henhouse or, worse, one of the windows. Twiss had always lacked the concentration—the stillness—to launch a ball with any real accuracy. She'd square her shoulders and position her feet, but the moment she went to swing the club, a gnat would land on her neck or a bee would buzz in her ear, and then the ball would lurch off in whatever direction it wasn't supposed to go. Of the two of them, Milly was the better golfer, though neither of them took after their father, who'd held a club as though it were an extension of himself. Twiss often wondered what would have happened if he'd lived his life as gracefully as he'd played golf.

She walked the length of the pond, up to the woodlot and shed, and back down through the meadow, which was crowded with prairie onions and bluestems that rose to the tops of her muck boots. Every day of her life Twiss had walked through the meadow, and still the beauty of it caused her to linger longer than she intended.

This morning, she broke off the stem of a prairie onion and chewed on it like the cowboys chewed on stalks of straw in her childhood adventure books. She loved the taste of onions; the bitter and the sweet on her tongue always brought her back to a vision of her father before the Accident, sitting at the kitchen table on Sunday mornings, sketching out strategies to shorten his game. In front of him would be a stack of scoring cards, which he used the way Milly and Twiss used flash cards in school. But instead of memorizing the multiplication tables or the meaning of the word "onomatopoeia," he memorized the steps to achieve a perfect hole in one. Most people believed holes in one were perfect by their very nature.

Their father believed differently.

On the days he wasn't giving lessons to the wealthy members of the golf course, members who came from Chicago and Minneapolis, who'd done well in the stock market or the steel industry and needed to learn how to play golf to make their money seem older than it was, Twiss's father would bring her along while he played the back nine. Though she wasn't strong enough to be his official caddy, he'd let her carry his old putter and whack at whatever mushrooms had popped up on the green. Rollie, the grounds-keeper, would give her a nickel for slowing their proliferation (except for the morels, which Twiss was supposed to save for Rollie's wife so she could make soup out of them). After she and her father had finished playing the course, Twiss would use the nickel to buy a cream soda from the clubhouse.

Milly would stay at home because someone had to stay with their mother, who didn't like to hear about golf, think about it, or dream about it. She said golf gave her heartburn.

While Twiss and her father drove to the course on Sunday afternoons her mother would listen to *A Day in the Life of . . .* , a radio program that was supposed to illuminate what it would be like to drive a train across Colorado or to sing on Broadway in New York City. She'd sit down at the kitchen table a whole hour before the program started. Every fifteen minutes, when the wooden bird sprang forth from the cuckoo clock, she'd jump a little.

"How would you like to climb Kilimanjaro?" she might say to Milly, if Milly happened to pass through the kitchen while the program was on. "I don't think I'd like to wade through all that snow, but it might be worth it to see the view from the top."

"I'd rather look up than down," Milly might say back, which would commit her to listening to the rest of the program.

Milly never said whether she liked *A Day in the Life of* . . . , but the way Twiss figured, she still had to sit down and not play golf for an entire hour, an eternal afternoon.

Countless ticks. Endless tocks.

Twiss didn't remember most of those Sundays with any real individual clarity, but she remembered one of them—when she was nine years old—photographically well.

4

That Sunday, Twiss was too sick to play golf, and her mother compelled her to listen to the program with her while Milly accompanied her father to the course. Once or twice a year Twiss caught a cold. To account for her sneezing, she'd pretend she had allergies. Ragweed, she might say. Hay fever, when she couldn't think of anything better.

On this particular Sunday afternoon, she said *just a little sick?* when she meant . . . she couldn't think of what she meant. Her head felt like a ball of dough.

"Oh, no you don't," her mother said, when Twiss dressed in her golf clothes and went to the front door to wait for her father. "I wouldn't hear the end of it at our next Society meeting. They already think I didn't donate enough fabric at Christmas."

"But I meant the yellow stuff," Twiss said.

"Pollen," her mother said. "If you'd said mold, I might have let you go."

Twiss appealed to her father when he came down the stairs in his golf shoes, which her mother was always trying to get him to put on outside since the metal spikes on their soles left polka-dot imprints on the wood floors.

"Looks like your mother may be right about this one," her father said.

"Milly thinks I look fine," Twiss said.

"What do I think?" Milly said.

"It's only *one* day," her mother said. "That's what I think."

Her father took the putter from her hand and replaced it with a cherry cough drop. "You can be a champion next week. Give your sister a turn."

After he and Milly drove off, Twiss tried to slip out of the kitchen and up to her room. When her mother asked her where she thought she was going, Twiss coughed a little.

"I should really be in bed."

Her mother motioned to a chair. "You should really sit down."

Before *A Day in the Life of* . . . began, she fixed a cup of tea for Twiss and one for herself. Into Twiss's cup, she drizzled honey. Into her own, she drizzled milk. Then she pulled out her secret stash of sugar cubes from the back of the cupboard, which Twiss had ransacked on more than one occasion because she liked to see how long the cubes would take to dissolve on her tongue.

"Looks like I have to find another hiding place," her mother said, amused rather than angry. She dropped a cube into her cup. She said that was the way the English took their tea.

Twiss wondered what people who spoke other languages did with their tea.

Her mother looked at the cuckoo clock, and then turned up the radio. "This one's about a man who lives with polar bears."

"With?" Twiss said, perking up.

"In the vicinity of," her mother said, and Twiss slumped back down in her chair.

The program announcer introduced the day's story by saying there were three kinds of people in the world: the kind that respected animals, the kind that got killed by them, and the kind named Hux. "No one ever dies on this program," her mother said. "Although there was a near death once." She took her tea bag out of her cup and placed it on the tiny plate beneath it.

"That's better than nothing," Twiss said, taking hers out too.

She looked out the window to make sure her father was gone before she crossed her legs the way her mother had crossed hers. She didn't altogether hate acting ladylike, but she could only act for so long before her instincts took over. In school plays, she was cast as a tree or a lamppost, whatever could appear or disappear without wrecking the show.

"It's called gunpowder," her mother said.

Twiss picked her cup up again. She liked the idea of being able to drink what you could load into a gun. "I should have been a boy," she said, puckering her lips at the bitter taste of the tea and letting her legs fly out in opposite directions.

Her mother uncrossed her legs and then crossed them again. "Being a girl takes practice. You have to learn how to do things boys never have to do."

"Like what?" Twiss said.

"Like painting your fingernails," her mother said. "Or holding your tongue."

The two of them stopped talking in order to listen to Hux talk about life in the Arctic Circle. Since the sun didn't rise or set at the normal hours there, Hux said it wasn't important when he woke up or went to sleep. Sometimes, he'd start his day with a cup of coffee at midnight. Other times, it would be four or five in the morning with a bowl of beef stew. Every day (or night) began with warming up his tundra buggy, which he'd drive over ice and snow and narrow crevasses to survey land for the Canadian government, which was hoping to uncover a bounty of natural resources, namely gold and uranium, to tap into.

Giddy up, old girl, Hux would say to the buggy before expeditions.

Queenie, he'd named it.

"What does it look like?" the announcer said.

"Picture a tractor," Hux said. "Then picture your best friend."

Twiss pictured the John Deere and then Milly.

Her mother looked around the kitchen as if a tractor might materialize from one of the cupboards or a best friend from the pantry.

"You'd be amazed how quickly you grow to love whatever you're capable of moving," Hux said. He lived in a government shack on the edge of the polar bears' habitat. He cooked on a kerosene stove and slept on a mattress made of straw (there must not be pine needles in the Arctic, Twiss thought). When the wind rattled the tin roof of his shack and he felt the most alone, he'd drive around with Queenie hoping to come across the polar bears.

One night, when the northern lights were swirling across the horizon like pink cotton, and he hadn't spoken to another person in three months, Hux found what he was looking for in a tundra meadow situated between a moonlit crevasse and snow dune. That night, he got out of his tundra buggy and walked over to the bears, who neither accepted nor rejected him, which Hux said was all anyone could really hope for in human company.

Together, he and the bears watched the northern lights.

"I believe that's called happiness," Hux said. "I only wish it had lasted longer."

"Amen," Twiss's mother said when the music swelled and the program ended, but she didn't say it in her usual religious way.

56

"I don't get it," Twiss said. "Why didn't they eat him?"

Her mother laughed. "Maybe you should have been a boy after all."

She put her hand on the back of Twiss's neck. When Twiss didn't pull away or lurch forward, her mother drew her into her arms the way she used to do when Twiss scraped her knee or fell down on the driveway. "You should stay home more. We had fun, didn't we?"

Which reminded Twiss of what she'd missed by being sick. By now, Milly and her father would have finished playing the back nine. They'd be walking back to the clubhouse. If her father had played especially well, he'd linger at each hole, retracing his steps so that he could repeat them the next time. Twiss wondered if Rollie had given Milly a nickel for a cream soda, even though she didn't know about the mushrooms and probably wouldn't have whacked at one if she did. Twiss imagined her father bursting through the front door with the same gleaming expression he usually reserved for her.

Who's the real champion? Twiss could almost hear him ask.

Me! Me! Me! She could almost hear Milly answer.

"Can I go lie down now?" Twiss said, slinking out of her mother's embrace.

She ran to the bottom of the staircase before her mother had a chance to respond. Before she climbed the first stair, she looked back at her mother, whose arms were wrapped around an empty space. *I did have fun,* she almost said, but that would have been the girl thing to do. She darted up the stairs instead, thumping each step extra hard with her heels and yelping like the cowboys in her books did.

The next Sunday was her mother's birthday, and to celebrate, Milly and Twiss hung a paper banner over the doorway in the kitchen that said CONGRATULATIONS! YOU'RE 32 IN '42! When their mother saw it, she frowned, but not as much as when she opened their father's gift.

Although their mother didn't golf, that year Twiss's father bought her a No. 1 Persimmon driver. The head was made from finely grained American persimmon wood, the hardest of its kind and, in her father's opinion, the most beautiful. The wood matched the jar of honey sitting on the counter, which her father dipped his fingers into even though he was supposed to use a spoon. Every time Twiss went golfing with her father, he'd tell her to wait outside the pro shop for him. When he came out, he'd wobble like a drunk.

"I thought you might want to start playing," her father said after Twiss's mother tore the brown wrapping paper off the driver.

"I don't want to know how much this cost," her mother said, placing the driver back on his lap. "What I know is, none of us will be happy until you try it out.

"Go," she said, neither kindly nor unkindly. "And take Trouble with you."

Twiss's father looked at Twiss and then at the dark patch of sky beyond the windows. "I'll bet a nickel the thunderclouds don't even thunder, Maisie."

"I'll bet a nickel they do, Joe," her mother said.

On their way out the door, Twiss took another swipe of coconut frosting from the cake Milly had baked for the occasion. Milly had decorated the top of it with four-leaf clovers, which she'd crawled through an entire field on her hands and knees to find that morning.

"Is my luck that bad?" their mother had said when the cake was presented to her.

On the drive to the golf course, Twiss rolled down her window to look at the cat's-paws on the river. She called the bigger ones tiger's-paws. The biggest ones were mastodon's-paws because mastodons were extinct and she liked to bring things back to life.

"One mastodon," she counted. "Two mastodons. Three. Four."

"One hole in one," her father said. "Two holes in one. Three. Four."

"I'm counting mastodons," Twiss said.

"Right," her father said. "And I'm counting holes in one."

He continued counting until he got to eighteen holes in one and they were over the bridge. Twiss could see the golf course in the distance, hemmed in by a row of pine trees and a stream that fed into the river. On humid days, while her father played the eighteenth hole, Twiss would walk to the stream. She liked to pretend she was Lewis, fording rivers and mapping new parts of the country. Her father was Clark.

"Clark!" she'd call when she found a native's spear (an interesting stick) or a new species (a one-legged frog). She kept track of her findings in a notebook at home. So far, she'd mapped four new rivers, five new species, and eighteen new weapons. Her favorite was the baby dragon that spit up fire instead of milk.

"Clark's crossing a mountain range!" her father would call back, which meant his ball had landed between the grassy moguls near the eighteenth hole. "He'll be there soon!"

On this day, there would be no Lewis and Clark because her father would be too busy with the new driver to play along. Plus, it wasn't hot enough to get wet. She'd have to amuse herself with the mushrooms, which she liked whacking at, but not as much as she liked when her father would surprise her. If it were really hot and he'd played a particularly good round of golf, he'd sneak down to the stream and jump into the water in all of his clothes.

"Here comes a grizzly bear!" he'd say, and growl his way over to her.

Her father was the one who'd taught her how to swim, though "taught" wasn't exactly the right word for what he'd done. Twiss would be so surprised by the growling that she'd close her eyes and start shoveling at the water with her arms and legs. When she opened her eyes again, she'd be on the opposite side of the stream. Part of the fun of the grizzly bear game was that she never knew when her father would play it. Whenever Twiss waited for her father to pop out of the tall river grass, he never would. And whenever she'd become invested in one of her discoveries, he'd trample her with his fearsome growling, his unpredictable love.

Twiss turned toward her father in the car. She was thinking about What If, the game she and Milly liked to play when they were bored. What if the sky was below us instead of above us? one of them would ask the other. What if you had a tail the length of your hair? A honeycomb instead of a knee? They would ask until one of them was stumped by a question.

"What would you do if you couldn't play golf?" Twiss asked her father, who didn't know about the game or the way to win it.

"Why wouldn't I be able to play golf?" he said.

"What if there was a flood?" Twiss said.

"I'd wait until the grass dried out."

"But what if it didn't?" Twiss said.

"I'd learn how to play in water."

"But what if you *couldn't?*"

"Then I'd forget how to swim."

They arrived at the course before Twiss could ask the question she really wanted to ask. Her father picked up the driver and the rest of his clubs. He was halfway to the clubhouse before he noticed that Twiss was still sitting in the car.

"Aren't you coming?" he said, grinning his special grin. He'd had his front teeth capped because that's what the most important members of the course did when theirs were uneven. Her mother was always telling him to chew his food twice as much as everyone else to justify the expense, which they were still paying for and would be for a long, long time.

For Twiss, all it took was a flash of those perfectly aligned teeth, and she was running after him, tripping on her shoelaces. They checked in at the clubhouse and came out with a scoring card and a freshly sharpened half-pencil.

Rollie was in the middle of pulling a dandelion out of the ground. "We just pulled everyone else off the course. Weather's coming."

"We're not everyone else," Twiss's father said.

"You keep watch for lightning, Button," Rollie

said, tucking the dandelion behind Twiss's ear. "You're too young to walk around with a streak of gray hair and a mixed-up mind."

Twiss wasn't afraid of storms, but she'd never been caught in a severe one either. There was a man who had, though, who lived in the woods by the river. People said if you saw him running in one direction, it was best not to run in the other. So as they walked along, Twiss kept watch for the lightning man while the clouds began to lump together like angry faces.

"Grumpy's getting grumpier," Twiss said, while her father teed off.

"Why are you grumpy?" her father said.

"I'm not," Twiss said, watching the treetops sway. "The sky is."

"That's just wind."

After her father putted the ball into the first hole, he started for the next one. Twiss followed him closely but not so closely as to test his concentration, even though he said the difference between a good player and a great player was how well the player could tune out his surroundings. Comparing the two, her father said, was like comparing a mule and a stallion; both could plow a field, but only one of them did so with grace.

Twiss lagged behind because she didn't want to be responsible for turning her father into a mule. Whenever he stopped to square his shoulders for a shot, she sucked in her lips to keep herself from speaking. Once, she'd asked him a question about bull snakes in the middle of a swing. Even though the ball went where it was supposed to go, he scolded her. "I don't like snakes," he'd said. "And I don't appreciate thinking one's near my golf ball either."

So Twiss stayed quiet even when, halfway between the seventeenth and eighteenth holes, the sky turned from grumpy to enraged and the fire station sirens began to sound. People would be closing their storm shutters and starting for their cellars. Most people kept emergency supplies in their cellars in case they were stuck beneath the ground overnight. Among Twiss's family's supplies were an oil lamp and a book of fairy tales, which her mother would read from when the cellar doors began to rattle. *Once upon a time,* she'd begin.

Twiss's father looked at the sky, but didn't seem dismayed. He studied the treetops and the sand blowing over the lips of the bunkers in the distance. A line of pink lightning flashed overhead. The wind howled.

"Run to the stream," he told Twiss, but he said it in the same steady way he explained the theory of wind and the physics of golf.

When she got there, she was supposed to crouch down low and put her hands over her head like they did in school when they were practicing for tornadoes. During the drills, kids would stick wads of gum to the bottom of the lockers in the hallway.

"Wait for me there," Twiss's father said, which Twiss took to mean *I'll be right behind you* since Twiss was such a fast runner.

Another flash of lightning. Another howl of wind.

"Run!" her father said, though it was he who started running, and not toward the stream. He took Persy, but left the rest of the clubs in the bag at Twiss's feet.

"It's the shot of a lifetime!" he yelled. "The shot of a lifetime!"

Twiss stayed where she was. The rain came before the lightning and the thunder, soaking her until her clothes stuck to her like a second skin. The wind sent the dandelion behind her ear flying toward the stream, but Twiss was too alarmed to follow it.

"Clark?" she said, after her father disappeared down the fairway.

Lightning! Thunder!

Whirrrrrrr, whir. Whirrrrrrrr, whir.

"Mom!" she screamed.

Right then, Twiss knew she should have loved her mother more for being right about the weather, but that would have meant loving her father less for being wrong about it. So with each snarl of thunder and each flash of lightning, each realization that her father wasn't coming back for her, she stuck to the safety of hating her mother, even though her mother would never leave her alone in the middle of a storm. Because her mother would never leave her alone.

"Milly," Twiss finally cried, since she didn't have to make a choice about loving or hating her. There wasn't a person in the world as worthy of love as her sister.

Though she'd never said so, Twiss knew Milly played halfhearted games of golf on her behalf. "Graceless," she'd overheard her father say to her mother one night about Milly's swing, which was perfectly graceful when she and Twiss were alone. "A mule could have played a more elegant round of golf than our elder daughter."

"So she had a bad day," her mother had said to him. "Even you've had a few of those."

"I'd jump off a bridge if I ever played like that."

In the end, when Twiss couldn't will herself to move or will her father to come back to her, it was Rollie who scooped her up as if she were a feather and ran with her all the way back to the maintenance shed, where they waited out the storm, which whirled things around plenty but never produced a tornado. Even after the sky cleared and the sun came out and a rainbow arched over the river, she wouldn't let go of Rollie.

"You're safe, Button," he kept saying. "You're safe now."

But Twiss didn't feel safe. None of her tricks had kept her from crying or brought her father back to her. As far as he knew, she was still crouching on the bank of the stream next to her baby dragon, whose gift couldn't protect her. Twiss realized just how much she'd counted on the history books being right; nowhere in the pages she'd read did Clark ever leave Lewis behind. The *and* always linked them together.

After her father returned, wild-eyed and wind-blown, Twiss ran to him, but not as quickly as she could have. It was as if he had inadvertently told her something essential about himself, a secret she would have to keep forever: You can't count on me.

5

Milly put down *The Curious Book of Birds* in order to pick herself up. She glanced at the bariatric walker—an affront to both her decorative tastes and her relatively small size—which was sitting in the corner of the room collecting old linens and scraps of fabric. She used to mend clothing for half the town of Spring Green when she could still sew without making a mistake. Despite her recent inabilities, she was working on a layette for a woman who lived by the river. The woman, a girl, didn't have a mother to sew one for her.

Not that people in Spring Green sewed much anymore; when they needed something, they went to the department stores in Madison. Milly had only been to a department store once, after her doctor recommended knee braces to treat her hip pain.

"But it's my hip that hurts," she'd said.

"Treating just the hip's like baking a cake without flour. You wouldn't do that, would you?" the doctor said.

Well, yes, she thought. *I would.*

But she and Twiss drove to the department store anyway and paid an astronomical price for what amounted to Ace bandages. And the walker, which could accommodate persons up to one thousand pounds. The salesman claimed that purchasing a bariatric was like getting two walkers for the price of one; plus, he'd said when they'd looked doubtful, it was the only walker left in stock. While they were there they also bought an electric mixer, which ended up in the attic because the sound of it made the chickens (and Milly) anxious.

Milly put *The Curious Book of Birds* back in its place on the shelf. She finished dusting the bookshelves and the hutch, twirling the duster around corners and spines until she saw a slight reflection of herself in the varnished wood. She didn't quite know when what had happened to her body had happened to her body. The sagging skin beneath her knees told one story. The liver spots on her hands told another. Though she'd never been the type of woman to fawn over her reflection, she wished she'd have taken a moment to appreciate her youth while she was still youthful. The one hip had already gone out, and the other was beginning to creak. One day, it would snap altogether and she'd have a body full of titanium, but nothing to propel her forward. And her chin! The pull of gravity had turned what was once one into two. The chins worked against each other like cresting waves.

Crash, they went.

You're old, they said.

So be it, Milly thought.

She pulled the drapes shut to keep out the heat and then drew a line through the task on her chore list. She looked over the way she spelled out each step like her mother used to because Twiss would feign ignorance that what was washed also needed to be dried.

MILLY'S CHORE LIST
Dust bookshelves and hutch
Dust and close drapes
Change bed linens

Wash bed linens
Dry bed linens
More dusting?
Supper?

The list struck her as both amusing and a little sad, and Milly wasn't eager to obey it this morning. She was drawn once again to the bird book as if it were a live thing, a wing beat of breath on an otherwise breathless day, which deserved her care—pleaded for it—more than some dusty old linens, worn-out threads. This time, Milly read about the different kinds of nests birds built, how some were well wrought and some carelessly fastened to branches. The smartest birds built their nests high up in the trees. Some birds, namely the wood pigeon, the clumsiest architect of all, began building their nests but never finished them.

6

That was the way the tree house went in the weeks leading up to Cousin Bettie's visit. By the end of May and the beginning of the trumpet vines and wisteria, the honeysuckle and hummingbirds, Milly and Twiss had collected enough scrap lumber to build the foundation.

They'd checked out a book from the library that taught them about basic woodworking, but Twiss didn't want to wait until they could afford to buy the materials they needed. She said they'd be dead before that happened. What was one more floor that leaned?

Together, they dragged the planks to the backyard. Twiss found two hammers in the attic. She didn't bother to wipe away the toadstool on the handles or the rust on the heads. She named her hammer Rust-O-Lonia and went to work. Milly called hers Hammer. After she washed the toadstool off him (*It's poisonous,* she told Twiss, but Twiss said, *Not if you don't eat it*), she tapped at the nails as if she were asking them for permission.

"Pretend the nail's something you don't like," Twiss instructed.

"You don't like snakes," she added when Milly didn't say anything.

"But I don't want to hammer them," Milly said.

"Cousin Bettie better be less of a humanitarian," Twiss said.

"Do you even know what that means?"

"It means we need a third person to finish the tree house."

Since they'd found out she was coming, Milly and Twiss had been making predictions about their cousin. They'd met her only once, and "met" wasn't the quite right word since Milly was two and Twiss was still a baby. Cousin Bettie was four then. According to their mother, they got along beautifully. Twiss was hoping for another her. Milly didn't know what to hope for, but figured their cousin would probably be wearing a bracelet with little charms in the shapes of horseshoes and tennis rackets like the other girls in Spring Green.

"Or worse," Twiss said. "A dress."

"*I* wear dresses," Milly said.

"But you don't act like you do."

At night, they'd talk until the shadow of their mother's feet appeared under the door, which meant *Not another word.* Their mother let their whispering go on longer than usual because she was eager to have another pair of hands around the house for the summer; a pair, she told Twiss, that wasn't as lazy as hers.

Mine? Twiss said, pretending to be outraged.

Their mother planned on repairing the damage living on a farm had done to her. She said that wives deserved a little mindless time and mothers deserved much, much more. Her sister, Gertrude, was sending their cousin with the understanding that if the three of them got on well together, Milly and Twiss would go up north next summer to help out. *If* was their mother's way of saying *when.* Each morning, she crossed a day off the calendar with a black X.

The day before Cousin Bettie arrived, Twiss flipped ahead three hundred sixty-five days to a Wednesday in early June, the day their mother decided they would depart for Aunt Gertrude's house in Deadwater, a day that would have been unremarkable if it weren't for the smiling sun their mother had drawn in the square with a yellow crayon.

Milly's father didn't notice the bath salts or the calendar.

After the Accident, which had taken on the weight of a proper noun somewhere between his coming home from the hospital and the appearance of the June bugs, he spent his time in the barn when he wasn't working. He'd even started sleeping up in the hayloft because he said their mother's snoring woke him, though a thick plaster wall separated their bedrooms and she didn't snore. Their parents had always kept separate bedrooms, but they hadn't always slept separately. When Milly and Twiss were little, their father had used his bedroom to store golf equipment, but would sleep in their mother's room. One day, though, for no reason the girls understood, a mattress appeared on the floor in their father's room and he started sleeping on it, now and then at first, then more and more regularly. Milly and Twiss would still occasionally catch him sneaking out of their mother's bedroom in the morning, which would hearten them. Other times, they'd find him asleep on his bed in all of his clothes, and their mother's eyes would be puffy, which would still hearten them because their parents were trying to work out whatever ugly thing had come between them.

Milly and Twiss couldn't find anything heartening about their father sleeping in the barn or him handing them notes scrawled on leftover scoring paper from the golf course when he had something to say to their mother. *You must be very happy, Margaret,* he'd written on the last piece of scoring paper. *You finally got exactly what you wanted.*

Like always, her father was talking about golf, with one significant difference: after he drove the car off the bridge over the Wisconsin River, and had recovered from his slight injuries, his swing had altered imperceptibly to everyone including him, though the outcome was clear; overnight, he'd become a player who duffed the same shots he used to sneer at for their elementariness. Overnight, he'd become average.

"We might have to face the facts," their mother said one evening when the pantry was empty but should have been full. Despite the sorry state of his swing, once again their father had spent most of his paycheck (which wasn't big to begin with since being a golf pro was more about prestige than money) buying rounds of drinks and cigars for members at the clubhouse. *You don't understand,* he'd said, when their mother handed him a stack of bills, the mortgage slip on top. *It's the only way to really be one of them.*

That afternoon, their mother had asked Milly and Twiss to go out to the pond to catch frogs, which she cooked for supper alongside a mountain of pink beans.

"Facts?" their father said, snapping off a frog's leg. "The fact is people pay big money to eat these. *French* people, Margaret."

Their mother pushed the beans around with her fork. Milly excused herself from the table. Even Twiss wouldn't touch one of the boiled frogs. She said it was immoral to eat something that hopped into her coveralls so willingly.

"It tastes like chicken," their father said. "Nobody gives a thought to eating those."

Mr. Peterson had given their father three weeks to get his swing back; he couldn't give him more than that because summer was upon them. Instead of readying the pro shop, Mr. Peterson let her father play the course every day. When her father's swing didn't return, Mr. Peterson opened the course up to him after hours.

"I can't add two and two when people are watching me," he said.

When his swing still didn't return, Mr. Peterson sent his personal doctor to their house, but after a lengthy examination, the doctor concluded nothing was wrong with their father.

"Then why can't I play golf like I used to?" their father said.

"Why do *you* think you can't play golf like you used to?" the doctor said.

Their father yanked the doctor's stethoscope. "You're the expert. You tell me."

When their father's swing (and the doctor) didn't come back, Mr. Peterson sat their father down to let him go. But he didn't let him go completely. He offered their father a job in the dairy division of his farm. He said, "Watching you golf was like watching the stars, Joe."

And though her father's accepting the job was an awful thing to be even slightly happy about, Milly couldn't help herself. Asa, Mr. Peterson's son, worked in the dairy too.

"What I wanted?" Milly's mother had said when she opened their father's note. She'd laughed the kind of hysterical laughter that Milly and Twiss had only seen unhappy people, namely their mother and father, achieve.

Since the Accident, the girls had been trying their hands at matchmaking.

"Mom wants you to have supper with us tonight," they'd say to their father, who'd look at them as if they'd said *Mom wants you to go to the moon.* "She's making steaks and potatoes."

To their mother, they'd say, "Dad wants you to visit him in the barn," which would produce the same disbelieving look.

One day, though, they convinced her they were telling the truth.

When their mother took off her apron and went out to the barn, Milly and Twiss smiled. They imagined their parents letting go of whatever invisible things they were holding on to so they could hold on to each other. But when their mother came back, her hair wasn't tousled the way they thought it would be and her lips weren't pink. She looked at Milly and Twiss very seriously before she put her apron on and went back to rolling out dough.

"Don't do that again," was all she said.

Milly and Twiss were hopeful their cousin Bettie would prevail where they'd failed. When relatives had come in the past, their mother and father would sleep in the same bedroom again without sneaking around in the middle of the night or first thing in the morning. A week would pass and they'd believe their parents had fallen in love again only to be jolted back into the fact of separate bedrooms when the relatives went home. Genuine or not, Milly and Twiss preferred the scent of cold cream mixing with aftershave in the bathroom.

What they didn't understand then was that love, or even the play at love, wasn't the same thing as forgiveness, which was what neither of their parents could offer. Their father couldn't forgive their mother for her background because it—the sprawling fairy-tale house in Butterfield, the glittering evening parties, the ladies in silk dresses and white gloves, the back patting, the cigars, and the golf, a game only gentlemen could afford to play then—was what he'd coveted his whole secondhand life. The only reason he'd been allowed on a golf course in the first place was to caddy, and the only reason he'd ever been allowed to swing a club was because a member had suspected his talent and had sponsored him. For her part, their mother couldn't forgive their father for wanting a lifestyle more than he wanted her.

Because Twiss didn't understand that then, the morning Cousin Bettie was due to arrive care of the postman, who ferried people from town to the country for extra pocket money, she ran back and forth between the house and the barn as if the distance had already narrowed.

"Race me!" she kept saying to Milly, who finally gave in and ran after her. The day was warm enough to go barefoot, but the mud puddles between the house and the barn were still cold enough to make them lose feeling in their toes.

"Stop dragging your sister around!" their mother called to Twiss from the front porch.

Twiss stuck her tongue out and ran toward the barn.

"I saw that!" their mother said. "Come back here and apologize!"

Milly ran after Twiss. When she reached the barn, she collapsed against the side of it, panting like the strays that came to the back door for scraps of food.

"How do you have the energy to love her and hate her so much?" she said to Twiss.

"I never said I loved her."

"Then why'd you want her to come out here?"

"For *him*," Twiss said.

Milly looked at her mother, who'd dragged the wash bucket onto the porch and was scrubbing her father's work clothes against the washboard, working at the milk stains with a bar of home-made lye soap. "You should be nicer to her," she said to Twiss.

"She should be nicer to me," Twiss said, and ran around the meadow again, stopping now and then to look at the end of the driveway.

Cousin Bettie was coming all the way from Deadwater, a fishing outpost in northern Minnesota. To make ends meet, her father had two jobs: during the week he was a fisherman and on the weekends a taxidermist. For Christmas, he'd sent them a buck's head, which their mother had put in the attic. That morning, she dragged it down the stairs and hung it on the wall in Milly and Twiss's room to make their cousin feel more at home.

To get to Spring Green, Cousin Bettie had to cross a bog, a prairie, and the Mississippi River. She was traveling alone because her family couldn't afford to go with her and their family couldn't afford to come and get her. In her letter, she said she'd be the one standing at the end of the driveway at eleven o'clock wearing black rubber hip boots.

"What is a bog exactly?" Twiss asked Milly between races.

"A swamp," Milly said.

"Then why don't they call it that?"

While Milly thought about the answer, Twiss took off running toward the barn.

"You tricked me!" Milly said, starting after her.

"You're easy to trick!" Twiss called back.

By the time the mail truck dropped their cousin at the end of the driveway with a paper bag for a suitcase and an armful of mail, Milly and Twiss were in the middle of a new contest down by the pond; whoever caught the least number of frogs had to wash *and* dry the dishes that evening. They'd decided to catch as many frogs as they could so they wouldn't end up on their supper plates again, although they were supposed to be clearing algae from the water so the fish didn't get sick again. Last summer, they couldn't swim without running into a floater.

Their mother walked out to the end of the driveway to meet Cousin Bettie, who was wearing hip
boots like she'd promised. She was taller than
they thought she'd be; she had to stoop to hug
their mother, who wasn't short. The boots, which
came up to the middle of her thighs, came up to
their mother's waist. When Cousin Bettie took
them off, they grazed the tops of the stinkweeds
at the side of the driveway.

After a while, their mother and cousin let go of
each other. Their mother carried the paper bag
and Cousin Bettie carried her boots. The two of
them walked toward the pond.

"She probably has Amazon blood in her!"
Twiss said.

"She can probably hear you," Milly said.

When Cousin Bettie and their mother passed
the pile of sand, which was supposed to have
become a beach but had sat all spring collecting
ground bees instead, Milly stopped pretending to
look for frogs, but Twiss kept going, croaking
and hopping after them.

"Put those frogs back this minute!" their
mother said to Twiss, when she and Cousin
Bettie were within shouting distance. "You're
supposed to be raking muck off that water."

When they got closer and she saw the mud
stains on Twiss's coveralls, their mother added,
"Stop making work for me!"

"Yes, ma'am," Twiss said, saluting.

"This is your cousin Bettie," their mother said. "She's got weak lungs, so don't run her around. If I even *think* you're up to something," she said, raising her eyebrows to Twiss, "I'll make you breathe out of a straw for a week and see how you like it."

"I have asthma," Cousin Bettie said.

"And I have a line of linens to take in, not to mention the tractor and the wheelbarrow. If it were up to your father, he'd let everything rust."

"The wheelbarrow's already rusty," Twiss said.

"Still," their mother said. "He ought to come out of that barn and help me."

"I'll help you, Aunt Margaret."

"I won't have you dragging a wheelbarrow around. We can't afford a trip to the general store, let alone the hospital. But I appreciate the offer. You won't hear that from this one," she said, motioning to Twiss. "You just tell me if she starts bothering you."

"I'm sure I'll be fine, Aunt Margaret," their cousin said.

"Just say the word," their mother said, and yanked a frog out of Twiss's pocket before handing Cousin Bettie the paper bag and heading into the house, leaving the three girls alone.

Milly and Twiss stared at their cousin, who was as thin and pale as the white asparagus growing in the vegetable garden. As unappealing, too. Except for the shock of red under her eyes and on top of her head, Cousin Bettie looked like the specimens Mr. Stewart preserved in formaldehyde at school. Dearly departed, or not so dearly.

"You look dead," Twiss said.

"Tired," Milly corrected.

"I am," Cousin Bettie said.

"Which?" Twiss said.

Cousin Bettie yawned. "Both, I guess."

Rarely did Milly and Twiss meet someone who could handle Twiss in full force without bursting into tears. The last girl they'd invited out to the farm walked all the way back to town after Twiss sprayed her with a hose and called her a water buffalo.

"You want to catch frogs with us?" Milly said.

"I have a better idea," Cousin Bettie said, and sat down to take off her shoes. On the outer edges of each big toe were scaly, protruding bunions. More striking than the bunions were the blood blisters that covered her heels.

"They're as big as silver dollars," Twiss said.

"Too bad they're not worth that much," their cousin said.

Beneath the blisters, the skin was purple. Cousin Bettie opened her paper bag and pulled out a sewing needle, which she'd stuck into a wedge of stale bread. She pushed the needle into the first blister until blood oozed out, and then she moved on to the other one. After the blood came white pus, then clear liquid, and then a look of relief.

"I've already popped them twice today," she said.

Milly turned away, but Twiss kept watching.

"I wish I had a blister," she said.

"Walk around in these for a while," their cousin said, handing over her shoes. "But you'll have to get your own needle. This one only takes my blood."

Twiss put on their cousin's shoes, the soles of which had been reinforced with squares of corrugated cardboard, which had been reinforced with construction paper and cushioned with brown felt. "What's it like to be eighteen?"

"Everyone gets married," Cousin Bettie said.

Twiss stood on her tiptoes. "Why aren't you?"

Cousin Bettie squeezed more liquid out of her blisters. After she peeled off the dead skin and tossed it into the grass, she wiped her hands on her housedress and stood up.

"What's it like to be so nosy?"

She didn't need to tell Twiss to follow her when she started walking toward the sandpile on the other side of the pond. Twiss adapted her gait to match Cousin Bettie's, which made her look like she was trotting. The two of them kept bumping into each other.

"Stop trying to hold my hand," Cousin Bettie said.

"I'm not," Twiss said.

A few more steps and they looked like they'd been walking along the bank together all their lives. When Bettie tossed a stick into the water, so did Twiss. When Bettie wiped sweat from her forehead, so did Twiss. It was as if their cousin had cast a spell on her.

Milly stayed with the hip boots, the dead skin, and the paper bag. She couldn't explain why the sight of Twiss and her cousin made her feel suddenly so alone, so useless. Twiss had left her behind plenty of times when she wanted to do something that Milly didn't want to do. But she'd always looked back at Milly for encouragement, and Milly had always given it to her.

"Aren't you coming?" Cousin Bettie said to Milly.

"Yeah, aren't you?" Twiss echoed.

The three of them walked to the sandpile, Cousin Bettie and Twiss weaving in and out of the murky water and Milly along the bank. Milly could already hear the hum of the bees, which surged, like her pulse, as they got closer to the other side of the pond. Since her father had paid a man to dump it beside the pond, Milly and Twiss had avoided the pile because the last summer a bee stung Twiss on her tongue.

When the three girls arrived at the sandpile, Cousin Bettie rolled her sleeves up to her elbows. "Let's see who can stick their hands in."

"That's dangerous," Milly said.

"People only get stung when they think things like that."

"There's no honey," Twiss said. "What's the point?"

Cousin Bettie walked over to the pile. "There isn't one."

Milly and Twiss watched as their cousin pushed her pale hands into the even paler sand. The bees came out in a giant black-and-yellow swarm, organized and armylike, and landed on their cousin's hair and dress, her face and neck, accumulating in such quantities that she began to disappear. She didn't flinch when a bee landed on her eyelid or when one landed on her nose. She simply closed her eyes and breathed out of her mouth, a maneuver that caused both Milly and Twiss to cover theirs. They'd heard of bee charmers, but it didn't look like Cousin Bettie was charming the bees. It looked like they were charming her.

"It's like being God for a minute," their cousin said.

Milly took a step back. Unlike Twiss, when they went to church, Milly paid attention. Miracles, Father Rice had cautioned them when he was still the priest, were contrary to the laws of nature, and whatever was contrary to nature came at a price.

"Your chicken may lay two eggs today," he said. "But what happens tomorrow?"

When Cousin Bettie pulled her arms out of the sand, bees occupied every inch of skin between her wrists and her elbows. Milly couldn't tell where the bees ended and the sleeves of Bettie's dress began. When Bettie backed away from the sandpile, Twiss stepped forward. She was still wearing their cousin's shoes, which were too large to cause any blistering, but had left marks on her toes where the felt ended and the cardboard began.

Milly took another step back, even though the bees had returned to the sandpile and her cousin's skin had remained intact.

"Why are you looking at me like that?" Cousin Bettie said.

"I'm not looking at you," Milly said, because she couldn't find a polite way to explain what she'd seen: a person so untouched by fear she was certain something terrible had happened to Cousin Bettie, or would. What Milly didn't know then was that whatever happened to Bettie would, in its own way, happen to her, too.

Milly looked at her mother, who was folding linens on the porch, and then at the front door of the barn, which her father had shut up despite the weather vane not spinning and the sky being perfectly clear. She hadn't seen her father since he took Rust-O-Lonia and the can of nails from its resting place beneath the oak tree that morning.

Cousin Bettie rolled down her sleeves, waving away the last bee and encouraging it to fly back to the sandpile. Out of the hundreds, not a single one had stung her.

"I guess I win," she said, moving closer to Milly to see what she was staring at now instead of staring at her. "By default, I mean. Since I was the only one playing."

Milly kept her eyes on the barn, trying to discern from the slivers of light between the wood slats what the woman at the town fair had discerned from a cup of tea leaves last summer. After Milly paid her nickel, she'd expected the woman to see a butterfly or a daisy, good fortune or love. But when it was her turn, the woman saw a raised finger: a warning.

"You'll fall in love like the rest of us," her mother had said, after the woman explained Milly's future. "It's what happens after that you have to worry about."

"Listen to your mother," the woman with the tea leaves said.

Milly's mother opened her change purse. "I'll pay you a nickel to say that to my other daughter. She's the one who deserves a warning."

Milly turned away from the barn, wondering what it would be like to be able to see into the future, wondering if she already could. Normally, she'd have asked Twiss her opinion, but Twiss didn't look like she could be deterred from her courtship efforts. It didn't take a woman with a cup of tea leaves to see that her sister was enamored.

"You're my hero," Twiss said to Cousin Bettie. She handed over their cousin's shoes as if they were made of glass. "How did you do that?"

Cousin Bettie—*Bett* she liked to be called—simply handed them back.

7

Twiss had paused in the meadow long enough that she couldn't remember where she'd intended to go. That happened often these days, remembering and forgetting. She'd get stuck somewhere old and have to wander around to find her mental footing again. The synapses weren't firing the way they used to. At first, she'd put a pitcher of milk into a cupboard or a clean plate into the refrigerator and remember a few minutes later. Now when she walked into a room looking for something and forgot what it was, instead of minutes later, hours later she'd lurch up from a chair and say My reading glasses! or The photo album! and then she'd be fooled into thinking her mind was intact until the next bout of chair lurching.

If Milly had noticed, she'd had the kindness not to say anything. Twiss had always been able to count on her sister for that. *You better be using that walker,* she thought, when Milly passed by the front windows, but she knew Milly wasn't. However gracefully her sister had aged—Milly's beauty hadn't been chiseled down to jutting cheekbones and withered lips, gizzards, fur—a part of her refused to admit she was old. *We're old,* she'd say, but her voice was caught between statement and question. What Milly didn't realize was that the bariatric walker wouldn't indict her any more than the floral print scarf she wore when they went driving or the housedresses with the removable lace collars, which she never removed.

"Guess what I am?" she'd said to Twiss, modeling a new scarf one day.

"Modern?" Twiss said.

When Twiss was feeling particularly obnoxious, she'd lumber around the living room with the walker, which was too wide to fit through the doorways. Neither Milly nor Twiss mentioned the fact that the price they'd paid for those tennis ball gliders in the medical equipment department could have bought them a car full of them in the sporting goods department. Twiss didn't know if it pleased her or displeased her that the people who designed walkers weren't able to come up with anything more advanced.

"We could mow a field with this thing," she'd say to Milly.

"If you mowed anymore," Milly would say.

Until last year, Twiss had made a point of mowing their property herself. Once a week, she'd ride the tractor around trying to look more defiant than she actually felt. The truth was, the tractor scared her with all its rotating blades and internal rumblings. In her lifetime, a handful of Spring Green farmers had lost their lives to steel blades. The less fortunate ones ended up in closed coffins because even with the best makeup the undertaker couldn't piece together a man out of the materials. Twiss didn't want to know what he'd do with a woman, so she gave in to Milly's ultimatum: either they let the grass grow like indecent people or pay someone to cut it for them.

"You still don't know me very well, do you?" she'd said to Milly.

"Why do you think I gave you one choice?" Milly said.

"You didn't. You gave me two."

"The chance to be indecent canceled out the other one."

"You sound like you should be sipping Jell-O from a straw," Twiss said.

"You love to be indecent," Milly said. "I love uncut grass."

But Twiss remembered the opposite. She remembered switchgrass clipped down to the earth, great upward sweeps of black field birds. She remembered Asa.

8

The week Bett came down from Deadwater, Asa came to mow their property for the first of many times that summer. Asa's father, Mr. Peterson, sent him over on the John Deere, which said property of the spring green golf course. Before the Accident, Mr. Peterson had joked about putting Twiss's father to work on his farm and must have felt sorry when his joke became a reality. Asa didn't mow anyone else's property for free.

That first Saturday morning, Twiss's father sent Milly out to Asa with a glass of lemonade. He vowed to bring home butter from the dairy by the next Saturday, so Milly could bake Asa something sweet. "One sugar cookie and he'll be hooked," her father said, as if he'd transferred his hopes of a better life to her. He and Twiss stood at the door of the barn and watched Milly walk out there, hand Asa the glass of lemonade shyly, and turn around.

"It wouldn't hurt you to linger," their father said when Milly returned to the barn. "You're about the right age now."

"The right age for what?" Milly said, her cheeks flushed. She kept looking over her shoulder at Asa in the field, as if he were the one talking.

"You're pretty is all," their father said. "You might use that to your advantage."

"My advantage?" Milly said.

While other people called her Goldilocks, Milly hardly noticed that her hair was more beautiful than anyone else's. Every morning she twirled it into a bun and pinned it the way their mother had taught her. What she never saw was the way it trailed down her back like yellow silk just after she'd brushed it out. Each morning Twiss would wake up to that view, which was like waking up to a bright sun—all the possibilities that came with fine weather. And that was just her hair.

"Beauty gives you choices," their father said to Milly. "Ugliness doesn't."

He glanced at the clothesline, where Bett was unpinning linens and dropping them into the wicker basket beside her feet.

"What about me?" Twiss said.

"Your hands belong around a golf club," their father said.

"What about my hands?" Milly said.

Their father drew them to him. "You both deserve more than this."

"I'm glad I don't have to get married," Twiss said. "The boys in my class have bat breath. One of them has warts all over his fingers. He wipes them on the girls he likes."

Their father laughed. "That sounds about right," he said, and went back into the barn to continue working on whatever he was working on. Though he no longer lived in the house, he still seemed to know what went on inside of it, as if he'd been looking through a window or listening on the other side of a door. He knew, for instance, that Twiss had chopped off the hair on the left side of her head one night when she was bored and that Milly had evened it out for her, creating a look their father called charming and a little boyish.

"Bye, Dad!" the girls said and went back to their chores, glancing over their shoulders whenever the grass around them stirred or a bird chirped or a frog hopped into the pond, although they never witnessed what they felt: their father watching over them.

In the afternoons, when they'd checked the last item off their lists, they were free to roam around as they pleased. Bett was free, too. On hot days, the three of them would walk down to the river to swim. Bett didn't have a bathing suit, so their mother lent Bett her black one, which Bett was too thin to fill out. Whenever it got wet, it bloused in the places it was supposed to be tight. Black did nothing for her pale coloring either, according to Twiss's mother, who said that against the material Bett's skin looked like ice.

Twiss liked that she could see the inner workings of Bett's circulatory system, the complicated patterns of blue webbing that kept her cousin alive. If you didn't know her, you'd think a puff of wind might knock her over, but when you did, you knew Bett was as capable as anyone else. She just didn't look good in a bathing suit. That was the beauty of her.

Twiss wore one of her father's undershirts over her bathing suit because she wouldn't normally walk around the house in just her underwear and didn't see why she should do so in a public space. She didn't like the idea of anyone seeing the little black hairs that had begun to sprout like wires beneath her underarms or the ones that marched up from her knees to her inner thighs to the other place she didn't like the idea of anybody seeing either.

Milly's was the only body that didn't merit hiding. Her bathing suit dipped in all the right places and hugged all the other ones. The suit was made of iridescent green crepe and matched the luminous color of her eyes.

Before the three of them worked up the courage to jump into the water from the wooden boat launch, they'd stand around in their suits. In June, although the air had already reached temperatures Twiss called *swimtastic!*, the water was still cold. The shock of it against their skin was something they could never prepare for, but always recovered from.

While they dawdled on the dock, warming their feet on the wood planks and hopping around to avoid the carpenter ants, men driving over the County C bridge slowed down to admire Milly. They tipped their hats in her direction.

"That's disgusting!" Twiss said one day. She put herself between Milly and the men on the bridge. "They're married. That one has three daughters."

"You can't blame them," Bett said.

"He's old enough to be our father," Twiss said.

"But he's not," Bett said, and jumped into the water.

Out of the three of them, Milly was the most graceful swimmer. Twiss always felt a little like she was drowning. She'd thrash and kick to stay above the surface, swallow a mouthful of water, and dip below the waterline despite her best efforts. Bett's swimming style fell somewhere in between theirs. She unsettled the water plenty, but moved through it in a quick, measured way. She said that's how people had to swim in Deadwater.

"There's a lake spirit," she said.

"What kind?" Twiss said.

"One that eats canoes," Bett said.

The three of them would swim out to Milly and Twiss's old sandbar, which still looked like an exclamation point or a question mark depending on the speed of the current, but no longer elicited corresponding modes of conversation from them. There were new, more interesting games to play.

Bett had introduced them to Truth or Consequences.

"Go outside, circle the house twice, and come back up," she'd said to Twiss for her first consequence on their first night all together. "Without clothes on."

"Naked?" Milly had said.

"It's more risky," Bett said.

Even though Twiss could have easily told a truth, she pretended she couldn't, although she didn't know why since she didn't get any particular thrill from tossing her robe on the porch and running a lap around the house without her clothes on, other than the thrill of impressing Bett and forcing her to think up other consequences for her.

"Go up to the attic," Bett said to Twiss for her second consequence. "Spend an entire minute alone in the dark and say 'Bloody Mary' three times."

At night, the attic felt strange and unfamiliar even though the boxes up there contained

97

familiar keepsakes from the past that had been deemed useless but not useless enough to throw away. Among the boxes was the wooden rocking horse she and Milly had played with as girls and the model airplane Twiss had abandoned building when she learned it would never fly. There was also her mother's serving platter from Hungary and her father's first complete set of golf clubs, which he'd worked three jobs to buy when he was fourteen.

He said he'd never worked so hard for anything except the institution of marriage, which had made Twiss's mother laugh heartily but not unkindly. "You've got quite the memory, dear husband. Dementia, I think that's called."

"You win, dear wife," her father had said, also laughing. "Someone gave me the clubs."

Standing up in the attic felt like standing in a graveyard. Twiss wasn't frightened, exactly, but she didn't feel like invoking the spirit of Bloody Mary and waiting for a chopped-off head or the body to which it belonged to pop out of one of the boxes either.

"Next time it's truth," Bett said when Twiss finally crept back down the stairs. "Consequences are obviously too easy for you."

For Milly, both options were difficult. She wasn't the type to prance around the yard without her underwear, nor was she the type to say the full truth of what was on her mind. Not that she was a liar; her explanations simply stopped where most people's began. And Bett wasn't all that fair to her. She'd ask questions designed to expose whatever secrets Milly kept.

"How old were you when you got your monthly?" she asked one night, which even Twiss didn't know the answer to.

The two of them didn't talk about what had happened to their bodies. One day, it was okay for them to walk from the bathroom to their bedroom in their towels and the next day it wasn't, just as one day they didn't wear brassieres and the next day they did. Twiss had never gotten used to the lumps beneath her shirts, the tops of which looked like root beer gumdrops. She hated root beer and knew Milly didn't like it either. When Twiss looked in the mirror, she saw two people: the person she used to be and the fleshy imposter who had taken her over. *Go away,* she'd say, pinching the soda-colored parts of her skin. *Leave me alone!*

"Well?" Bett said to Milly. "How old were you?"

Milly hid her face in her pillow. "Fourteen," she said, and started to sniffle.

"Miss Milly Prim," Bett said.

"I got mine last year," Twiss said. "When did you get yours?"

"When I was nine," Bett said. "I had to tell my dad."

"Where was your mom?" Twiss asked.

"On a time-out," Bett said.

"Like when you're little?" Milly said.

"No," Bett said. "Like when you're unhappy."

When Milly and Twiss didn't say anything, Bett said, "Right then, my dad stopped kissing me good night. He said I wasn't his little girl anymore."

"We have an outhouse," she added. "You can imagine the difficulties. Not to mention the wolf spiders that live in there. They're as big as birds. They have *fur*, for God's sake."

"Fur?" Milly said, letting go of her pillow a little bit.

"Hair, if you want to be technical about it," Bett said.

So far, Deadwater was the most exciting place Twiss had ever heard about. She couldn't wait to go up there the next summer and marked off the days on her mother's calendar before her mother had a chance to; instead of an X, she drew a canoe in the square allotted to each passing day. "Do you have a canoe?" she asked Bett.

"We live in the middle of a chain of lakes. How else would we get anywhere?"

Bett added a stick figure to Twiss's drawing.

"I was born in a canoe," she said. "I'll probably die in one too."

"That's bad luck," Twiss said.

"No," Bett said. "That's Deadwater."

Twiss didn't know how much of what Bett said about Deadwater was true, but she chose to believe her cousin's stories the same way she chose to believe that the family who drowned in a boating accident last year was actually living at the bottom of the Wisconsin River.

Last June, the family was on a day trip when a storm came up on the river. The whitecaps swamped their johnboat and overturned it. The two children, girls in elementary school, were sitting on their orange life preservers instead of wearing them; either they weren't very smart or they didn't go out on the river very often. The parents didn't see the necessity of having life preservers for themselves and swam as well as you'd expect people to swim fully clothed. The father was wearing steel-toed boots. The mother was wearing heeled oxfords. The children were barefoot and stayed afloat the longest.

When Twiss imagined the family at the bottom of the river, she didn't see willowy spirits swaying like river grass; she saw a rosy-cheeked family sitting at a kitchen table made out of driftwood, discussing the day's plans.

"What shall we do today, dearest?" the mother would say to the father.

"Let's ask the children what they'd like to do," the father would say.

"We shall go for a walk," the younger girl would declare.

"And then we shall bake a cake!" the older one would add.

There were a lot of *shalls* in the river family's dialect. *Ice cream,* they'd say, when they were on the verge of negativity. *Moon pies.*

Twiss didn't share her exact imaginings with Bett (or Milly)—the outward part of her knew they were silly, but the inward part insisted they weren't. She decided to tell Bett the basics: that four people had drowned in the river.

"People are always drowning," Bett said. "Do you know how many people went under and didn't come back up when my town flooded? Deadwater wasn't always called Deadwater. It used to be Two Rivers. Before hydroelectric power came up north, when I was twelve."

Bett said that was before the government men in charge of constructing the dam got control of the water, when the lakes were still rivers and converged just above the town, careening like enemies. One day in late spring, after a week of torrential rain, the temporary dam broke and flooded everything within a twenty-mile radius. People crawled out of their windows and lived on top of their houses. They ate whatever happened to float by.

"My family was lucky," Bett said. "A jar of

beef jerky got stuck in our gutter one morning. Another family got a rocking chair."

"Did they eat it?" Twiss said.

"Well, they didn't rock in it."

Bett said most people took what they could and left. Bett's family and a handful of others stayed on. Bett said her father wasn't the type of person to leave a place just because it was underwater. After the water withdrew, they became unincorporated, which Bett said was another way of saying officially irrelevant. She said, "You're lucky to live where you do."

Which Twiss did feel lucky about. She didn't know how she could do without pine needles and black soil on a daily basis. And those were just two of the things that worked to complete her. Her overall feeling about Wisconsin had less to do with the obviously pleasant things about the state: the picturesque apple orchards in the fall, the spotted cows grazing on hillsides in the summer, and the lazy river oxbows that turned into skating rinks in the winter. She was one of the few people who loved Wisconsin for the mosquitoes and the blackflies, the leeches and the water snakes, the scent of manure rising on a still day.

Other people, namely Father Stone, the new priest, didn't see it that way. Father Stone had come from Illinois, which he said (and often) was more civilized than its northern neighbor.

Whenever he came out from behind the pulpit, he brought along his cross as if to ward off people. Twiss missed Father Rice. And even though Father Stone had read Father Rice's postcard out loud to make a point about the nature of sin, the words had made Twiss smile.

To the faithful folks at Lilly chapel, Father Rice had written from the Baja Peninsula. *I've had my first margarita today. Oh, the frosted glass! Ah, the salt! If only limes grew in Spring Green . . . Yours, Father Rice.*

After the first postcard, Father Rice sent a letter, this one from the south side of Chicago. According to Father Stone, who summarized the letter at the end of mass one day, Father Rice had lost all of the Sunday school money, as well as one of his legs, in Mexico. Father Stone said they had to decide if they wanted to raise the money to bring Father Rice back to Spring Green for his convalescence. Doing so, he said, would probably be the Christian thing to do, but he also said, "If one offers up his body to sin, he deserves to get stung by it."

"But he lost his leg!" Twiss had said, to which Father Stone had said, "A lost leg doesn't take away the sins of the rest of the body, my child."

"I'm not your child," Twiss said.

She spent a lot of time wondering which leg Father Rice had lost, in addition to the always-pressing activity of wondering how he'd lost it.

Twiss decided she'd let go of her left leg before her right one. When she was bored, she dragged it around like a cripple.

"That's not funny," Milly would say. "He probably can't walk the normal way."

But even she would eventually start laughing.

Bett didn't find Twiss as funny as other people did. It was as if she knew the outcome of whatever high jinks Twiss had begun before Twiss knew it. Twiss was always trying to come up with more daring ways to get Bett to notice her. Usually she went around trying to impress people merely for the sake of impressing them; with Bett, her motives were not altogether clear to her. To start, Bett was the only person she knew who wasn't afraid of something. Twiss's father was afraid of snakes. Her mother was afraid of the checkbook. Milly was afraid of being afraid. Even Twiss admitted a fear, however minor, from time to time. At the moment, she possessed a fear of earwigs. She'd also had a sinister feeling about crab apples lately.

One day when the three of them went to the river, Twiss came up with a way to test Bett by pretending to drown on their way to the sandbar. She wanted to see if Bett would save her and what it would feel like if she did.

When the three of them were halfway to the sandbar, swimming in their usual configuration (Bett in front, Milly in the middle, and Twiss trying her best to keep up in the back), Twiss started flailing more than usual, inhaled as much air as she could, and slipped beneath the surface. Twiss knew Milly would try to rescue her immediately, and had compensated by putting as much distance as she could between herself and Milly before she went under. "Help!" she gurgled on her way down.

Twiss was in the middle of congratulating herself when Bett grabbed hold of her waist and pulled her up to the surface. Twiss didn't even have a chance to run out of breath.

"I thought you knew how to swim," Bett said.

"I do," Twiss said, and started swimming toward the sandbar again.

Bett couldn't see that she was smiling.

Milly was still under the water. They didn't know it then, but her bathing suit was caught on something that was dragging her toward the bottom of the river. When she tried to call for help, she swallowed a mouthful of brown water. Bett and Twiss made it all the way to the sandbar before they realized she wasn't with them.

"Where's Miss Prim?" Bett said, wringing out her hair and tucking it behind her ears.

A sand crane circled over the middle of the river. The air smelled of fish.

"Your *sister,*" Bett said.

"Maybe she got her monthly," Twiss said.

She put a hand on her hip like she'd seen girls

do in school when they wanted a boy to notice them, but let it fall to her side just as quickly because Bett wasn't a boy and because Twiss wasn't the type of person to fawn over boys or girls.

Also, because Bett had frowned.

Twiss scanned the surface of the river. When she saw the branches from a fallen willow reaching up out of the water like fingers, she said, "I don't know" more seriously, and dropped the milkweed thistle she was twirling in her hand.

Twiss and Bett walked to the edge of the sandbar. They began calling for Milly in a leisurely way at first. Neither of them wanted to appear to be gullible if Milly were playing a trick on them. They expected Milly to pop out of the water just like they had a few minutes before, especially since she was the best swimmer out of the three of them. When Milly didn't answer them, they became more certain of themselves.

"Milly!" they said. "Mmmmiiiillleeee!"

When Milly still didn't answer, Bett jumped into the water.

Twiss didn't move. She was so stunned by the possibility that something bad was happening to Milly that, for the first time in her life, she couldn't move. The idea of Milly drowning in the river made Twiss think of an angel falling from the sky; Milly had two pink birthmarks the

107

size of dimes on her back, which always made Twiss think of wings.

"Aren't you coming?" Bett said from the middle of the river.

When Twiss didn't answer her, she yelled, "She's your *sister!*"

Bett didn't have any siblings because she said her father had preserved what was dead for too long to be able to create life. When Bett was younger and had begged for one, her father gave her a marmot he'd stuffed for a man from Wyoming.

"This is your brother, Christopher," he'd said, placing the marmot on Bett's pillow one night. "He doesn't talk much, so you'll have to pick up the slack there."

"You can love pretty much anything," Bett had told Twiss.

Usually, Twiss's body would tell her what to do, and her mind would trail along behind her like a loyal farm dog. Her instincts would bring light and speed to whatever was dark and slow, so that her body could navigate the terrain that unfolded in front of her. This time, her thoughts kept edging out her instincts. There was the word "sister," and there was Milly.

Without Milly, her father's *No, I will nots!* and her mother's *Yes, you wills!* would seem hopeless instead of hopeful (Milly said that exclamation points meant they still cared). That was one of the benefits of having such a positive sister; together, they made one regular person.

By the time Bett finally grabbed hold of Milly and pulled her to the surface, Twiss couldn't hear herself saying Milly's name, which made her wonder if she'd been saying it at all.

Bett had draped Milly across her back like a shawl.

That's when Twiss remembered Bett's asthma and her mother's threat to make Twiss breathe out of a straw for a week if she played a part in rousing it. Something about visualizing her mother allowed Twiss's body to take over once again. She pictured her mother with a hand on her hip, shaking her head. *Stop doing whatever you're doing! Don't, don't, don't,* which made Twiss want to do, do, do. As if by magic, her feet carried into the river. She followed Bett's instructions and grabbed hold of Milly's arms. Together, they dragged her onto the sandbar.

"What happened to her?" Twiss said, after they'd laid her out on the warm sand.

Milly's bathing suit was torn. Her legs were scratched raw.

"She isn't breathing," Bett said.

Bett put her mouth over Milly's—the way people did in the movies, except that no orchestral music swelled in the background and no stars fell from the sky. There was only the occasional low rattle from the sand crane perched on the beaver dam downriver and the unadorned expanse of blue above.

Bett exhaled until a swampy breath leaped back at her, and Milly opened her lovely green eyes. In a croaky voice, quite unlike her usual melodious one, Milly said, "Am I dead?"

"That depends," Bett said. "Did you see a white light?"

"I saw you," Milly said.

That night, the three of them sat in their bedroom in the quiet way they'd sat on the sandbar that afternoon while Milly got her breath and bearings back, which she was still doing and Twiss was still watching her do. Bett was sitting cross-legged on the rollaway cot between the beds combing out her tangled hair.

"Two sisters in one day," she said. "I should get a medal. One of those Bronze Stars."

"Those are for valor," Twiss said.

"I know," Bett said, glancing at Milly, who'd pulled a thick wool blanket up to her chin, despite the fact that the evening air was so humid the walls were sweating. The buck's head was also sweating; tiny yellow drops gathered like dew at his brow line.

Milly wasn't sick, but she wasn't well, either. Even though Bett had pulled her from the river hours ago, she was still shaking. Her scratches had turned bright red, then purple, then black where the blood had dried. Twiss had dabbed them first with salve, then with the sprigs of cooling witch hazel she'd found at the edge of the woods.

I'm sorry, her fingers said, but they wouldn't say what for.

"Truth," Bett said to Milly. She tore a knot out of her hair with her comb and placed it on the pillow beside her. "What did it feel like to almost die?"

"Consequence," Milly said in a voice still not quite her own.

"You just came back from the dead," Bett said. "Are you sure?"

"It's a game," Twiss said. "You don't have to play."

"The *dead,*" Bett said.

"Consequence," Milly said again, this time with more certainty.

Bett set down her comb. "You're going to regret saying that."

9

Milly and Twiss still occupied their childhood bedroom. They still slept in their old twin beds, the ones with fleurs-de-lis carved into the headboards, Milly with a plywood board under her mattress and Twiss without. When their parents died, they'd entertained the idea of separating, but neither of them had wanted to sleep on the bed their parents had once shared or the one they didn't. Besides, Milly had thought, there were worse things than sharing a room with Twiss, even if she did thrash around like a wild woman.

The summer Bett came to visit, she called Twiss "the tiger" and Milly "the lamb." Bett would throw her pillow at Twiss to get her to settle down. She'd throw her pillow at Milly to rile her up. "Are you even alive under there?"

Milly would hand Bett's pillow back as her reply.

"Now if we could only get your sister to stop growling," Bett would say. "I keep thinking she's going to turn over and bite me."

"She only does that when she's hungry."

Bett liked to get Milly to participate in her style of verbal banter, and whenever Milly did, Bett would congratulate her. "I knew it! No one can be that nice!"

Milly didn't see herself as being either nice or mean, but sometimes it was hard to know who you were without someone telling you.

"I'll tell you who you are," Milly's mother would say to Twiss when she'd done something wrong. When Twiss ate a handful of their mother's sugar cubes and denied doing it, for example, their mother said, "You're a thief and a liar, and it's only seven in the morning!"

When Twiss used their mother's nightgown to carry potatoes, she said, "You're like that farmer who harvested Mr. Peterson's alfalfa field. You take what isn't yours."

People were making predictions about what Mr. Peterson, the rightful owner of the field, was going to do about the misappropriation of his property. Mr. Sprye not only had harvested his field but also had bought a three-piece suit from Italy with the earnings. Mr. Peterson's delaying taking action made people believe blood might be spilled, even though he seemed like a good man—he'd helped their father, after all.

"Maybe there'll be a public hanging," Bett said.

"Or a shoot-out!" Twiss said.

"This is Wisconsin," Milly said. "If anything, there'll be a fair and speedy trial."

In eighth grade, she'd studied the Constitution. So had Twiss, though she'd balked at the idea of a bunch of men getting together to decide people's rights. "Where were all the women?" she'd said to her teacher.

"Betsy Ross sewed a *very* nice flag," the teacher said.

"At least we have the right to vote," Milly said.

"Hang voting," Twiss said. "I want to be the president!"

Milly liked to picture Twiss in the Oval Office, handing down orders and smoking cigars with foreign ministers. Twiss had a good voice for politics, a dramatic timbre.

"Good morning, my fellow American!" she'd say to Milly when they got out of bed each day. She'd use the carafe of water as a microphone. "How did you sleep, fairest senatoria?" After Bett came to stay with them, her morning announcements changed to include their cousin. "How did you sleep, Senatoria 1? Senatoria 2?"

"You're worse than an old man!" Bett said one morning in late June. "Have you seen the circles under my eyes? The red balloons? No one will ever want to marry me like this."

"Cucumbers help puffy eyes," Milly said, while she brushed out her hair at her dressing table. "Cold cloths, too."

Twiss started for the bathroom. "Why does everyone want to get married?"

"Because I don't want to be sleeping next to you for the rest of my life," Bett said.

She took the cold cloths Milly offered her, but they didn't bring down the puffiness beneath her eyes, nor did they take the redness out. No matter how many hours she spent on what she called the Great Beautification Project, Bett couldn't get her hair or the skin beneath her eyes to submit to her desires.

"Here," Milly said, offering Bett one of the

silver butterfly combs her mother had given her for her birthday. The combs came from the small stash of items in the bottom of her mother's jewelry box that had belonged to her mother since she was a girl. Before she and Aunt Gertrude had married for love and were cast out of the sphere of their immediate family, their father had given them each a set of sterling combs and dainty oval lockets with the words "For my darling" inscribed on the back. Her mother said she missed that—being called darling.

"It'll keep your hair out of your face," Milly said to Bett, who took the comb, but frowned when she saw the result in the mirror.

"You have no idea how pretty you are, do you?" she said to Milly. "You can have anyone you want." Bett stared out the south window at the green of the front lawn and the garden, the spread of clover and crabgrass, the twists of yellow squash vines. Then she looked out the north window at the pitchfork and the pile of brown manure, which was steaming in the morning light. "I'm going to be stuck with that."

Milly fixed Bett's hair for her and filed her nails like the women who worked in the beauty salon in town did. "This is the way the movie stars do their hair," she said, after she'd swept Bett's hair into a loose chignon. "At least in the magazines in the general store."

Bett looked at herself in the mirror. She didn't smile, but she didn't frown, either.

The two of them sat on Milly's bed and talked about their futures, how many children they wanted, whether they would be boys or girls and in what order. Milly wanted six and Bett wanted two. They laughed at the names the other one came up with.

Jacob was Milly's favorite for a boy. She pictured him having Asa's wheat hair and sky eyes. When Asa had come to mow and she'd handed him a glass of lemonade, a part of her, which she didn't even know existed until then, had wanted to jump onto the tractor with him.

Jacob Peterson. Milly Peterson. Mother. Wife.

Bett's favorite for a boy was Donaldio Maurice Winterberry III.

But when Twiss came back into the room, Bett jumped off Milly's bed and declared that Jacob was a stupid name. Whenever the three of them were together, Bett found a reason to dislike Milly. And quickly.

"You're the most passive of the passive people I know!" she said, biting one of the nails Milly had just filed for her. "I'd give up my firstborn to see you get angry just once."

"Milly doesn't get angry," Twiss said, while she rifled through the closet for her coveralls. "You could cut off her leg and she'd still ask if she could get you anything."

"Her lack of anger makes *me* angry. She'll never make it in Deadwater."

"I will, too," Milly said, though she'd begun to doubt the truth of that statement.

Bett's last story about Deadwater gave Father Stone's sermon about the difference between Civilized places and Uncivilized places some credence.

"There was a man who got lost in the bog, once," Bett had told them. "He walked for six days without food or water before he collapsed beside a badly injured bird."

With the last of his strength and because he was very, very hungry, the man began to devour the bird. He worked at the wings first, swallowing a tuft of black feathers without chewing before he moved on to the body and the legs, which snapped like matchsticks in his mouth. He continued to eat until he got to the bird's head, which was still quivering the way a chicken's head did on the butcher block just after it was chopped off. The bird cooed, which gave the man pause but did not stop him from putting the bird's head into his mouth and clamping down on the bones and feathers.

After that, the man was able to walk again. He found his way out of the bog and went home to his wife and children, who'd kept a candle burning in hope of his return. The man was overjoyed to see his family, and his family was overjoyed to see him. All of them were hoping to put the episode behind them.

"Daddy didn't die!" the children said, jumping up and down. "Daddy didn't die!"

That night, the man slept next to his wife as peacefully as a well-fed baby. He fell asleep with his arms around her, his lips pressed against the back of her neck, whispering some sweet and some not-so-sweet things into her ear.

In the morning, the wife woke up to a soft trilling sound, which she thought meant her husband wanted to embrace in more elaborate ways than the night before. She pinched her cheeks to give them color. She was glad she'd thought to put on her pretty white nightgown instead of the ragged brown one, but the eyelets in the white lace made her cold, and her husband's feet, which were entwined with hers, made her even colder. She felt a tug at one of the buttons at the back of her gown and heard another trill.

"Oh, Bill," she said. "Go and put some socks on. Your feet are freezing me solid."

Bill wouldn't put socks on, namely because he was dead; neither would the bloody head of the bird that had crawled out of his throat and across his lips onto the pillow.

"Oh, Bill," the bird said.

The woman shrieked, and then fainted. When

she came back to the world of consciousness, she was relieved because decapitated birds that talked were the stuff of dreams, and dreams didn't come true in Deadwater.

"Put some socks on," the bird said. "Your feet are freezing me solid."

The woman was so afraid that she followed the bird's instructions. She didn't know what else to do since her children were too young to protect her and her husband was too dead.

"Kiss me," the bird said, so the woman kissed the bird.

"I love you," the bird said.

"I love you, too," the woman said.

After a while, she got used to the bird cooing to her in the morning and cooing to her at night. Her husband had never been particularly romantic. He'd been the type of man who saved his affection for special occasions. The bird was more effusive.

"You look beautiful," the bird told her. It raised its eyebrows. "Embraceable."

Months passed in this way, and the woman grew to love the bird even more than she'd loved her husband. The children grew to love the bird, too, since he let them ruffle his feathers.

"We love you, Bird Daddy!" they'd say, while he made them pancakes or tucked them in at night. All the while, the husband was tucked away in the bedroom closet, turning as black as the feathers he'd swallowed in the bog.

• • •

In church that week, Milly said several prayers, all of which included the words *Please God, don't make me leave Spring Green.* She brought along a penny in case Father Stone was right and a cash donation was the only viable avenue to salvation.

Ever, she added when the basket came around.

Father Stone had begun to skip the part of the service where people turned to one another and said, "Peace be with you." He didn't light incense, either, though it was true his feet didn't smell. Although he always read from the Bible as smoothly as if he'd written the words himself, he chose menacing passages.

" 'Every living thing that moved on the earth perished—birds, livestock, wild animals, all the creatures that swarm over the earth, and all mankind.' "

That day, after Father Stone finished reading, he signaled to Mrs. Bettle to play "Thee We Adore, O Savior," which seemed to Milly too cheerful a hymn to follow the mass destruction of human life. He thanked Mrs. Bettle ahead of time for her rudimentary twanging.

"I'd like to see you play the organ," Mrs. Bettle said. "I don't care how Civilized you think you are. One note would expose you."

Mrs. Bettle got up from her seat at the organ. She put on her wide-brimmed, silk-flower-adorned hat and sat down heavily in the first row of pews. Her white stockings bunched around her ankles. Her ankles bunched around her shoes. She was younger than Milly and Twiss's mother, but dressed and moved like a grandmother.

"I'm tired of minor chords," she said. "For once, I'd like to sing about something other than God and His works. I'd like to sing about the streets of Manhattan or my parrot, Henry."

" 'Upon the wicked He shall rain snares!' " Father Stone said. " '*Fire and brimstone*, and a horrible tempest—this shall be the portion of their cup!' "

"What is brimstone exactly?" Twiss said.

"Damnation to hell," Milly whispered.

"It's like she's been waiting for someone to rescue her," Bett said, "and just today realized no one was going to do that."

"She's as ridiculous as the rest of them, if you ask me," Twiss said.

"Nobody's asking you," their mother said.

Father Stone smacked his Bible against the side of the pulpit. "Don't any of you care that you're going to hell?"

"So this one's kind of a pessimist then," Bett said.

Their mother, who was sitting next to Bett, started laughing. Usually, she had a high-pitched, floaty laugh. This morning, her laugh turned deep and guttural, the kind Milly had heard walking by the saloon. Their mother kept laughing until her entire body shook and she dropped her Bible and everyone stopped looking at Father Stone and started looking at her. When she finally regained her composure, after a short spell of hiccups, she picked up her Bible with one hand and reached for Bett's with the other.

"I haven't laughed that hard since—"

She squeezed Bett's hand.

"My God, I don't think I've ever laughed that hard."

After mass was over, Bett and their mother invited Mrs. Bettle back to the house for supper, which Milly offered to make since her mother was tired of sticking her face into a hot oven in a hot kitchen in a hot house.

"It's weird," Twiss said to Milly. "They're two letters apart from being the same."

"Who?" Milly said.

"Mrs. Bettle and Bett."

Milly put her hand on her sister's shoulder. "You're just jealous."

"Aren't you?" Twiss said.

While two of them waited outside for their mother, Mrs. Bettle, and Bett, Twiss gathered a handful of brown tulips and amused herself with the petal game.

Supper will be good. Supper will be lousy. Supper will be good.

Milly was trying to think of what she could make out of milk—their father had been told he was allowed to take home as much as he wanted from the dairy (as well as butter), which made him want a lot of it, although he claimed he only wanted it so Milly could bake for Asa. "What would you make with it?" Milly asked Twiss.

"I'd pour it in a glass and drink it," Twiss said.

If they were alone, Milly and Twiss would have taken their usual shortcut through the field and across Mill Creek, although it really wouldn't have been a shortcut because Twiss would have wanted to hunt down the leeches that lived beneath the stones and play with them, maybe even stick one to the milkiest part of her body for a joke. Milly would have bit her lip to keep it from quivering as she stepped over the bright green algae, the slippery black stones; like most people, she was afraid of having anything suck her blood.

So today, thankfully, they stayed on the road, and watched the wavery heat mirages that formed in the dips ahead. They listened to their mother, Mrs. Bettle, and Bett talk about why women should be allowed to be priests.

"We're a lot warmer than men," their mother said.

Mrs. Bettle fanned herself with her hat. "At least when we have our monthlies."

"What about the sausage fingers?" Bett said. "I get to feeling so fat."

"I bet *you* were never fat," Mrs. Bettle said to Milly.

"She's always had just the right amount of everything," their mother said. "That's why I named her Milly. Pretty women always do better with ugly names."

Mrs. Bettle nodded as if she knew what the consequences of their father's selection would have been. "I never cared for dainty names myself. I'm originally German. We like more stoic arrangements of the alphabet."

"What about me?" Twiss said.

"One of the nurses in the hospital named you."

"You don't even know which one?" Twiss said.

Twiss kicked the ochre-colored gravel on the road with the tips of her church shoes, which were badly scuffed from previous occasions of hurt feelings. "What was Dad doing?"

"It was a Sunday afternoon," their mother said. "What do you think he was doing?"

Everyone knew the answer, but nobody said it out loud. "Golf," a word that used to roll off their tongues as easily as water, now got stuck in each of their throats like phlegm, which women were taught to swallow instead of cough up.

"I bet he played the best game of his life in honor of me!" Twiss said to their mother with her chin pointed high up in the air, just after they'd turned onto their driveway.

"Ask him," their mother said, as if it were a consequence.

Twiss stared at the barn. "Milly needs help with supper. It'd be selfish to leave her alone in the kitchen to wait on all you trolls!" She ran all the way down the driveway to the front porch and into the house.

After the screen door slammed, their mother said, "No one wants to know the truth around here."

Mrs. Bettle took her hand. "No one wants to know the truth anywhere."

Milly and Bett walked behind the two of them, their hands fixed to their sides.

"What's wrong with your dad?" Bett said.

"He can't play golf anymore," Milly said. "I mean not as well as he used to."

"So can't a million other people," Bett said. "But they don't lock themselves in barns."

"It's not locked," Milly said.

While Milly and Twiss made supper inside, Mrs. Bettle, Bett, and their mother sat at the table on the porch. Their mother opened a bottle of apple brandy that one of the members of the golf course had given their father after he'd helped shorten the man's game. The label said MADE IN FRANCE—which was the only reason their mother allowed it in the house.

"Fire and brimstone!" Mrs. Bettle said, gesturing wildly.

"No salvation for you!" their mother said.

"Or you!" Bett said. "He sure has got a stick up his—"

"Arse!" Mrs. Bettle said, and then covered her mouth with her hand. "You'll have to excuse me. Those are my roots speaking."

"I thought you were German," Bett said.

Their mother poured another finger of brandy for Mrs. Bettle and another fingernail for Bett. "I've seen the Eiffel Tower!" she said. "I've been to France!"

"Here we go," Twiss said.

While their mother told Mrs. Bettle and Bett about her trip to France when she was a girl— *Oh, Champs-Elysées!*—Milly hauled out a bottle of milk from the refrigerator and a sack of dried kidney beans from the pantry. She opened her recipe book, looking for something to make out of the available ingredients: milk, flour, butter, and kidney beans. When she didn't find a recipe, she decided to do what every woman in the country did when she lacked materials: bake a pie. Not every woman would have made a kidney bean pie, though.

Milly sent Twiss out to the garden for tomatoes, which were still small, hard, and a little bit green but would do all right in a baked dish. The robins were already going after them, clearing pathways for the fruit worms. Protective coverings, which most women in Spring Green made out of stockings, would have kept both away, but Milly's mother said there were only enough stockings to go on legs in their family, so the plants would have to bear the indiscretions done to them while they bore fruit this summer.

"I'd rather go to the guillotine," Twiss said, on her way out. "How can Bett stand it?"

"The apple brandy?"

"Her," Twiss said, letting the screen door slam shut.

Milly went to work on her piecrust. After she'd rolled out the bottom layer and then the top one, she moved on to the kidney beans. She didn't know that the beans had to be soaked in warm water overnight and then cooked for several hours otherwise they'd upset the digestive tract —*to the point of tears,* Milly would read later in the cookbook. She plucked a sprig of thyme from her herb box on the windowsill and dropped it, along with the beans, into the pie.

Poor things, she said to her herbs, stroking their leaves, which were soft as feathers.

Twiss had knocked over the herb box when their father came into the kitchen unexpectedly the day before. "Don't mind me," he'd said, swooping in like nothing had changed. He ignored the soil on the floor and opened the cupboard.

"I came for a cube of sugar!" he said in a voice louder and more dramatic than his regular one. Milly and Twiss still saw their father every day, but they hadn't seen him enter the house except to say that he wouldn't be entering the house anymore the day before Cousin Bettie arrived from Deadwater. If they needed him, they were supposed to go to the barn.

"What do you do about your clothes out there?" Twiss asked, as their father took down the tin of their mother's special sugar cubes from the cupboard. She was scooping up soil from the floor and dropping it back into the herb box. "Your silk golf shirts."

"They're hanging in the rafters," their father said. "It's a lot easier to locate things that way. It's also nice because everything smells like hay."

"What about bathing?" Milly said.

"A rusty wash bucket suited our forefathers fine," their father said. "Lincoln was from Kentucky. Nothing but forests back then. The future."

"Actually, our forefathers had bathtubs," Milly said, because neither she nor Twiss could scrape together the courage to ask their father why he'd decided to live in the barn. They couldn't help but feel implicated since the house was where they, too, resided. *I'd live in the barn if I had to be married to her!* Twiss had said. Their mother had said that men were at their absolute worst when they were in the process of losing something, which Milly suspected was the observation closest to being right. None of them knew how bad his worst would get, though.

"I'll bet the servants didn't have bathtubs," their father said.

He was speaking even more loudly than before and was looking toward the staircase, toward the door to their mother's bedroom, their parents' old bedroom, the recollection of which seemed as far away now to Milly as the words "once upon a time." She didn't know if she should tell her father that her mother had gone into town.

What she wanted to say was, *Sarcasm doesn't become you.*

"I'm not too proud to join the ranks of a servant," he said. "I work with a man who has no teeth and another who drinks milk right from the udder. It's my ambition to end up in one of the shacks by the river. That's the only way I could be happy."

There was that word again.

The pantry door opened, and Bett stepped out from behind it with a broom and a dustpan, which she handed to Twiss. "Aunt Margaret's not here," she said to their father.

Their father returned the tin of sugar cubes to its place in the cupboard. He smiled at Bett, but frowned at his girls. "Why didn't you two say so? I wouldn't have gone on like that."

• • •

The kidney bean pie turned out worse than Milly expected; eating it felt a little like eating gravel. "I think I broke a tooth!" their mother said.

"I hope it falls out," Twiss said.

"Contrary for the sake of contrary," Mrs. Bettle said. "I don't envy you that, Margaret."

Bett looked toward the road. "Praise the Lord!" she said to Milly. "I've been waiting and waiting for your consequence to come, and here he is shifting gears on the hill right now."

"Who's coming where?" Milly's mother said.

"There!" Bett said, pointing to the road.

The moment Milly saw the John Deere cresting the hill, she felt like she might tip over even though all the legs of her chair were planted firmly on the porch. She knew what was coming, what had been coming ever since Bett pulled her out of the river.

Bett had made her sign an IOU.

I, Milly, hereby promise to follow through with whatever consequence Bett thinks up for me, even if I deem said consequence unsuitable to my personality or my personal values. X (signed) Milly

Bett walked over to Milly. The others kept talking, but Milly couldn't hear what they were saying anymore. All she could hear was the consequence Bett whispered into her ear, and all she could smell was Bett's breath, which reminded Milly of the scraps of vegetables she spread over the garden as fertilizer.

"I can't do that," Milly said.

"Too bad," Bett said, wheezing a little between each word.

Ever since church that morning Bett had been coughing. Humid places weren't supposed to be good for her asthma. Neither was exercise. In lieu of a trip to the doctor, Milly's mother had offered Bett her drawer of handkerchiefs and her wool shawl.

"He only runs on so much credit before he stops running," she'd said. "It's the same with the butcher. Last week, he suggested I take in his wash to pay for a roast. All the lye in the world wouldn't get the blood out of those aprons."

"Let's go," Bett said to Milly.

"I'm going by myself," Milly said as firmly as she could.

"Then I want proof."

"What kind?"

Bett whispered into Milly's ear.

"I don't like secrets," Mrs. Bettle said. "That's why I live with a bird and not a man."

"That's the reason?" Twiss said.

Milly put on her muck boots. When no one was looking, she took one of Bett's handkerchiefs from the table and walked out to the meadow.

• • •

Asa had parked the tractor and had climbed down to adjust the blades. As she got closer to him, Milly saw the lines of sweat streaking his shirt, the pale fuzz on the back of his neck. The muscles in his arms and shoulders grew taut as he lowered the blades to the level of the grass, which made her blush though she didn't know why.

"Hello," she said, hoping that Asa wouldn't hear her, but also hoping that he would.

As much as Milly loved seeing Asa on that tractor, a part of her dreaded the days he came to mow, not only because her father made her go out to him with cookies and lemonade and watched her closely the entire time, but also because on those nights, Bett and Twiss would trick her into talking about Asa, and Milly would fall for their tricks. Milly understood Twiss's reasons for teasing her—Twiss didn't want to lose her—but she never understood Bett's.

Bett would start innocently enough. "I heard Milly was talking to someone in the meadow the other day. I heard she baked him a red velvet cake shaped like a heart."

"I heard she did more than that," Twiss would say.

"With Mr. Peterson."

"She likes them old, yep, she does."

"Wrinkly," Bett would say.

"Hairy."

"Pruney!"

When Milly could no longer stand the teasing, she'd pull her blanket over her head and say, "It wasn't Mr. Peterson I was talking to, it was Asa! And it wasn't red velvet cake; it was butter cookies! They weren't shaped like hearts, either."

And then the laughter would come, and Milly would know she'd been fooled into giving up another part of herself that she preferred to keep secret. The night she first told them about how much she admired Asa's work ethic (when she really just meant him), Bett and Twiss had made fun of her, and of Asa's slight stutter.

"M-M-May I eat one of your cookies?"

"Y-Y-Yes, you may."

"M-M-May I love you like coconut flakes?"

"L-L-Love me like coconut flakes, you may."

They laughed when they said the word "love," but that was the word Milly had begun to think about—the possibility of it—whenever she was with Asa and, even more often, when she was without him. The word was with her when she pinned clothes to the line, or scrubbed the linoleum, or baked a pie. Sometimes, when no one was looking, she'd trace an A into a well of flour or hold a mop as though she were holding Asa's hand.

"Hello," Asa said, shading his eyes against the sun.

Milly thought about what Bett had told her to say and knew that she couldn't make her tongue do what Bett wanted it to do—her brain wouldn't allow her tongue to get stuck on a hard consonant for the sole purpose of amusing her cousin—but she also knew now, as she looked back at the porch and saw Bett doubled over the railing at the beginning of another coughing cycle, what she could do.

"My cousin's sick," she said to Asa, holding out Bett's handkerchief so that he could see it. Even though Milly had folded the handkerchief into a neat square, the drops of blood on the inside were still visible. "Will you do something for me?

"For her," she added.

"I guess I mean for both of us."

Milly whispered her request into Asa's ear, even though there was no one else around to hear. "Thank you," she said when she'd finished speaking, accidentally grazing his ear with her lips, after which Asa started the tractor and drove back through the meadow and back down the road as quickly as he'd come up it. He kept touching the ear that Milly had whispered into, which made her wonder about her breath.

When Milly returned to the porch, Bett snatched the handkerchief out of her hand.

"What did you do?" she said.

"Nothing," Milly said.

"You're a worse liar than Twiss. You still owe me a consequence."

The others were plotting ways to dethrone Father Stone and restore Father Rice to his former position as the priest of Lilly chapel. They'd need money, for certain.

"The Sewing Society's raised more than I've made in my entire life," Mrs. Bettle said. "It's too bad they're the ones who helped choose Father Stone. He's a cousin of a cousin."

"It would truly be a shame to have to go against them," their mother said, smiling.

"They tried to give me a winter coat last year," Mrs. Bettle said. "A great big, feathery thing. I looked like a chicken. My cats attacked me. Henry started to cluck. It took me the rest of the winter to undo that. Parrots are smart, you know."

"How do you think Father Rice lost his leg?" Twiss said.

Their mother set down the bottle of apple brandy. "The Society has his latest letters. They're supposed to be quite blasphemous."

"I *love* blasphemy," Twiss said.

"I know you do," their mother said, patting her hand.

Milly got up to get a plate of pie for her father, who still ate whatever was prepared for the rest of the family, just in the privacy of the barn. After everyone went to bed, he'd walk from the barn to the house and leave his plate on the top step of the porch like a drifter between railroad stops. Even when Milly's mother cooked milk and vegetables down to a soggy mess, his plate would be cleaned and his silverware set neatly aslant like people did in fancy restaurants when they were finished with their meals.

"I made you supper," Milly said when she reached the front door of the barn. She knocked twice before her father appeared at the entrance.

"Let me just wash up," he said, wiping grease from his hands onto his good trousers.

Usually, Milly left his plate on the tree stump next to the barn door and went back to the house. Today, she waited for him to rinse his hands and face at the water pump beside the barn because she knew what was coming. Even though she knew asking the favor of Asa had been the right thing to do, she didn't want to see the look on Bett's face when what she'd asked for finally arrived. She thought about her lips grazing Asa's ear and touched them with the tip of her tongue. She was surprised to find that they tasted like salt.

When her father returned, the collar of his shirt was soaked through but his hands and his face were still black. He glanced at the container of turpentine just inside the door, but picked up the plate of food instead.

"This looks delicious," he said.

Milly sat on the maple stump while her father

worked at his piece of pie. The sun was beginning to set, stretching pink fingers of light across the sky. The air was hot and wet and unlikely to cool much overnight; they were beginning to reach the point in the summer where heat stopped leaving the walls at night. Theirs was one of the few houses that didn't have a screened sleeping porch attached to the second floor. At least once every summer, Milly and Twiss would haul their blankets onto the regular porch, bed down, and be back in the house a minute later. Like the wolf spiders in Deadwater, by the end of June the mosquitoes in Spring Green were also as big and furry as birds. By August, their bites did as much damage to the flesh as the bites of beavers to logs. The people who used lemon oil to repel them had welts up and down their arms and legs. The people who used camphor did a little bit better.

Milly walked over to the pump and filled the tin cup hanging from it with water. "You won't hurt my feelings if you say the truth," she said, handing the cup to her father.

"The truth?" her father said in his old tone of voice. He scraped the last bit of kidney bean pie onto his fork and drew it to his mouth. When he finished, he laid his silverware across the plate horizontally and picked up the cup of water, which he drank from until it was empty.

"I'm miserable," he said, wiping his mouth with the sleeve of his favorite golf shirt.

10

When Twiss saw the goldfinch peeking out of her pocket, she remembered what she was doing in the meadow, but didn't feel the kind of relief that one might expect from knowing where you are and where you're going. Reorienting herself to the present moment, the ordinariness of it, felt to her a little like being robbed. According to her chore list, she was supposed to feed the chickens. Milly had already retrieved the eggs. She'd mentioned something about egg salad, if she could round up a jar of pickles in the cellar.

"A change might do us good," she'd said, which had made Twiss laugh.

"Nothing like old pickles to oust us from routine."

Twiss fed the chickens, each of whom she called Raoul because she couldn't tell them apart, and swept up the droppings on the floor. Under the feed trough, she spotted a golf ball and slipped it into her pocket. Twiss had broken the main window so many times that neither she nor Milly saw the use in repairing it anymore. Twiss had covered it with plastic and secured the corners with electrical tape. The lattice of wood was the only element still in place, bisecting the frame like a crossword puzzle—another game Twiss had never possessed the patience for.

She'd flip through the newspaper until she got to the answers, which were positioned upside down on the last page to deter the person prone to cheating.

Hinge: A five-letter word for a movable joint used to fasten two things together.

"I'd like to know who makes these things up," she'd said to Milly that morning.

Milly said the key to the answers, more than the clues, was the arrangement of the squares. "You have to think like the puzzle maker to know how everything fits together."

"I don't want anything to do with a person whose thoughts fit into neat little squares."

Milly took the crossword puzzle from Twiss. "A five-letter word for a musical instrument typically found in churches? *Organ.*"

"I'd have gotten it if you'd have said Beetle," Twiss said.

"How can you still call her that?" Milly said.

"How can she still be alive? She's got to be on her ninth life by now. Tenth, if you count the time she fell in the tub."

"Poor Henry," Milly said.

"Yes, poor Henry," Twiss said. "He had to see her naked. Who wants to see an old body?"

"You've seen me naked, too," Milly said.

Which was true. When Milly got her hip replaced with a titanium one, the nurse had made her wear a cotton gown without ties. The hospital in Madison was supposed to be better than the one in Sauk, although neither of them was convinced.

"Go home," Milly had said after her surgery, which didn't go as smoothly as planned. Her heart rate had dipped down so low that the doctors warmed up a defibrillator and shocked her twice to keep her going. When Milly's heart had stabilized, she was transferred to a room that overlooked a playground. Children came and went all day, jumping on the bright yellow slide and hanging from the swings, laughing in the delicious way only children are capable of.

"They'll shock me if my heart gets out of line again," Milly said.

Twiss was sitting on the edge of Milly's bed, giving her the first of many pedicures in the weeks to come. She'd never painted her own nails, and her lack of skill was reflected in the uneven globs of pale pink polish that adorned each of Milly's toenails.

"Really," Milly said. "Stop fussing. I'll be fine. Go home."

Twiss blew on Milly's toenails one by one. "I am home."

What an unsatisfactory little word! Now that

she was old, Twiss understood why people her age stopped speaking and started sitting on porches. Language failed to describe the simplest of phenomena; a fine sunset, for example, was more than fine. There were no words, or Twiss couldn't find them anymore, for the way the colors made her feel. She'd say to Milly, "It's an especially pretty one tonight," when she meant that it reminded her of other sunsets, and years, and people who had nothing to do with sunsets: pinks and reds and blues.

"It is," Milly would say. Or she might add a word like "lovely" or "otherworldly" and then Twiss would know that Milly, too, was thinking about something else entirely as they passed a glass of iced tea back and forth and gazed at the changing colors of the sky.

11

When Twiss was a girl, language was language as a sunset was a sunset. There was no need or time to give either much thought once a word came across her lips or the sky emptied of color for the night. Words were vehicles that got her where she wanted to go. She didn't pick them for their nuances. She picked them for their shock value.

"Father Stone's a pigheaded bigot!" she'd said to Mrs. Bettle, Bett, and her mother the night Milly made kidney beans and, for the first time in her life, made everyone suffer. "If anyone should *ferme sa bouche*, it's him!"

"C'est vrai!" her mother said that evening on the porch, on one of the rare occasions she and Twiss were getting along.

That night, Mr. Peterson and his doctor arrived in a shiny black car, which seemed like the kind of car a king would drive. In the early evening light, the fender shone more brightly than the silver serving platter her mother polished every week, though she never used it.

Bett had gone upstairs complaining of a stomachache, but it was Bett whom Mr. Peterson and the doctor wanted to see. The doctor fingered the stethoscope around his neck. Mr. Peterson fingered a tiny ring that would no more fit his fingers than it would a woman's.

"I can't abide a child being sick," Mr. Peterson said. "Where's the little girl?"

"She's *eighteen,*" Twiss said to him.

"You must be younger than that," Mr. Peterson said, smiling lightly.

"Twiss is fourteen," her mother said.

"That's an unusual name," Mr. Peterson said.

"A nurse named me," Twiss said, smirking.

Her mother showed him and the doctor up to the bedroom Bett was sharing with her and

Milly for the summer. Her mother kept picking up stray items as they went along—Twiss's Sunday dress, which Twiss had thrown on the stairs the moment they got back from church, her Sunday shoes, and the blue ribbon she'd been forced to wear in her hair. Mrs. Bettle, who was still tipsy from the brandy, attempted to level the crooked pictures on the wall and knocked over a glass paperweight that crashed to the floor, but didn't break.

If Twiss had been the one to drop the paperweight, she would have had to stay in her room until she'd pieced it back together or come up with the money to buy a new one, but her mother ignored Mrs. Bettle. She explained to Mr. Peterson and the doctor that Bett had come down from the North and was staying with them for the summer, which led to her admitting that they couldn't afford a doctor's visit, but she knew Bett needed one.

"My sister Gertrude didn't send her down with any money," she said. "Her husband's out of work right now. They live in the bush."

"No, they live in Deadwater," Twiss said.

"Deadwater is the bush," her mother said.

"I lost a child once because I was poor," Mr. Peterson said. "I won't lose another."

He smelled like bay rum, which Twiss's father used to wear when he still worked at the golf course. The scent was the only link Twiss could detect between the two men, other than their link of boss and employee. Mr. Peterson was taller than her father, and broader in the shoulders, but it wasn't just his body that took up the majority of the hallway; it was his unwavering resolve, as well as his finely tailored suit, which Twiss wasn't positive stemmed from having so much money, but suspected was the case.

Twiss's mother knocked on the bedroom door, a courtesy she didn't usually grant any of them. When Bett told her to come in, she swung the door open wide enough so that Mr. Peterson and the doctor could fit through at the same time.

Though Twiss was standing behind Mrs. Bettle, who was standing behind her mother, she was still able to see Bett curled up on the cot, coughing into one of the handkerchiefs her mother had given her. Bett was wearing the nightgown Milly had lent her when hers disintegrated in the wash bucket the day before. Whatever color Bett's face lacked, the tiny purple lilacs, which trailed from the bodice of Milly's nightgown down to the hem, made up for. In the dim light of the bedroom, Twiss couldn't see the red half-moons beneath Bett's eyes or the puffiness in Bett's face, the wonderful sprawling veins she'd seen at the supper table. In this light, her cousin looked syrupy sweet. Pretty even, which disappointed Twiss since beauty wasn't the beauty of her cousin; ever since Bett had stuck her hands into the sandpile and the ground bees had swarmed all around her, Twiss had had trouble describing what was, although she knew one thing for certain: anyone else would have been stung.

Mr. Peterson went to Bett's side. Once Bett granted him permission he stroked her forehead. "I've brought my personal doctor," he said to her. "He wields his stethoscope like a magic wand. May he have a look at you, my dear?"

"It's my stomach," Bett said, casting her covers aside and uncurling herself. "It feels too full or too empty, I don't know which."

"We'll fix that," Mr. Peterson said.

"My lungs are bad, too," Bett said. "They won't let me do anything I want to do."

Which was news to Twiss. So far, Bett's lungs had allowed her to go swimming and stick her hands into a giant beehive and drag Milly from the river as if she were as light as a dime.

The doctor came forth and placed his stethoscope over the lilacs at the back of Bett's nightgown. After that, he motioned to everyone except Mr. Peterson to exit the room.

"In the interest of privacy," he said, which no one in their house had ever benefited from. He opened his medical kit and laid out several instruments that Twiss didn't recognize on the night table beside the cot. One of them looked like a shoehorn.

Mr. Peterson and the doctor stayed an hour with Bett before the door opened and they emerged from the bedroom. Twiss's mother had made Twiss and Mrs. Bettle go downstairs with her, so that they didn't seem like they were trying to listen in.

"Why won't you let me put a glass to the door?" Twiss said.

"Because fourteen's too old for that," her mother said. "What I'm wondering is how Mr. Peterson knew Bett was sick. Could people be talking about it?" She glanced at the chair that Milly usually sat in, as if its emptiness had answered her question before she'd finished asking it. "That boy better marry her if we're to endure this."

Mrs. Bettle yawned.

"Go tell your father to take Mrs. Bettle home," Twiss's mother said.

"But I'll miss *everything*," Twiss said.

"Then you better hurry," her mother said.

When Twiss heard the bedroom door open, she ran to the barn as fast as she could. Milly and her father were sitting on two tree stumps outside of it.

"That was smart what you did today in the meadow," her father said to Milly, which made Milly blush and then blush all over again.

"I did it for her," Milly said. "Not for myself."

"Everything we do is for ourselves," their father said. "That doesn't take away the goodness of the act, though. I'm sure Asa didn't mind the attention at all."

"Mom wants you to take Mrs. Bettle home!" Twiss said, because she was sick of hearing about Asa. "Mr. Peterson's here with his doctor. They're listening to Bett's lungs."

"We saw Mr. Peterson drive up," Milly said.

"Then why didn't you come?" Twiss said.

Before Milly could answer, their father stood up. "I'll drive Mrs. Bettle home on one condition," he said to Twiss. "That you come with me."

"What about Milly?" Twiss said.

"She needs her rest."

"I'm the one who's had to listen to the Beetle all night!" Twiss said.

"Then twenty more minutes won't hurt you," her father said.

Even though their parents no longer spoke to each other, they had a similar way of speaking when they wanted Twiss to do something she didn't want to do. She didn't know if all parents spoke this way or if, despite their current (and forever?) dislike for each other, her mother and father's linguistic habits had rubbed off on each other.

"You sound like her," Twiss said.

"That's because I didn't say what you wanted to hear," her father said, brushing pie crumbs from his pants. "We'll be home before you could sprint to the front door."

• • •

But they weren't.

After they dropped Mrs. Bettle off, her father drove into town. When Twiss asked where they were going, he said, "I want to see something."

Twiss hadn't been back to the golf course since just after the Accident, when her father had played his first round of golf back like an amateur. After that dismal round, he didn't invite her along again and she didn't ask to go with him. Twiss had felt a kind of embarrassment for him that she couldn't explain then, but understood now as they entered the course by way of the maintenance road when they used to drive through the front gates like everyone else.

People had always looked up to her father when he was playing golf—they asked him for advice about the game and looked him in the eye when they shook his hand; at those times, it didn't matter that the members had more money than he would ever have, because he knew how do something that they didn't know how to do. Twiss had always held her head as high as her father's. *That's my dad!* she'd think, when people stopped their own games to admire his.

That day on the course, after he'd missed several easy shots that even Twiss could have made (well, at least Milly could have made them), she averted her eyes.

"I don't understand," he kept saying.

Twiss didn't understand either. Even though he squared up for the shots the way he always had, the ball didn't go where it usually went. By the seventeenth hole, he'd lost his swing and his temper. When his ball landed between two of the moguls, he threw his club so high in the air that Twiss thought it might never come down.

"Golf was the only thing I was good at," he said, when the club, his beloved Persy, finally landed in the stream and sank to the bottom.

Twiss understood then that it was his singular vision that had made him such a skilled golfer, the way he lived and breathed in terms of it. She also understood that without it, he would be regular, which neither Twiss nor her father was ready to accept.

"Maybe Rollie changed the moguls while you were in the hospital," she said.

"Of course!" her father said.

He grew cheerful. "Changes are supposed to be cleared through me. No one else has the authority. I'm still the only one who's ever played a perfect game around here."

Of course Rollie hadn't changed anything—they both knew that—but the idea that he might have instilled in them a kind of hope that what had been lost could be recovered.

When her father turned off the headlights and began to motor over the course illegally, whatever hope Twiss had been maintaining dissolved once again. She slumped down low in her seat. "We could get in trouble," she said to her father.

"You sound like Milly," her father said.

They drove over the neatly clipped grass, the rhythmic dips and rises of earth that had been constructed to make the course more challenging.

"Do you feel that?" her father said. "Every two seconds. Unless it's just rained. Then it's three." He inhaled and exhaled deeply. *"God, I've missed this—"*

Before her father drove off the bridge, he was working on a design for the eighteenth hole. The Grand Finale, he called it, and he had left intricate sketches all over the house. Hole by hole, he wanted to create a course that would attract players from around the world. He imagined the expensive gifts he'd be given for having the nerve to design such a beautiful—here, he meant difficult and ingenious—course.

"Moisture collects in the dips," her father said, motioning to the patches of fog the headlights illuminated when he turned them on. "They have their own weather patterns."

Twiss knew the weather didn't work quite like that, but she'd forgotten the exact words her textbook used to describe where rain came from and she didn't want to discourage her father, who parked the car next to the seventeenth hole, which had no flag pin in it since the course was closed for the evening. There was something sad about the way that empty hole shone in the orange headlights that a golf ball wouldn't fix. Inside the car, the air smelled of freshly cut grass and the fertilizer Rollie used to ensure no brown spots appeared in August. Even in drought years, the greens glowed like emeralds.

"I love her," Twiss's father said. "Just so you know."

He took a tape measure from the glove box and got out of the car. Why, then, had he moved into the barn? Why did he send the notes he sent? The last one, which he'd addressed to Twiss's mother, had said, *Because I don't love you!*

Twiss sat in the car until her father opened her door.

"Hold this end," he said, handing her the tape measure.

Twiss did what she was told, but hoped Rollie would discover them. This time, though, she didn't crave cold cream-soda fizz on her tongue. She craved the presence of someone who understood the importance of golf to her father, and who understood the importance of her father to her. Rollie had a way of putting things. If he saw them on the course, he might say, "Go home, Joseph. Button should be in bed by now. She needs her sleep."

"I am home," her father might say.

Rollie might pat her head like he used to when she was little.

He might say, "You only think you're home."

But Rollie neither appeared out of the shadows cast by the pine trees at the edge of the course nor told her father what he would not have wanted to hear. The maintenance shed was dark, save for the moon, which illuminated the wavery old window glass and the mowing equipment stored just beyond.

"I'm tired," Twiss told her father. "I should be in bed by now. I need my sleep."

A long piece of white measuring tape connected them. The sweat on Twiss's neck had dried, and her clothes no longer stuck to her skin. For the first time all summer, and even though the temperature hadn't changed, she had goose bumps.

"I'm cold," she added.

"Put one of my shirts on," her father said. "There's one in the car."

Twiss set her end of the tape measure on the ground and went back to the car for her father's shirt, which she found crumpled in the backseat. The shirt was made of slate blue silk, soft as the down pillow stuffing she'd replaced with pine needles the moment her mother had relented. Though it fit her father perfectly, the ends of it hung to Twiss's knees. On her, the shirt resembled the smocks her art teacher made them wear so their clothes would stay clean.

"My art teacher says I have talent," Twiss told her father, thinking of her last piece. Although she usually preferred to draw gory things like bloody axes and pus balls, for the last project of the quarter her teacher had asked them to draw a picture of what happiness felt like. Twiss drew a flock of all different kinds of birds—red, blue, gray, green—taking flight from the top branches of an old-growth pine tree. When her teacher asked her to explain the drawing, Twiss said to her happiness felt like freedom. Sadness felt like the opposite.

Once, when Twiss was six years old, she was walking through the woods and came upon a cardinal with only one wing. Though she'd seen plenty of injured animals in her life, none made Twiss sadder than that bird, that loss of flight. She'd run to the house to make a wing for it, which she fashioned out of red construction paper, but by the time she returned it had died.

"I thought you wanted to be a champion golfer," her father said.

"I do," Twiss said, when she meant *I used to.* Ever since her father had taken the job with Mr. Peterson and had stopped playing golf, she realized golf wasn't what she'd loved.

"Art could be a backup," she said.

"You can't have a backup if you want to be a champion," her father said, motioning for her to pick up the measuring tape again. "What does the tape say?"

"Thirteen feet, two and a half inches."

"Excellent!" her father said.

In his excitement, he let go of his end of the tape. Before Twiss could let go of her end, the tape snaked its way back to her, hissing as it entered the metal casing. The end of it snapped at her fingers like teeth and drew blood the same way.

Twiss and her father were mostly quiet on the drive home, Twiss sucking blood from the cuts on her fingers and her father glancing at the measuring tape the way he'd once glanced at Persy on her mother's birthday all those years ago.

"Why didn't you let go?" her father said.

Though the car was warm, and her skin sticky again, Twiss didn't take off her father's shirt. "I tried to," she said, holding her fingers away from the material so she wouldn't bleed on it. As they went over the bridge and the river, Twiss stuck her fingers out the window. On the black water, the moon looked like a giant silver coin.

"The older you get, the more like your sister you become," her father said. "Milly's incapable of seeing what's in front of her."

"I'm the one who needs glasses," Twiss said.

"You have my eyes," her father said.

When they arrived home, her father parked the car in front of the barn. The car had been cleaned and repaired after the Accident, but the engine still made mysterious noises after it was shut off and it still smelled like fish even though the last of them had been removed.

Twiss and her father got out of the car.

"I was just joking about Milly," her father said, opening the door to the barn.

Twiss had heard more jokes after the Accident than she'd heard her whole life, except that the post-Accident jokes weren't really jokes. None of them was funny.

"You could come in for a while," Twiss said, but her father had already said good night.

Or I could, she thought as she walked across the grass to the front door.

Inside the house, her mother was listening to opera music on the radio and putting dishes away in the cupboards. The woman on the radio was singing in a language Twiss couldn't understand but made her think of the color red.

When Twiss tried to slip past the kitchen to the stairway, her mother whipped around and ended up dropping a plate in the process. Twiss expected her mother to scold her for being sneaky. Instead, her mother knelt on the floor and began picking up pieces of the plate, which was the last of the ones from her childhood, and placing them in her apron. She cut her finger on one of the shards of porcelain.

"Mr. Peterson said he'd only take a penny to help Bett," she said, wrapping her apron around her finger. "I don't know how we'll ever repay him."

"We have plenty of pennies," Twiss said.

"We'll be shack people," she said. "Maybe we already are."

"My stomach hurts," Twiss said.

"Mine does too," her mother said. She emptied her apron into the trash bin and went back to putting dishes in the cupboard. "Your sister forgot to soak the beans."

"He took me to the golf course," Twiss said, wanting to tell her mother about the trip but also knowing she wouldn't because she felt responsible for protecting her father.

"I figured that's why you were gone so long," her mother said. "He can't let it go."

Twiss looked around the kitchen, wondering if her mother had ever felt about it the way her father felt about the golf course. Being a woman in Spring Green, and probably anywhere in the world, seemed so unfair to Twiss sometimes— that was the having to compare a golf course to a kitchen, a golf club to a soup ladle, which to her knowledge her mother had never held like it was the love of her life.

"Well, good night," she said to her mother, turning for the door.

"Good night," her mother said.

Upstairs, Milly and Bett were already in their beds. Bett was snoring lightly, inhaling in the language of pigs. Her feet dangled over the edge of her cot. Milly was as silent as the buck's head on the wall above her bed, whose blue eyes glowed when the moonlight caught them. Bett's father had run out of brown glass eyes when he was preserving it and had used a pair of eyes meant for wolves instead. Bett had helped pick them out. She said the object of taxidermy was to make the specimen look as lifelike as possible, and though bucks didn't have blue eyes, she felt they captured a quality of their spirits that people didn't often think about.

Twiss climbed into her bed without changing into her pajamas. She wondered what had happened with the doctor and Mr. Peterson, what was ailing Bett besides the dust and the damp, and the beans in her stomach.

Twiss tossed her pillow onto Milly's bed, and Milly tossed it back.

Usually, Twiss would have made Milly tell her everything that had happened, what, exactly, she'd said to Asa in the field and her father at the barn, and why. In return, she would have told Milly about the measuring tape and her fingers, her father and the moonlight on the river. The look of the seventeenth hole without its flag pin.

That night, she and Milly lay in their beds without speaking, Milly in her less lovely nightgown and Twiss in her father's silk golf shirt. Their silence, the absoluteness of it, announced the damage long before the future did.

12

Milly set the bird book on the coverlet in her mother's room—she didn't know why she kept dragging it all over the house this morning other than its weight made her feel steadier.

Twiss was no longer in the meadow, but when Milly was changing the linens in their bedroom, her sister had been standing there, looking as bewildered as the black swan they'd nursed back to health last year. Lately, Twiss would stand whole hours in the thigh-high grass and stare at the barn as if it had been the one to hurt her when they were girls. A part of Milly wanted to go to her sister, but rescuing Twiss would have been the same as condemning her.

With a little brass key she wore on a chain around her neck, Milly opened her mother's jewelry box, which contained her mother's plain silver wedding band and a pair of equally plain silver earrings. Since her mother had come from a family of jewelers, the contents of the box seemed paltrier than they would have been otherwise; when Milly and Twiss were young, their mother told them stories about her and Aunt Gertrude playing catch with a ruby.

So it was a little bit sad that the jewelry box was made of oak when all the nice ones from that era were made of African ebony. Milly lifted the tray out of the jewelry box and set it on the dressing table. A dusty and time-yellowed letter, folded in half, was pinned to the plush red velvet lining the box. As if she were a child again, Milly looked toward the light of the window and the dark of the door before she pulled the sewing pin out of the velvet and opened the letter, which in her lifetime she'd opened at least hundred times.

In it, she looked for what she always looked for: the beginning of the end, which was the only reason she could come up with to explain why her mother had kept this letter and none of the others she'd received in her life.

Beyond the windows and the twists of this year's drought-stricken trumpet vines, the birds chirped and the insects hummed and time tick-tocked by.

To my (formerly speaking, that is) lovely little country chapel and all of the people who have graced its pews over the years, as well as those who grace them now:

At this point, you must surely know that I'm no longer who you thought I was. I'm no longer who I thought I was, if that is any consolation to you good people. The trouble here is Faith, which I lost temporarily, along with my leg and several other unmentionables (which, unlike my Faith, though it has altered, are not likely to return to me any time soon). I'm writing another letter to ask for your forgiveness, which still may be more than you can offer me and more than I deserve.

Enclosed is a small, but important, part of what I've taken from you: the first installment of the money necessary to build a new Sunday school room for the children of Lilly chapel as was planned by the Ladies' Sewing Society, money which I've worked honestly in the paper mills to procure and will continue to work honestly to procure until I have settled my debt.

All day, I am stationed beside a man named Beardsley, who lost his hands as a result of his goodwill and bravery. They have us working in what they call the invalid sector; a host of us here have lost limbs or are stricken by some other mysterious illness or disease. Last year, there was a fire in the north mill, a great blazing beast, which some said resembled the devil himself. Beardsley rescued three poor tubercular souls who had lost consciousness from exposure to the billows of black smoke that poured into the room where they were sifting pulp.

I wish I could say that I had lost my leg in such an honorable way, but alas, I cannot. Perhaps that is why my leg pains me so on this lonely night, in this lonely room, and in this lonely city where the stars never make themselves visible long enough to close your eyes and wish on.

Yours sincerely,
Edward Rice

13

Milly's mother took Father Rice's letter out of the Sewing Society's vault (a picnic basket that sat on the top of a bookshelf in their meeting room) during the emergency hedge maze meeting, a mere day after the sparkler debacle meeting on the fifth of July. Her mother said she'd latched on to the first thing her hand touched; the other members were deep into conversation about the hedge maze proposed for the outside of the town hall—Uniformity is the essence of Civilization! they said—but as her mother had learned, they were never too invested in philanthropy to notice a button missing on her coat or her hand in a picnic basket.

"It was like having an alarm in my purse," she said. "I kept waiting for it to go off."

She read Father Rice's letter aloud to Milly, Twiss, and Bett in their bedroom, although nowhere in Father Rice's words, or between them, did blasphemy resound. The cheerful margaritas in Mexico had made way for the black liquor mills in Chicago. Milly couldn't help but wonder whether the paper he'd written the letter on came from the mill he sifted pulp in all day. Though she knew nothing about Chicago, she visualized smokestacks and soot, a slate-colored lake, bowls of porridge thick as dough.

"I'd like to know where the money went," Twiss said.

"I can't very well ask, now can I?" their mother said.

"Who's the envelope addressed to?" Bett said.

"Father Stone," their mother said.

"Then that's who took it," Bett said from her bed.

Bett was supposed to rest as many hours of the day as was possible. There was to be no heavy lifting, no laundry washing, and absolutely no gallivanting around the countryside.

Twiss asked if Bett was allowed to skulk around it.

"Let's try to stay away from anything that ends with *ing*, shall we?" her mother said, slipping Father Rice's letter into her apron pocket. "I'll be downstairs getting lunch started."

"We shall," Twiss said, with just the right amount of smartness for her mother to know she was being smart, but not enough to elicit punishment from her.

Twiss had gotten over whatever was bothering her about Bett (the root of which was no doubt jealousy and a pinch of something else Milly couldn't put a name to), and they were back to dreaming up ways to cause trouble, even if that trouble was limited to the confines of Bett's new bed. In addition to paying for the doctor's visit, Mr. Peterson had sent over a proper bed for Bett, which took up half of the room and looked like a ship with all of its freshly varnished wood. Bett called it the SS *Forest*.

Milly disliked the bed for its blatant waste of tree life, but liked it because it had come from Asa's home, which Milly had never been inside of but imagined was full of furniture with clawed feet, waiting to be softened with swatches of lace.

According to Bett, who said Mr. Peterson had told her his story the night he brought the doctor to examine her, Asa's mother had died on the passage from Germany to America, and his little sister had died shortly after. Both had come down with scarlet fever, which had blinded them before it made their hearts stop beating. To ease her transition to darkness on the ship, Bett said Mr. Peterson traded his wife's shawl for a pair of reading glasses that belonged to an Albanian-German immigrant, who gave the shawl to his wife to relieve her of the heartbreak of having to leave yet another place against her will. The rest of the voyage, whenever Mr. Peterson took a turn around the steerage deck and saw the shawl, he'd think his wife was feeling better and had come up to join him. He'd wind his way through the masses of people, the crying children, the wash buckets filled with barnacles. Whenever he'd reach the shawl, the Albanian woman would clutch it with the same force she clutched her children when they leaned over the railing to look at the water. *Mine,* she'd say in a language he couldn't understand, but understood completely.

Ava was his wife's name. Arielle, his daughter's. The glasses did nothing for them.

"I guess they liked A's," Bett said. "Mr. Peterson's first name is Aubrey."

"That sounds like an old professor's name," Twiss said, starting to laugh.

"Aubrey's a fine name," Milly said.

"Of course you think so," Bett said.

"His wife and child died," Milly said. "Doesn't that mean anything to you?"

"We wouldn't even know his name if it wasn't for you," Bett said.

"No, we *w-w-wouldn't,*" Twiss said.

"There was blood on your handkerchief," Milly said.

"From shaving my legs, dummy," Bett said.

Before Milly could put together the question forming in her mind—*If you're not really sick, then why are you pretending to be?*—she heard the clock downstairs, followed by the sound of her mother's footsteps on the stairs and jingle of the plate on the tray she was carrying. At the end of his visit, Mr. Peterson's doctor wrote out a complicated list of dietary recommendations for Bett, which included meat, meat, and meat, and also plenty of butter and cream. He said she was lacking animal proteins, what Bett called *grrr.* Now instead of washing and ironing all morning, their mother spent that time preparing meals—*A carnivore's delight!* Twiss said—for Bett. She'd fry ground beef, bake it, or boil it until it was hard and gray.

"Look!" Twiss said on boiled meat days. "A brain!"

Milly was now in charge of the washing and Twiss was in charge of the ironing, which meant that all of their sheets were clean, and either badly burned or wrinkled. Twiss was supposed to dust the buck's head, too, because it was making Milly congested. Lately, she'd sneeze so much that everyone stopped taking the time to bless her.

"Time for meat!" their mother said, when she entered their room.

When Bett saw the lump of meat on the tray, which Milly's mother had garnished with a scoop of equally lumpy gravy, she said, "I'm starting to look like a biscuit."

"Meatballs are for lunch," their mother said. What she didn't say was what all of that meat was costing her. Only Milly knew that she'd traded her mother's antique crystal brooch for a week of roasts and her gold promise ring for the promise of more.

Twiss swiped a finger full of brown gravy from Bett's plate, and their mother smacked her hand. "Food isn't your deficiency," she said. "How is it I have one daughter who can only think about herself and one who never does? You two are going to end up old and alone."

"What's so bad about that?" Twiss said, licking her finger. "Besides, I'm not even thinking about myself right now. I'm thinking about Father Rice. I don't understand how his address could be 6 1/3 Steele Street. Does that mean it's one-third of a house or one-third of a room?"

"What are you thinking about?" their mother said to Milly.

"I'm thinking about him too," Milly said, although she was really thinking about Asa and the loneliness he must have felt growing up without his mother and his sister, and also how much she wanted to take him in her arms and comfort him. The last time he'd mowed their property, she'd made him butter cookies and seen the tiny blond hairs at the back of his neck stand up and the drops of sweat trickle down and she'd felt faint, in the best possible way.

"I liked it better when he wrote about margaritas and lime juice," Twiss said. "He didn't sound like himself at all in that letter. He sounds so—"

"Helpless," Milly said.

"His life doesn't sound that terrible to me," Bett said, which made everyone look at her. "At least he has a job and a room, or one-third of a room, he can go back to at night. He even has a friend. That's more than anyone has in Deadwater. Since they dammed the rivers, there aren't any fish to fish for. The lakes are all algae. If you put your hand in the water, it'll come out green."

"Father Rice has a *stump* for a leg," Twiss said. "His friend doesn't have *hands*."

"Everybody loses something," Bett said.

Their mother looked out the window at the barn. "That's true."

Still, the four of them decided to try to help Father Rice, if for no other reason than it gave them

167

something to do on the long summer days and even longer summer nights, when the clouds balanced on the horizon like the moon but would neither vanish during the day nor bring relief from the heat at night. All week, the weather vane had behaved like a still life; the arrow had turned to a north-facing position, and there it had stayed, although it still predicted the weather better than that morning's *Gazette*, which advised people to bring along umbrellas to the Saturday market despite the sky being perfectly blue. *Don't forget to take home a watermelon,* the article said. *The kids will amuse themselves for hours with seed-spitting contests! Whole hours!*

"We can't afford to follow the doctor's recommendations, but we can't afford not to," their mother said, when Bett asked if she could go with them to the Saturday market.

"I get lonely when I'm alone," Bett said.

"Eat your meat loaf," their mother said gently. "We won't be gone long."

"Does Mrs. Bettle have to come?" Twiss said. "Her voice makes my skin itch."

"She has to get more food for Henry," their mother said.

"Holy, holy, holy," Twiss said. "Henry in the highest."

After they picked up Mrs. Bettle, who had one of Henry's green feathers pinned to the front of her hat, the four of them drove into town. The moment their mother turned the engine off, Twiss ran away, and Milly followed her. Twiss said she wanted to see the eggplant that was supposed to look like Saint Augustine, when she wanted to do anything but be near Mrs. Bettle, who'd debated the qualities of different birdseed mixes the entire way into town.

"I can't decide who I want to kill more: Mrs. Bettle or Henry," Twiss said to Milly as they walked past the fruit and vegetable vendors, the stand of kettle corn, and the chocolate éclairs, which the baker had lined up like bullets. The air smelled of burnt sugar.

"You shouldn't be so mean to Mrs. Bettle," Milly said. "She doesn't have anyone but that poor old bird to talk to."

"Do you think he'd stay with her if he had the chance to go?"

"He's a bird," Milly said.

"Exactly," Twiss said. "He doesn't belong in a cage."

Milly didn't mind Mrs. Bettle, though she knew Twiss was right about the one-way aspect of her and Henry's attachment, which made her feel even sorrier for Mrs. Bettle because her love was requited insofar as Henry instinctively desired to stay alive, and perhaps to live well. Wasn't that how most people lived, though? Surely their family wasn't all that different.

People just expected more from each other than they expected from birds.

Milly and Twiss walked along the outer edges of the Saturday market to avoid the rush of people tromping over to see the eggplant, which did look a little like Saint Augustine. The eggplant had a pointy protrusion, vaguely resembling a nose, raisin-sized indentations for eyes, and a white beard, which sprouted mysteriously from its base.

"Step right up!" the farmer said to everyone that passed. " 'Hope has two beautiful daughters. Their names are anger and courage; anger at the way things are, and courage to see that they do not remain the way they are.' "

"That's an eggplant with corn silk stuck to it!" Twiss said.

"Only if you see it that way," Milly said.

"If you become a philosopher, I swear I'll have to kill you *and* Mrs. Bettle *and* Henry."

Twiss stalked off in her own direction while Milly continued walking along the perimeter of the market. Her mother and Mrs. Bettle were standing in front of the birdseed stall, examining the different varieties in the careful way that jewelers examined diamonds for inclusions. Milly walked past them and the potato sacks filled with seeds, past the stand of summer squash and zucchinis. She stopped when she got to the stall that was usually filled with tomatoes but was filled with paintings today.

Mr. Stewart, her old science teacher, was admiring a landscape of the river.

"How strange," he said. "I was just thinking about you."

Milly felt her cheeks getting warm.

"And fossils," Mr. Stewart said quickly. He reached into the pocket of his tan trousers. "I found this one by the river just before I came here. You're the only one who was listening to my lecture on our field trip. I thought you might be interested in my discovery."

"I am," Milly said, her cheeks cooling. "What is it?"

"A fish, as far as I can tell. At least that's what its bone structure suggests to me."

Mr. Stewart handed Milly the fossil, which fit neatly into the palm of her hand. She turned it over carefully, so that the sandstone wouldn't crumble; even so, cinnamon-colored dust clung to her skin. Mr. Stewart said the fish in her hand had probably perished during the glacial floods that swept through the Wisconsin River valley, or maybe it was from a time when Wisconsin was an ancient sea where jellyfish and anemones floated freely over coral reefs.

"What you're holding is probably two hundred fifty million years old, and the Cambrian sandstone's even older than that," Mr. Stewart said, writing something down in the notebook he kept in his shirt pocket. "That it's intact is something of a miracle. You can't teach that kind of antiquity from a book." Mr. Stewart turned his attention to the landscape he'd been admiring. In it, a sandhill crane soared on an updraft over the river. Its tawny wings spanned the length of the brush-stroked sky. "Maybe you can't teach that at all."

Mr. Stewart took a long look at that landscape before he reached into his pocket for his wallet and said, "I'll take it," to the artist who had painted it. To Milly, he said, "You can't imagine what it's like to stare at white plaster. I don't know why I didn't notice during the school year. I guess I was too busy grading lab reports."

"We have wallpaper at my house," Milly said, trying not to think of the F in laboratory that had marred her otherwise perfect report card. "There's also a buck's head mounted on the wall above my bed. It sweats on me sometimes."

"You be careful that sweat doesn't have formaldehyde in it," Mr. Stewart said.

Milly handed the fossil back to Mr. Stewart while the artist wrapped the painting of the river in brown paper and secured it with twine. After Mr. Stewart paid the woman, he placed the fossil in Milly's palm again. "Color deserves color."

While it was almost always appropriate to say "thank you" when someone gave you a gift, the sentiment didn't seem personal enough for a two-hundred-fifty-million-year-old fossil. If Mr.

Stewart had been his buoyant classroom self, the right appreciative words might have come to Milly more easily. But today, Mr. Stewart seemed unhappy and out of place at the Saturday market, in the midst of people haggling over the price of peppers and onions, tubs of freshly churned butter turning in the sun. He kept looking around, as if now that he'd purchased the painting he didn't know what else to do with himself or the rest of the morning.

In the distance, Twiss was making faces at the eggplant.

"My sister and I are trying to bring Father Rice back from Illinois," Milly said. "We were hoping you could help us."

"I'm not Catholic," Mr. Stewart said. "I'm not really anything. Not since I was young. And then I was Episcopalian, mostly to please my mother and father. I think I might be an atheist. I've sure been working at it lately."

"You don't have to believe in God to be a good person," Milly said.

"You sure?" Mr. Stewart said, looking at the paper covering around his painting and then at Milly. "I'll tell you what. I'll do what I can to help if you promise me one thing."

"What?" Milly said.

"Don't ever ruin your life over a broken heart."

Milly turned the fossil over in her palm, imagining the ancient sea that the fish might have swum freely in, among jellyfish and anemones, vibrant coral reefs. Then she imagined the rapidly melting glaciers, the rising water, and the flood that might have killed him, though the second of Mr. Stewart's theories seemed odd to her. Fish were supposed to be at home in the water. Could they also drown there too?

After Mr. Stewart took himself and his painting home, Milly set off to find Twiss to tell her about his promise of help. She passed the Sewing Society's stall, where the members were selling slices of cherry pie and lemonade for a nickel to raise money for their hedge maze.

"Come have a piece of pie!" one of them called to her.

"You look absolutely famished!" another one said.

"Ravenous!" said another.

They were all wearing their yellow Society hats and resembled a swarm of bees.

"I just ate breakfast," Milly said.

She didn't know if they were aware that Father Rice's letter was missing, but she didn't want to stay to find out. Milly wasn't a good liar—the truth would show on her face. She didn't know what would happen to her mother but knew enough to understand that crossing the Sewing Society was like crossing God; in a town like Spring Green, they could sink you.

"Oatmeal isn't enough for a girl your age."

"You need eggs. Maple ham."

"Honey cured is better for the complexion."

"Actually," Milly said, "I ate a piece of meat loaf this morning."

"For *breakfast*? Has your mother lost her mind?"

And off the Sewing Society ladies went, huddling together like bees, and gaining strength in the same way. . . .

"Readjusting to new circumstances must be difficult."

"I heard he works in the dairy now."

"Milk is good for the bones."

"Oh yes, excellent."

"I could snap her in half she's so thin."

"But pretty."

"That hair."

"Those eyes."

"I'd have her engaged by now if she was my daughter!"

"I'd be planning her honeymoon to Europe!"

The women stopped talking for a moment and looked at Milly. They tilted their heads the way people did when a stray puppy or kitten crossed their paths.

"Poor girl," they said, as if they'd memorized the same script. "Are you sure you don't want a piece of pie? A glass of lemonade? We won't charge you a penny."

"No, thank you," Milly said, which was more gracious than it was genuine. Like a chicken, they'd cornered her and plucked her clean. A moment more, and they might also chop off her head with questions about her monthly. Milly thought of what Twiss or Bett might have said in the same situation and divided the fierceness of their imagined words in half, so that she ended up with something between honest and smart.

"My mother's making meatballs for lunch."

"Tell your mother she still owes us her monthly dues," they said after Milly had excused herself, but by then she was far enough away that she could pretend she didn't hear them and keep moving forward. "She hasn't paid for her hat, either!"

Milly walked until she could no longer hear their voices. She understood why her mother loathed these women, but not why she needed their approval. Milly continued past the kettle corn and the fruit vendor. She stopped when she saw the sign above the city council's stall. cake-baking contest. $25 first prize.

One of the councilmen handed Milly a yellow flyer.

"I've heard about your apple crisps," he said.

"The clerk at the general store must have exaggerated," Milly said.

"That's not who I heard it from."

When Milly saw Twiss bounding in her direction, she folded the flyer and slipped it into the pocket of her dress. She didn't want Twiss to chime in with her opinions about the irony of the city government holding a cake-baking contest when they'd just raised the taxes on sugar.

"Really," the city councilman said, just before Twiss reached for her hand and pulled her away from the stall. "You could win."

"Dr. Greene agreed to help us bring Father Rice back," Twiss said, when they were alone. "Mrs. Collier said she would, too. I don't know if we want her help, but she offered it."

"So did Mr. Stewart," Milly said, patting her pocket to make sure the fossil was still there. It occurred to her then what she should have said to Mr. Stewart, what he probably needed to hear more than anything else. *You're a good teacher.*

Milly and Twiss walked until they found their mother, who was helping Mrs. Bettle carry a sack of birdseed to the car. After Twiss told her about Dr. Greene (the oldest of the old town doctors), Mrs. Collier, and Mr. Stewart, their mother said, "We need to raise money."

Mrs. Bettle wiped the sweat from her forehead with a handkerchief. Before she put her hat back on, she stroked the green feather pinned to it.

"Henry can sing 'Ave Maria' in Latin. People might pay to see that."

"At your *house*?" Twiss said, imagining a recital of sorts.

"At the town fair," Mrs. Bettle said.

The town fair, which took place over the last weekend of August each year, was just over a month away. If their family agreed about any-thing, it was the town fair. Twiss loved the Wild West game and the spun sugar; their father loved the putting game and the caramel apples; their mother loved the bean counting game—last year she'd guessed 1,245 beans and won a forty-pound sack of kidney beans—and the Ferris wheel; and Milly loved what everyone else loved, except the livestock show and the amateur rodeo, where boys from the 4-H club wrestled calves to the ground for giant gold belt buckles.

Milly also loved how the fair transformed the abandoned field behind the high school from twenty-five dandelion-inhabited acres that went unnoticed most of the year into a kind of fairy-tale place, where people sucked on cherry-flavored ice chips and honey-roasted peanuts, and the Ferris wheel went round and round, and the firecrackers reached higher and higher. Milly was always sorry to see the field revert to weeds again.

"That's perfect!" their mother said to Mrs. Bettle, with more enthusiasm than she'd said anything in a long time. Since she'd taken Father Rice's letter out of the Sewing Society's vault, she'd been cheerfully embittered instead of just embittered; thievery became her. "Henry will be like the man who puts nails through his tongue. We've all paid to see that."

"It's a religious song," Mrs. Bettle reminded them.

"I only meant he might be as popular," their mother said.

"Well then, *carpe diem!*" Mrs. Bettle said.

The four of them got into the car, Mrs. Bettle and their mother up front, and Milly and Twiss in the back, the sack of birdseed between them. After they'd driven out of and beyond the Saturday market, their mother turned left instead of right; she said she didn't feel like going over the County C bridge again. She was in too good a mood to see the skid marks that had changed their lives twice in one day.

"Do we have to talk about him right now?" Twiss said. "The girls in my class do the same thing. They'll spend the whole lunch period trying to figure out what some boy meant when he said, 'Will you throw me the kickball?' "

"Henry's *very* straightforward," Mrs. Bettle said.

"That's our nature," their mother said.

"To analyze what someone probably doesn't even feel to death?" Twiss said.

"Exactly," their mother said.

They drove along the road out of town and

into the country, past the cornfields and the Clydesdale farm, the petting zoo and the underground house with grass for a roof, where a goat was grazing on the blue fescues that sprouted from the trestles.

Milly slipped her hand into her pocket. She thought about showing the fossil to her mother the same way she'd thought about showing it to Twiss, but didn't. Neither of them understood how she could like Mr. Stewart after what he'd done to the uniformity—A, A, A, A, F—of her report card. She'd even gotten an A in leadership, though she'd never led anything.

"There's such a thing as leading by example," her teacher had said, when she asked about her grade. "You're the only one who does what people tell you to do."

Milly didn't know if that merited an A or not; doing what she was told seemed a lot easier than not doing it. But it wasn't just that; along with saying no to Bett the day that Asa had arrived to mow their property, it didn't occur to Milly not to do her homework or dutifully recite an answer when her teacher called on her.

Q: Whose job is it to be pleasing?
A: Mine.

"The Sewing Society offered me a free piece of pie," Milly said to her mother.

180

"You didn't accept one, did you? Tell me you didn't."

"I know better than that," Milly said.

Her mother looked in the rearview mirror and smiled. "Maybe you won't end up old and alone after all."

Milly smiled too. She wasn't quite where Twiss was yet—Twiss said the word "spinster" with a kind of affection most people reserved for the loves of their lives.

"I'm going to be the world's most interesting spinster," Twiss said again now.

"You'll need a house," their mother said.

"Not if Milly lets me pitch a tent in her back-yard!"

"You'll have to ask her husband."

"I don't have a husband," Milly said before Twiss could interrupt with her thoughts on why women shouldn't have to ask permission for any-thing, particularly from their husbands. After all, she might say, sisters have a stronger bond than spouses.

"But you will," her mother said.

Milly was looking forward to the town fair for the usual reasons, in addition to whatever they were going to do there to raise money for Father Rice and the cake-baking contest, but there was another reason too: she wanted to visit the woman who read tea leaves again to see if her fortune had changed. She wanted the woman to tell her what everyone else had been telling her all along: you will be loved.

Milly didn't know if being loved by someone outside of her family had become important to her before or after she'd met Asa; she only knew that he amplified the desire so much that she'd felt envious when she saw a young family at the market this morning.

The parents were carrying their two children on their shoulders, stopping from time to time to reach into a bag of kettle corn. The children had hair the color of corn silk, the color of hair Milly imagined her own children having. As they bounced along on their parents' shoulders, they leaned back and forward, left and right, playing a version of Simon Says. The mother and father gave the impression they weren't paying attention, but the moment either of the children wobbled, the parents' hands tightened around their children's ankles.

Milly could only remember herself and Twiss playing that kind of game once. Twiss had just learned to climb and took great pleasure displaying her new talents by climbing up people who allowed her to. Their father had taken them to the golf course that day, and their mother had come along, which wasn't rare at that time.

Milly was five and Twiss was three.

Their father lifted Milly onto his shoulders

first, after he'd gotten a hole in one and they were walking on the course to the next hole. "You're light as a feather," he said, spinning her around like the helicopters that fell from the trees in the spring.

Their mother was waving to the members who passed, doing her best to be charming, which Milly remembered she was. Her mother was wearing a dress the color of vanilla frosting that day. In the sunlight, Milly could see the outline of her slim, sun-freckled legs.

After her father put Milly down, he picked up Twiss.

"You're heavy as a stone," he said to her, which made her giggle. Everything made Twiss giggle when she was a toddler. You could hand her a pinecone, and she'd act like you'd handed her the funniest thing in the world.

"I'm not a stone!" Twiss said, thumping the back of their father's head with her thumb, which she sucked despite the bitters their mother put under her fingernails. "I'm a baby!"

"You're the future female golfing champion of the world, that's what you are," their father said. "What do you want to achieve more than anything else?"

"Wwwweeerrrlllddd," Twiss said, still giggling.

"Holes in one!" their father corrected.

"She'll probably want to be a ballerina, Joe," their mother said, smiling.

Their father covered his ears, but he was also smiling. "Don't say that, Maisie. You're the only one I want to plié for me."

"*Tendu,*" their mother said.

Twiss was thrashing around on their father's shoulders.

"I'm a bird!" she said. "Watch me fly!"

When Twiss started to lose her balance at the same time that her father leaned over to kiss her mother's cheek, Milly started running. Halfway to them, Twiss tumbled down her father's back and landed headfirst on the grass, where she lay looking up at the sky, deciding whether or not she wanted to go through the trouble of being hurt.

That day, she did.

"I'm still a bird," she said, and began to cry.

"Of course you are," their mother said. "You just had an accident."

"You can still be a champion," their father said. "You can still get a hole in one."

Twiss squirmed past their parents on the ground. She rolled across the grass until she got to Milly's feet, which she hugged close to her chest.

"Milly saw me fly," she said.

And Milly did.

Though sometimes, she wished her parents had been the ones to lift Twiss onto their hips and ask her where she flew that day, to smile when Twiss said she'd been to the moon and eaten a piece of lacy white moon cheese before the moon king made her come back down.

Milly stared out the window as her mother drove the four of them farther and farther into the country. The corn was rising along the river; the river was falling. When Milly was certain Twiss wasn't looking, she pulled out the yellow flyer. Aside from all of the practical things that twenty-five dollars could buy—flour, sugar, butter, meat—Milly thought of the handsome silver lapels shaped like tractors she'd seen in the general store. She couldn't think of anything more pleasing than being able to give them to Asa after the fair.

"You could win," Milly heard the man say, but she didn't yet believe it.

She folded the flyer and slipped it back into her pocket.

When her mother turned onto Mrs. Bettle's road, the watermelon she'd bought at the market, unbeknownst to either Milly or Twiss, rolled out from under the seat. Twiss took out her pocket-knife and cut into the rind of the watermelon, exposing the bright red flesh, the hard black seeds. She lifted one of the seeds out of the watermelon and positioned the seed on the tip of her tongue. Then she sucked in her cheeks, stuck her head out the window, and spit the seed as far as the air in her lungs would allow her to; the seed landed first on the window and then bounced onto the road, where it quickly disappeared into the gravel.

Twiss stuck her knife into the watermelon again and scooped out another seed. This time when she tried to spit it out the window, the seed landed on the front of her shirt. She laughed, plucked it off, and began the process again. After they'd dropped Mrs. Bettle off and were turning into their own driveway, she handed Milly a seed.

"I was thinking a guest room might be nicer than a tent," she said. "Tents let in rain."

Milly placed the seed on her tongue.

"What rain?" she said, and spit the seed out of her mouth and out of the open window. The tiny black seed sailed away from the car on a wave of hot white air, where it rose and fell like the prow of a ship, gaining momentum and then losing it, rising and falling, skipping and spinning, before it finally lost all its forward energy and landed in the meadow of bluestems and prairie onions beyond the car.

I could win!

14

The day had become what the *Gazette* had predicted: hot and humid, without a cloud in the sky or a cooling patch of shade to stand in. When Twiss finished cleaning out the coop, she walked to the barn. She lingered outside the utility door, deciding whether or not to enter. All these years she'd been walking into that barn trying to make things right and all these years that barn had neither resisted nor yielded to her. Twiss picked a black-eyed Susan and tucked it behind her ear. Though the sun dangled like an ornament high up in the sky, the heat was above and below her, radiating from all directions. She walked over to the water pump and the white lilac bush. She didn't feel like playing golf just yet.

When they were young, she and Milly would take turns pumping for water on days when the temperature crested into the triple digits. The pump was rusty even then, which made the coaxing of water all the more difficult and yet all the more rewarding. One of them would pump until the other one got tired or until the water sputtered yellow drops then ran clear. After they'd quenched their thirsts, they'd run around the pump, filling up the tin coffee mug that hung from the pump's handle and splashing each other in the face.

"For the love of water!" they'd say, and go round and round.

Twiss began the slow business of working the water pump now. Though her arms were puckered with age, they were still strong from swinging a golf club nearly every day of her life. As the pump rose, she could almost feel Milly standing by her side when they were young, both of them anticipating the first drops of water that would fall into the cup.

That was one of the few marvelous things about aging—Twiss could travel from here to there without having to go anywhere at all. Her memories were her suitcases, and her mind her passport, only she didn't need to leave Spring Green to see one of the world's seven wonders; all the wonders that she needed were located in the Wisconsin River valley. True, she'd wanted to see the Taj Mahal and the Great Wall of China, Machu Picchu and the Egyptian pyramids (what were the others?); she just must not have wanted to see them enough.

Standing on the Continental Divide was the only experience she felt she'd missed out on by staying in Spring Green. When she was young, she'd planned on positioning herself astride it and taking a photograph. She liked the idea of being in the exact middle of two watersheds. She'd planned on sending a postcard to Milly.

From the Divide with Love, Your Sister, Twiss.

While Twiss was on her trip, Milly would have been snugged into her life with the two children and the husband she'd always wanted to have. She'd be engaged in the time-consuming activity of darning socks or preserving jam when the postcard arrived. And for a moment, just a moment, amid the shrieks and tugs of her children on her shirtsleeves—Milly would be making chicken and dumplings for supper: their favorite—and the press of her husband's boots on the porch steps, she'd wish she were standing on the Divide with Twiss.

From Spring Green with Love (and a smidge of envy), Your Sister, Milly.

When they were kids, Milly used to draw pictures of her future family. There was a son named Jacob and a long-haired daughter named Molly Blue.

"Why blue?" Twiss would ask her.

"Because it's pretty," Milly would say. Her future husband, tall and pencil-line thin, didn't have a name.

"Why didn't you pick a name for the daddy?" Twiss would ask.

"Because he hasn't told it to me yet," Milly would say.

Twiss would draw pictures of the species

she'd captured on the golf course. She had the idea that she would not only become a great explorer like Lewis or Clark, but that she'd also write textbooks filled with her own kind of science.

While I was digging for a pot of gold in the Amazon, she'd written as the opening of her first textbook, *I came upon the world's first flying beetle. It has one hundred three and a half legs and uses them to fly to the sun to gather sunspots. This explains the shiny yellow dots all over its body!*

Although Twiss didn't become a scientist or an explorer like she'd planned, rescuing birds was a little like being both at the same time. In order to repair a wing properly, she believed you had to understand what it was like to have one, which led to much mental soaring around the countryside, much unskilled flapping in the bathroom. A bird's wing, though it contained several distinct bones, functioned as though it contained only one. You couldn't fiddle with even the tiniest bone without repercussions in the larger ones.

Twiss's bird books said as much about avian anatomy, though the authors didn't suggest that ornithologists take up flight as a mode of diag-nosis. "Take up your disinfected stainless-steel scalpels," the books said. "Your impermeable latex surgical gloves."

What words for restoration!

Sometimes, Twiss wished she could be the one making vanilla drop biscuits in the kitchen, while Milly was in the bathroom guessing at the steps that would bring a bird back to full chirping life. Sometimes, she'd have rather been responsible for fixing breakfast than fixing what often, with her skill set, could not be fixed. There was nothing quite as depressing as running up against your limitations before you had your morning tea.

That had happened with Father Rice—Twiss had believed she could save him. What she didn't understand when she was fourteen, but understood very well now, was that not everyone in the world could be saved or, for that matter, wanted to be.

15

I forgive you, Twiss wrote in the first of the batch of letters she addressed to 6 1/3 Steele Street during the month of July, because that's what she thought Father Rice wanted to hear. Twiss expected Father Rice to say "thank you," which he did, and be back to his old, fish-eating, tarnished-silverware-accepting self, which he wasn't.

Dear Twiss,

I was greatly cheered when I came home to find your letter beneath my door this evening. I can almost see you skipping along the long dusty road into town to mail it, although you might be too old for skipping now. Perhaps you've always been too old.

When I left Spring Green, you and your sister, Milly, were the last people I saw. Your sister looked frightened from the pew where you two were sitting that morning, but you . . .

All I can advise is read your Bible, my dear. If I remember right, you were quite a fast runner. As you know, it's impossible to run without a leg.

> *Sincerely,*
> *Edward Rice*

Father Rice's letter prompted Twiss to write a second letter, which began indignantly, even for her.

Dear Father Rice,

I'm not a child! Please tell me what comes after these three dots . . . and before the words "All I can advise." I can handle it. I'm fourteen now.

> *Sincerely, Twiss*

P.S. I don't read the Bible anymore, but I do still skip. ☺ ⇐ *Not because I'm young, but because I'm me.*

Dear Twiss, Father Rice wrote back,

You caught me.
What I meant was that you have a certain spark of life, which I would hate to see go out because of your own stupidity (which, in this case, is really my stupidity since you have not done anything to endanger your general well-being, yet).
What I love and appreciate about you—what I've always loved and appreciated about you—is your ability to be truthful. Forgive me?
    Sincerely,
    Father Rice ☺ ⇐   *Not because I am trying to be conciliatory.*

P.S. Well, maybe a little. The truth is writing this letter has been the first activity in months during which I've temporarily forgotten to feel sorry for myself. Thank you.

I forgive you, Twiss wrote, among other things. Again.

She hadn't received a letter back from Father

Rice yet, which she was a little disappointed about since he'd already sent another letter and another payment to Father Stone, which Father Stone had handed over to the Society without the payment, and which her mother had attempted to steal during another emergency meeting, this time about the blight of Back Bend on the river landscape.

Mrs. Merrykind, the president of the Society, had caught her mother with the letter and had smacked the back of her hand. When Twiss's mother attempted to defend herself—*Father Stone is the real thief!* she said—Mrs. Merrykind called her a liar of the worst sort. Instead of voting to evict the people of Back Bend, the Society voted to evict Twiss's mother.

"I wasn't forced to do anything," her mother said, after the meeting and after she'd brought Mrs. Bettle over to the house for moral support. She looked toward the barn as if for further validation. When she didn't find it in the view, she said, "I renounced my membership."

The afternoon was slipping into early evening; the sky was beginning to look like cotton candy, which was nice enough to look at but made Twiss's tongue feel fuzzy.

"You're braver than I am, Margaret," Mrs. Bettle said. "I might have kissed their feet."

"It was embarrassing, though," Twiss's mother said. "To have all of those women staring at me like I was the Antichrist or the devil—what's worse?"

"The devil, I think," Mrs. Bettle said.

Why are you even here? Twiss thought.

Thank the Lord that Henry was the pickiest parrot that ever lived—*Henry despises drafts!*—or else Mrs. Bettle probably would have moved in by now. Twiss had begun to love that spoiled old bird. She had fantasies about teaching him to look directly into Mrs. Bettle's eyes and plead, *Don't leave me alone, Mum-Mum.* The danger with this lesson was that Mrs. Bettle might bring him along with her instead of staying home. Twiss decided that teaching Henry to say something like *You sure are ugly!* or *You sure are fat!* was better because it would make Mrs. Bettle cry, and no one Twiss knew liked to do that in public, or at all.

Ah, fantasies.

Maybe Milly was right that Mrs. Bettle's aloneness made her more annoying and more ottoman shaped than she would have been. The longest Twiss had ever gone without talking to another person was when she'd gotten stung by a bee, and that was only because she couldn't talk, although she remembered having plenty to say. When Mrs. Bettle finally went home—*Oh Lord, Henry must be starved!*—Twiss decided to construct an experiment to see if she should stop fantasizing about Henry making diminutive comments and feel sorry for the Beetle instead. For one whole day, from sunset to sunset, she vowed not to speak to anyone.

"Does that include writing?" Milly said, after she and Bett had finished unpinning that day's wash from the clothesline, folding what needed to be folded, and ironing everything else because they didn't want Twiss's burn marks on their clothing.

Twiss picked up a pencil. *Yes,* she wrote, and then added a smiley face.

"You might not want to smile just yet," Bett said. "You're a person who likes to talk."

Bett was right; after only an hour of silence, Twiss had an incredible desire to say something hateful to someone, simply because by her own design she was not allowed to. Without her voice, everything else ceased to seem real to her. Or everything else was still real, but she wasn't. And if she wasn't real, then how could everything else be? People often asked the question: if a tree fell in the forest and there was no one around to hear it, would it still make a sound? For Twiss, the more pressing question was: Why did the tree have to fall in the first place?

At supper, Twiss tried voicing her desires without voicing them, first by pointing to the bowl of mashed potatoes, then, when no one passed it to her, by reaching across the table.

"All you had to do was ask," her mother said cheekily. Bett had told her about the experiment after she'd scolded Twiss for not participating in that evening's grace.

"It certainly is peaceful this way," her mother said. "How long will this feeling last?"

"Twenty-four hours," Bett said.

Twiss smacked the table.

"I mean twenty-two," Bett said, smiling at her.

"It'll be a short vacation then," her mother said. "But a vacation all the same."

Twiss smacked the table again.

"Stop acting like an animal," her mother said.

I'm not an animal!

"Yes," her mother said. "You are."

By the time supper was over and the plates were cleared, Twiss was beginning to get the hang of expressing herself without words, although her modes of expression invited ridicule from everyone except Milly, who'd positioned all the food in front of Twiss.

That night, as they did almost every night, the three girls played Truth or Consequences, which ended up being more like a game of charades. The first question Bett asked Twiss was *Have you ever kissed a boy?*, the answer to which was easy to convey since it only required Twiss to shake her head. The same was true of Bett's second question: *Have you ever wanted to?*

Twiss jumped onto the SS *Forest* and pretended to vomit.

Bett's third question was not as easy to answer: *What is your father doing in the barn?*

Twiss looked at Milly, who was huddled under her covers despite the heat and the heavy evening air, pretending to be asleep since it was her turn to play the game next. Even asleep, she could be induced to play if Asa's name were mentioned.

Twiss got off Bett's bed and walked over to her own. The moment she got under the covers, Bett pulled them off her.

"If I have to be sick," she said, "then you have to answer the question."

You're not that sick, Twiss thought, feeling betrayed by Bett's question even though she knew it was a reasonable one. Twiss had begun to tell Bett things she wouldn't have told anyone else—*I'm actually scared of leeches,* she'd said earlier that day. *Every time I cross the creek in the summer, I stick one on my body so that over time I'll be less afraid.*

"It's a perfectly reasonable question," Bett countered, as if she'd heard Twiss's thoughts.

Earlier, Bett had responded to Twiss's fear with a fear of her own: *I'm afraid I'm going to be all alone my whole life.* And also, *Once, I heard my mother tell my father it was too bad I was ugly.*

Bett put on the robe Mr. Peterson had sent over for her. Against the soft blue chenille, her hair looked even more red. That afternoon, Milly had brushed it out for her, working at the tangles with the same concentration she reserved for knitting, until it fell halfway down Bett's back, not quite like silk, but no longer like horsehair. Now, Bett looked as unremarkable as every other girl, which Twiss thought was worse than being ugly because it was average.

"I don't see what he has to complain about," Bett added, about their father. "At least he has his health." She coughed to illustrate that she still didn't have hers, and left the room.

Twiss and Milly didn't need to speak to each other to know where their cousin was going, or to know that they were both jealous of her determination to find out what their father had been doing in the barn all of this time. Though he'd never said they couldn't come in, and though he came out plenty, Twiss and Milly felt a zip of unbridled electricity whenever they stood outside the utility door; don't go in, the zip said, unless you want to be shocked.

All they knew was that he'd taken their tree house materials and their dreams of scatter rugs and evenings alone under the stars. The pile of sand and the ground bees at the far end of the pond had been disappearing, too.

"What do you think he's doing in the barn?" Milly said.

Twiss emerged from beneath her covers but didn't open her mouth.

"You can talk," Milly said. "I won't tell."

"I don't know," Twiss said, exhaling as though it was her breath she'd been holding.

Milly hugged her pillow. "Neither do I."

Though Bett was gone, they kept looking at her bed as if she would pop out from beneath her covers at any moment and ask another question—*Would you drink your own blood if you were starving?*—or scold them for feeling sorry for themselves by telling another one of her stories. Twiss was still excited to go to Deadwater, but now she was afraid she wouldn't want to come home. Or that while she was gone, she'd start to hate the very things she loved about Spring Green, the things that made home *home*.

That's what happened in her adventure books. Once the boys became men and the men became cowboys, they couldn't go back to their old ranching lives. They couldn't be happy with three home-cooked meals a day, foursquare lives. Always, they had an itch to gallop away on their horses and shoot off their guns. Always, the horizon line pulled them to it.

As much as Twiss craved adventures in other places, she didn't want those places to change how she felt about home. Travel, she'd noticed, had a profound effect on people in Spring Green. When they came back from weekend trips even to places as close as Lake Geneva or Mill Valley, suddenly the colors of their houses were all wrong, or the style of their curtains. What had satisfied them before now offended their sensibilities.

Every house in Lake Geneva is steeple-white, they'd say, or, *You should have seen the striped valances on their windows. Breathtaking!*

Although Deadwater wasn't a place people seemed to choose for their vacations, and curtains were a waste of money when you lived where there was no one to see you, Twiss was afraid she'd come back home thinking *How absolutely insignificant the pond looks! How ridiculously small!* Would the snapping turtles hold up against a live-dead bird, a dead-live man in a closet?

Of course Twiss would want to come home, but she was worried that home wouldn't be what it was before she'd left. When her parents were still merely annoyed with each other, sometimes her mother would look around the house and say, *I wonder where I'd be if I weren't here.*

Father Rice was the only person Twiss knew who'd left Spring Green for more than a weekend or a weeklong vacation, and he was also the only one she knew who'd left the state of

Wisconsin proper. Twiss longed for another letter from him, so that she could send another letter too. She wanted to ask him about Mexico, and his leg, although she didn't want to be predictable or rude. Nearly every person he'd encountered on his travels must have stopped to stare at the one-legged man from Wisconsin, and nearly every one of these people must have eventually broken down and asked the question that had come into their minds the moment they saw him: *How did you lose your leg?* Maybe it was easier to tell your life to someone you didn't know than to tell it to someone you did.

Twiss and Father Rice weren't strangers, but she did wonder about his leg. While she and Milly waited for Bett to come back from the barn, Twiss imagined him losing it in a hand of high-stakes poker, which seemed as likely as any other scenario she'd been able to think of.

Because Father Rice had bet the Sewing Society's money and lost it, Twiss imagined that he'd been forced to make a deal with a man who sported a thick black mustache that curled at the ends, a man who carried a machete instead of a gun.

Twiss called the man Carlos Vidales of Rosarie. She imagined him looking out over the length of his hacienda (Twiss's history teacher said that hacienda was a fancy way of saying plantation, which was a polite way of saying indentured servitude, which was a more acceptable way of saying slavery), content in the knowledge that his land rolled on for miles, but also not so content since people didn't hold on to such estates by forgiving debts.

"Pick the part you want to lose," Twiss imagined him saying to Father Rice.

"Take my heart," she imagined Father Rice pleading.

"If you were still a priest, Señor Rice. Then it would be worth its weight in gold."

Twiss imagined Father Rice kneeling before one of the women standing on the periphery of the poker table, the one who was the most covered up despite the hot weather and the one who also looked the most like the Virgin Mary.

"I am still a priest," she imagined him saying, growing more certain of himself.

(This, Twiss thought, must have been the moment Father Rice regained his Faith, although, as he said in his letter, it would have been an altered form of Faith, but Faith nonetheless. As he looked out onto the orchards of fruit trees and coffee fields—here Twiss imagined neat rows of porcelain cups filled with the warm, brown liquid—he wouldn't have been able to stop thinking about the slow curve of the river, the black earth smell of home.)

"Then you won't mind if I take your leg," she imagined Carlos Vidales of Rosarie saying, wielding his machete like a sling blade. "*Tus Dios* will grow you another one."

Twiss pictured Father Rice drinking down his margarita and sucking his wedge of lime and licking the salt sprinkled around the rim of his glass.

"To the Glory of God!" she imagined him saying heartily, just before Carlos Vidales of Rosarie took from him what he owed. "To happiness in all its forms!"

"I have an idea of how we could raise money at the fair," Twiss said to Milly, who'd opened a gardening book but had failed to turn a page since Bett left the room. It was too late in the season to plant anything anyway—the garden was beginning to look like a jungle.

"How?" Milly said.

"What does everyone want?" Twiss said.

"I have a feeling you're going to tell me," Milly said, closing her book.

"Happiness," Twiss said.

Milly raised her eyebrows. "You're going to give that to people?"

"No," Twiss said, visualizing the meadow, a place she couldn't remember being unhappy in. The sound of it in the summer—of the crickets and the frogs, the blades of grass and weeds brushing against each other—felt holy somehow. Although Twiss didn't pray in church, she'd pray in the meadow. She'd listen for the sound of the earth in acorns the way people listened for the sound of the sea in shells.

Twiss jumped up so that she was standing on her bed.

"I'm going to give them Twiss's wonderfully stupendous momentous illustrious unforgettable Purple Prairie Tonic!"

She imitated the announcer who rattled off prices and particulars about cattle and sheep at the livestock auction with a speed that most people's voices couldn't achieve.

"You don't have money? You don't have health? You don't have love? You don't have a leg? An arm? A child? A parrot named Henry? Any of the aforementioned materials? Try Twiss's wonderfully stupendous momentous illustrious unforgettable Purple Prairie Tonic. Drink it down, drink it up, drink it sideways, if you like. It's genuine goodness in a bottle. That's Twiss's wonderfully stupendous momentous illustrious unforgettable Purple Prairie Tonic. One hundred percent guaranteed to cure what ails you!"

"Purple Prairie?" Milly said.

"It sounds better than Purple Meadow," Twiss said.

"How much is it?" Milly said.

"A nickel," Twiss said. "Remember, that's Twiss's wonderfully stupendous—"

"You can stop saying that," Milly said. "I'll buy some of your tonic. So will everyone else if you badger them."

"I bet Dr. Greene will help me make it," Twiss said. "He still has a whole cabinet of cure-alls. I'm pretty sure he already gave one to Mrs. Collier. Mold-Be-Gone."

Milly tossed her pillow at Twiss. "You have the eyes of a crazy person."

"What would your home economics teacher say about your behavior?" Twiss said.

"Pillow throwing shows too much independence on the part of a young woman!"

"You sound like *me*," Twiss said.

"You sound like Bett," Milly said.

"That's only because Bett sounds like me."

"Then you must be easy to sound like."

After that, the two of them lost their laughter.

What had Bett been doing in the barn all this time?

Milly stood up on her bed and draped her sheet over the buck's head on the wall the way people did after the first snow, when they closed off entire sections of their houses to conserve heat, and money, for the winter.

"I don't like how this thing looks at me," she said. "Sometimes I swear it winks."

"Sometimes I think it does too," Twiss said.

When they heard the screen door open and close, the two of them stopped speaking. This time, they didn't toss pillows at each other or pretend to be asleep. Milly opened her gardening book again and Twiss reread Father Rice's letter.

Dear Twiss, You caught me . . .

You caught me . . .

As if Father Rice were a fish and her letter a lure.

When Bett came in, she took off her robe and placed her slippers at the side of her bed. "Neither of you told me how funny your dad was. I thought he'd be the bitter type. The life-isn't-a-bowl-of-cherries kind of man after that stunt in the kitchen the other day. But he wasn't. He invited me right in and set out a milk pail for me to sit on. He was charming."

My milk pail? Twiss thought. *Charming?*

"He told me a story," Bett said to Twiss. "About the day you were born. He wasn't playing golf like your mother thinks."

Twiss covered her ears.

"Don't be such a baby," Bett said, gently pulling Twiss's hands away from her ears. "Your father was at the river, helping a group of other volunteers look for a man who was thought to have drowned."

The man, Jester Johnson, had disappeared the night before—willfully, Bett said, because he'd spent an entire month's earnings on a bronze compass and was shamed by his lack of will-power to walk past the shopwindow where it was displayed and continue on to the general store like he was supposed to. Jester had promised to bring home a bottle of milk and a loaf of bread for supper and had brought home the compass instead.

When Jester showed her the compass, his wife didn't look mad like she usually did, nor did she place her hands on her hips. As if she'd known the outcome of his trip to town before it came out, she'd gone ahead and scraped together enough flour for a miniature loaf of bread, which she'd baked into the shape of a heart.

"Sit," she said to Jester. "Put your feet up."

Jester pulled off his boots and sat in the chair at the head of the table.

"Tell me about your day," his wife said.

Jester was waiting for his wife to ask about the milk and the bread—she always asked about the milk and the bread. "It was all right," he said.

"You have circles under your eyes," his wife said.

"I'm a little tired, I guess," Jester said. "What about you?"

"I feel better than I have in a long, long time," his wife said, smiling. "No more cramping today. No more pain."

"Good," Jester said. "That's good."

What had changed? That morning when he'd left for work, his wife had made his breakfast, but she hadn't kissed him good-bye or wished him well—she hadn't wished him well in a long time, although he supposed he didn't deserve to be wished well or kissed good-bye. Jester was selfish—he knew that; only a selfish man came home with a compass.

But he loved her. Sometimes he'd be walking down the street and be struck down by this love so cruelly that he'd have to stop to steady his breathing, his legs. (True, that didn't happen as often as when they were first married, but it still happened. Not everyone could say that, could they?) After he'd steadied himself, he'd think *Go home, Jester, go home,* but his legs would rarely carry him there. The distance between what he wanted and what he needed was too great; often he'd forget where he was standing. He'd bought the compass so that even if he forgot where he was standing, he'd always know how to get home.

"That's good," Jester said a third time.

The house was quiet, peaceful. His wife was round again. She took her little loaf of bread out of the oven and set it on the plate in front of him.

"This is the last time I'm going to give you my heart, Jester."

That night, after his wife had put the one child to bed and quieted the other one, who, unlike the first child, was overly rambunctious in its soupy habitat, by rubbing her belly, Jester took a walk.

He walked and walked and kept on walking until he reached the river.

Go home, Jester. Go home.

Jester stood at the edge of the river a long time before he unwrapped his handkerchief and dropped the loaf of bread into the dark water. The moment it disappeared beneath the surface, he regretted he'd let it go.

Bett said that after searching all day, Milly and Twiss's father and the other volunteers finally found Jester on a sandbar in the middle of the river late that afternoon, weakened but alive, with a handful of soggy breadcrumbs in his hand.

"So that's what he was doing the day you were born," Bett said. She pinned her hair up so that sleep wouldn't tangle what Milly had worked so hard to untangle.

Was it true? Was it false?

Was it better to pretend not to know for sure what you surely knew?

Bett set down Milly's brush. She tilted her head the way she did whenever she was genuinely concerned about something or someone. "I thought you'd be thrilled, Twiss. Your father saved that man's life. In Deadwater, nobody ever saves each other."

Why did Twiss's father tell Bett that story, and why had Bett been taken in by it? Twiss was about to go to the closet to look for the bronze compass, which her father had given her as a birthday present when she was eight years old and no money was left to get her a real gift.

Jester—that was what her father always wished he'd been named; it was the name of the most heroic hero in his old adventure books, which now belonged to Twiss.

"You're supposed to be gloriously happy right now," Bett said to Twiss.

Happy? Twiss thought, and slumped back down on her bed.

"Maybe she is," Milly said. "Only she can't say so for nineteen more hours."

Bett eyed the sheet on the buck's head, and Milly's pillow on the floor.

"You can't fool me. I know you've been talking."

16

Milly hated herself a little for opening her mother's jewelry box. Why couldn't she let the past stay where it had landed? Why all of this meddling today?

A woman had singled her out for not being a mother—that was all.

By now, the woman wouldn't even remember what she'd said to Milly or what Milly had said in front of her daughter. She'd have dropped her children off at the school, gone to the grocery store, and vacuumed her toxic carpeting. "You must have a lot of time on your hands if you're still thinking about that," she'd have said.

Yes, Milly thought. *I do.*

"Old people are hopeless clingers-on," the woman would have continued. "They can tell you what happened during the Depression— The dust storms they had to endure! The mealy potatoes! The loaves of bread on credit!—but they can't tell you what Fruit Roll-Ups are."

"I know what Fruit Roll-Ups are," Milly would have said back, although she didn't know why they were sold as healthy snacks for children when they were heaped full of preservatives that were engineered in laboratories hundreds of miles from the nearest fruit tree.

Before the processed-food craze, a health-food craze had hit Spring Green when they were in the last years of middle age. One of Milly's doctors at that time had recommended eating bricks of gray tofu instead of red meat and mashed yeast instead of mashed potatoes. Another had recommended a colonic cleansing, which Milly had submitted to because she'd thought the doctor would merely send her home with a bottle of pills, maybe some hemp.

"What did you think 'cleansing' meant?" Twiss had asked her on their way home from the doctor's office. She kept biting her lip, so that she wouldn't laugh.

"You'd think they'd have warned me."

"Miss Milly Prim, I'm afraid you're about to be probed now!"

"They didn't cover me with a sheet," Milly said. "I could tell what they were thinking."

"You're crazy?" Twiss said.

"You don't count anymore," Milly said.

Twiss steered the car to the side of the road. When a dark blue truck approached on the opposite side of the road, she got out of the car. She walked around to the front.

Milly knocked on the windshield. "What are you doing?"

"Testing a theory!" Twiss called back.

When the truck was a hundred yards off, Twiss turned to face Milly. She smiled as she unbuckled her belt and dropped her trousers, followed by her underpants.

"Have you gone mad?" Milly said.

The driver of the truck honked several times in a row, waving emphatically as he passed them. "That-a-girl!" he said, continuing down the road.

When the truck disappeared, Twiss pulled up her underpants and her trousers, buckled her belt, and got back into the car.

"You're right," she said to Milly. "You're never too old to be embarrassed."

"I think that was the Sprye boy driving that truck," Milly said, smiling.

"No," Twiss said. "It was Asa's boy's boy."

"Oh?" Milly said, trying not to frown.

"He looks just like her."

"Does he?" Milly said as if she hadn't noticed the resemblance. She glanced at the side mirror, at the writing engraved in the glass.

Objects are closer than they appear.

Curtis. When he was in high school, he appeared in the sports section of the *Gazette* every Saturday during the fall. Curtis had won a scholarship to the university because he could throw a football farther than any other boy in Wisconsin. But it was his sister's career that Milly had really been interested in and had secretly followed.

Every Saturday, heat or cold, rain or shine, Milly would see Avery running up their road, her long blond ponytail swishing in time with her legs, just as the sun was making gemstones out of the fields and the hills and the bales of hay scattered across the landscape. Twiss would still be snoring away upstairs. Years of sleep remedies had failed to subdue her; she still slept like a wild animal and woke like one, too.

On warm mornings, Milly would take her cup of tea out to the porch to watch Avery run by. Though she'd never been a runner herself—she didn't like the sensation of breathlessness, or the hard thunk of her heart—she'd loved to watch Twiss run. And Avery was an even better runner than Twiss had been, and certainly more graceful. She'd run first on the Spring Green high school team and then on the university team and now was training to run the marathon in the Olympic trials.

In an interview, when a reporter from the *Gazette* asked her why she ran, Avery said, "Why does anybody do anything?" which had made Milly like Avery even more.

Each Saturday morning, after she passed the driveway, Avery would pick up speed in order to crest the upcoming hills. Sometimes she ran with a yellow music player and matching headphones, but most of the time, she ran without them.

"Something comes in and something goes out," Avery had added in the interview, as if she'd been playing at being coy but couldn't really play when it came to running. "I'd keep running forever if my legs would let me."

"Tell me about the routes you run in Spring Green," the reporter had said.

"My favorite is my Saturday route," Avery said. "There's this little purple meadow I pass on my way up into the hills. When I was little, my grandpa used to say it was enchanted. He said if you walked through it, you'd never be the same person again."

"Where did he hear that story?" the reporter asked.

"I guess he used to know the people who lived in that house," Avery said.

"The bird sisters?" the reporter said.

"All I know is, when I pass that meadow, suddenly I can run faster," Avery said.

"Are you superstitious?"

"I visualize the meadow during all of my races, if that's what you mean."

"Have you ever walked through it?"

"I believe in it too much," Avery said.

"Can you be more specific?" the reporter asked.

"No," Avery said.

17

The meadow did possess a kind of magic, at least on the day Milly and Asa had walked through it together, both nervous, shy and young, and grateful for the owl-shaped cookies Milly had baked that morning (inspired by the barn owl that had sung in the oak tree and in her dreams all night), which provided an entrée into what she'd come to think of as the conversation of her life, a conversation unremarkable in every way but one: She'd had it with Asa.

Mr. Peterson had taken Bett to the doctor's

office to get her lungs X-rayed; Twiss was off in the woods, searching for ingredients to put into her happiness tonic; her mother was canning the vegetables she'd harvested from the garden that morning so they would be able to have milk-braised wax beans in the winter. Her father was in the barn.

For once, Milly was left alone enough with Asa for her feelings to materialize into something more tangible than salt on her lips.

"The owls are my favorite," Asa said, as they walked the perimeter of the meadow. Asa had just parked the tractor in the middle of it when Milly came out with the plate of cookies and a glass of iced tea garnished with a mint leaf she'd plucked from the garden when her mother wasn't looking. The mint was supposed to be for a special jelly her mother planned on making for the following Christmas supper. By then, she said, they might be able to afford the roast of lamb it traditionally went with. By then, everything sad and black might be buried under a thick layer of fresh white snow. Her mother was hoping for an early blizzard that would go down in the history books. *Forty feet of snow in September! Some say a miracle! (Others can't find the front doors to their houses. Still others can't find their houses at all.)*

"I like that they have pecans for beaks," Asa said about Milly's cookies. To get the pecans,

Milly had had to barter with the clerk at the general store. A small batch of her sugar cookies —his favorite—for a small bag of pecans, which seemed fair enough.

"The only thing I ever made was mud pie," Asa said.

"Mud pie's delicious," Milly said, more cheerfully than she meant. "But it's basically just chocolate pudding," she added to compensate.

"I mean with real mud," Asa said. He covered his mouth the moment he began to trip over his words. In school, Asa had worked with a woman every day on his speech. Now that he had graduated, he simply worked. "*M*'s are hard for me. If you can't understand—"

Milly thought of what Bett or Twiss would have said—*m-m-m*ean *m-m-m*ud *m-m-m*outh—and drew Asa's hand away from his face and into her own. "I understand you perfectly."

They walked that way, hand in hand, until Twiss darted out of the woods, jumped up and down yelling "hoo-hoo" on a bed of pine needles for a straight minute, and darted back into the woods again. Even though Twiss had disappeared, they could hear her laughing.

"I'm sorry," Milly said. She was suddenly conscious of how sweaty her hand was. Girls weren't supposed to sweat, let alone sweat on a boy they liked. "My sister has to be the center of attention or she'll die."

"Jumping out of the woods is like a survival mechanism then," Asa said.

"Now she'll live another five minutes," Milly said, smiling at him.

The two of them continued circling the meadow, and the mower, but didn't leave it for the pond or the woods or even the spotted monarch butterfly that flitted back and forth between the two. Above them was a patch of blue, blue sky. Below them a series of snake holes, which Milly stepped carefully around since the snakes they belonged to had already laid the first of the season's leathery-shelled eggs and the snakes were as long as she was. She didn't want Asa to know that she shared her father's fear of them, or that once, when Twiss put a garter snake in her bed, she'd sprained her ankle trying to get away from it.

Asa pointed to Twiss, who was hanging from the branch of a pine tree. "Has it been five minutes already? Your sister's persistent."

"Even when she's not doing something," Milly said, "she's doing something."

"I don't have a sister," Asa said. "I mean I used to, but she died when I was four. My mother did too. Before we came to Wisconsin."

"Do you remember them?" Milly said, thinking of the story Bett had told her.

"Sometimes I think I do," Asa said, scratching his cheek as if he didn't know what else to do with his free hand. "But then I realize they're my father's memories, not mine. It's sort of like losing something you never knew you had, but always knew you wanted. All I know is my sister used to call me *Afa* because she couldn't pronounce *s*'s. She'd stick her tongue out at me if I wouldn't pick her up. Her hair was red as an apple—like your cousin's."

"What about your mother?" Milly said.

Asa glanced at the tractor. The field birds were pecking at the owl cookies Milly had left on the seat. They were bathing in the glass of iced tea. "It's hard just having a father."

Milly meant to reach for Asa's hand, but she pressed her lips against his lips instead. She didn't close her eyes like the actresses did in the movies, nor did she tilt her head or lift her foot off the ground romantically, flirtatiously. This was a practical kiss, a kiss meant to accomplish what she didn't know how to say meaningfully: *I'm so sorry.*

The two of them stood that way, still as the grass around them—for a second? a minute? an hour? forever—before Twiss leaped down from the branch of the tree she had climbed and a snake leaped up from the hole it had burrowed into and both of them hissed and hissed.

Milly jumped onto Asa's back, and Asa did his best to hold her there.

"It's just a rat snake," he said, shooing it away

with one hand and holding Milly's bare leg—
her dress had twisted and shimmied up her thigh
during her jump—with the other.

"They don't bite," he said. "Even if they do,
they're not poisonous."

"How can you tell?" Milly said, aware of his
hand on her leg, which felt practical yet
impractical at the same time. If he let go, she
would fall.

If he let go . . . *Don't let go.*

"His tail," Asa said. "Look how pointy it is."

Once the snake had gone back into its hole,
Milly stopped clutching Asa's back and let her
feet touch the ground again. She could hear
Twiss cackling from her place at the edge of the
woods. Milly was glad that Bett was gone;
there was a chance that Twiss wouldn't tell her
about the kiss and the snake, depending on how
generous she was feeling that evening and what
the doctor had discovered or not discovered
about Bett's lungs.

"Your heart thumped me," Asa said, after
they'd started walking again.

Milly untwisted her dress and smoothed her
hair. Her leg was back to being just her leg
again—functional. "Your heart thumped me,
too," she said.

Bett took much longer to come home than anyone expected, so that when Mr. Peterson finally

dropped her off in front of the porch, and kissed both of her cheeks like French people did, they were certain she'd walk through the screen door bearing bad news.

"Iron lung!" Twiss kept saying.

"That's for people who can't breathe on their own," Milly said.

"Iron lung!" Twiss said again anyway.

Their mother had just finished setting supper on the table and the three of them had bowed their heads to say grace, when Bett walked through the front door on her tiptoes, a brown paper package tucked under her arm. She was wearing different clothes than she'd left the house in. Her hair was different, too.

"Mr. Peterson took me to the salon," Bett said, and set her package on the chair she usually ate her meat in. "I had my first real haircut today. My first manicure, too." She waved her fingers in the air. "The woman said French girls paint their fingernails this way."

"Why are you walking on your toes?" Twiss said.

"I'm practicing," Bett said.

"For what?" Twiss said.

"They're pretty," their mother said about her fingernails.

"I could show you how to do it," Bett said.

"That dress—," Milly said.

"Is it silk?" their mother said.

Milly had seen the dress on display in one of the shopwindows in town. She'd also seen the price tag and had forced herself to keep walking.

Bett twirled around as if for the first time in her life. "Mr. Peterson thought I needed a new one. He didn't believe me when I told him I'd never worn something new."

"What about the old one?" their mother said.

"He bought me a pair of shoes, too." Bett went out to the porch and came back with another brown paper package and a rectangular box. "I don't even know how to walk in them."

"They look like sapphires," their mother said.

"Crystals actually," Bett said. "They're from London."

"Those are—," Twiss began.

"Magnificent," Milly said. "I didn't see them in the shop."

"They were in the bridal shop," Bett said.

"What about the old one?" their mother said again, about the dress she'd lent Bett.

"The shopkeeper wouldn't let me bring it home," Bett said.

"Wouldn't *let* you?" their mother said.

Bett opened the package she'd placed on the chair and handed their mother a light green day dress with an even lighter green floret at the back.

"She sent me home with this instead."

"For me?" their mother said, draping the dress

over one of the kitchen chairs and then walking around that chair, admiring the fine fabric with her fingers, and smiling girlishly—she said she hadn't been in such close proximity to a dress of this quality since she was sixteen—until one of her nails, which the washboard had made jagged, pulled a tiny green thread loose.

"Mr. Peterson thought you'd like it more than your other one," Bett said.

Their mother took a step back from the dress.

"It's from Europe," Bett said.

"No matter how much I'd like it to be otherwise, and believe me I would," their mother said, "when I look out the window, I see cornfields, not the Eiffel Tower and cappuccino."

"What's cappuccino?" Bett said.

"It's a nice gesture," their mother said. "I just don't think it would fit me."

"Hello! Dresses are boring!" Twiss said. "What's wrong with your lungs?"

"See for yourself," Bett said, and handed Twiss an oversized envelope.

Twiss ripped the X-ray films out of the envelope and held them up to the light, although she had no idea what she was looking at. "I don't see anything," she said.

"That means I just have asthma," Bett said.

"Do you still have to eat meat?" Milly said.

"Not if I don't want to," Bett said.

"Do you have to stay in bed?" Twiss said.

"Only if I feel like it," Bett said.

Their mother put her plate beside the sink. She hadn't eaten a single bite of the supper she'd spent the afternoon preparing. Her napkin was still folded neatly on the table.

"I'm glad you're all right," she said to Bett. Even though it was only six o'clock, she yawned and slipped quietly upstairs.

After their mother closed her bedroom door, Bett said, "Why wouldn't your mother take the dress? It was the right size. And even if it wasn't, we could have altered it to fit her."

"Would your mother take the dress?" Milly said.

"What does my mother have to do with it?" Bett said.

"They're sisters," Milly said.

"Tell me everything about the doctor's office!" Twiss said. "What kind of instruments did he use? Did he take a sample of your lungs? With a scalpel?"

"This is the twentieth century," Bett said. "Not the Dark Ages."

"What did you and Mr. Peterson talk about?" Milly said.

"You, actually," Bett said. "He wanted to know what you were like."

"What did you say?" Milly said.

"I told him you were the meanest person I'd ever met. I also told him you made sacrifices to pagan gods with pigs' hearts, but that you were just biding your time with them until you got a human one. Everyone knows how powerful they are in comparison."

"You didn't," Milly said.

"You're right," Bett said. "I told him you were nicer than the word 'nice.' "

"What did Mr. Peterson say?" Milly said.

"He said, 'That's nice.' "

Before Bett regaled Twiss with details about the doctor's office—no, there wasn't a giant jar of pus on the counter, but there was a book with sketches of different kinds of skin and bone diseases—she told Milly that Asa had come to town, too.

What are you trying to do? Milly thought.

"I was in the bridal shop," Bett said, "standing on the fitting pedestal entranced by the sparkle of the shoes in the mirrors. I guess Asa didn't recognize me in the new dress and the new hair and all. He came in with grass stuck all over him and looked at me like he was about to really look at me—like I was someone worth stopping to admire—but then it was like he remembered something suddenly because he opened the shop door and left."

"That's all?" Milly said, happy and sad at the same time.

"He had a little purple flower sticking out of his front pocket," Bett said. "I'm guessing some-

226

one came over to mow the property today and someone else brought out more than a plate of cookies and lemonade this time."

Milly stared at Twiss. *Hold your tongue.* Which Twiss did.

After that, Milly went upstairs to look in on her mother.

"I'm so jealous you got X-rays!" Milly heard Twiss say as she opened her mother's bedroom door. "I would kill for X-rays, especially when people claim I don't have a heart."

Me too, Milly thought concerning the jealousy part, but for much different reasons.

Although she had pined over the blue silk dress that now belonged to Bett, that wasn't what she was really jealous of. Or the shoes, although they were stunning. Wanting the dress and the shoes was a controllable desire; though it was difficult, she'd walked away from the dress when she saw the price tag dangling from the material like a lock. Her desire for Mr. Peterson's affection was different; that he so obviously preferred Bett hurt her terribly.

Milly thought of how Asa had held her up in the meadow and wished he was in the room with her now, doing exactly the same thing. She touched her leg on the place that Asa had touched it, but there was no magic in the pads of her fingers, just as there was no magic left in her lips. That she would have to wait until it rained again to feel what she'd felt that afternoon in the meadow was unthinkable. That was the difference between yesterday and today, perhaps the only difference between then and now. Yesterday, she had hope. Today, she had relief. She didn't know what she would have tomorrow.

"Mom?" she said, a few steps into the darkened bedroom.

"I'm just tired," her mother said from beneath the covers.

The room smelled of dust, of light that had been abruptly cast out by the drawing of the shades. "I'm tired too," Milly said.

Her mother made a space for Milly in her bed. That night, the two of them slept side by side in their clothes without supper in their bellies or pillows beneath their heads (her mother had given her pillows to Bett). When her mother finally fell asleep, her breathing became less labored than it was when she was awake. According to Twiss, everyone dreamed whether or not they wanted to. What her mother was dreaming about Milly didn't know; she'd drawn her knees to her chest like a baby. Beyond the windows, Milly heard the sound of nails being driven into wood. Her father, no doubt. Trying to find a way to live without golf.

Before Milly fell asleep, and dreamed whatever she was meant to dream, she unfolded a thin cotton blanket and covered her mother with it.

Even at the height of the summer, the room had a draft. Milly kissed her mother's neck—*I wouldn't have taken that dress either*—and rolled over so that as she drifted off to sleep she'd be facing the windows and, though the shades were drawn, the little purple meadow, which would never again be to her what by its nature it was: grass and dirt and weeds.

18

When the water ran clear, Twiss stopped pumping and drank a mug of it down. As she bent to put the mug back in its place on the rusty handle, the goldfinch fell out of the front pocket of her work shirt onto the wooden platform, which their father had built around the pump when they were young so their shoes wouldn't get muddy every time they were thirsty. The boards were as slick and black as the stones at the bottom of Mill Creek, although this summer, because no rain had fallen, the boards dried too quickly to grow mold.

Twiss picked up the goldfinch. Like Milly, she didn't know if she could muster the energy to find the trowel and go back to the gladiola bed, where she'd have to get on her hands and knees and dig down into the earth far enough that the squirrels and field mice wouldn't pull the gold-finch back up and make a postmortem meal out of her hard work; she didn't know if she could muster the energy for another disfigurement, another little death.

Twiss had read stories about native people who stuck their dead up in the trees, suspending their souls like ornaments so that whatever god they believed in could pluck them up into the heavens and the afterlife, if there was such a thing.

For most old women in Wisconsin, only two choices were available: to believe in God so as to thwart the fear of the inevitable—*God will lift me up so that I will still be me, just me in a different place, an airy place with fine table-cloths and even finer silver settings*—or to believe in God so as to thwart the inevitable itself—*God, spare me another year, another month, another day, another hour, another minute, another second.* Twiss had created a third choice: to believe in the inevitability of fear on the eve of one's death. Good old-fashioned debilitating fear; that's why she'd made Milly agree to wheel her onto the porch when death knocked on their bedroom door.

Give me lightning! she thought. *Give me thunder! Give me the storm of my life!*

Should the air be still and the sky be blue like it was today when the reaper came for her, she'd simply refuse to die. If you could live through a walloping tornado, shouldn't you also be able to live through a sedate, if blistering, summer afternoon? If the weather (and the reaper) wouldn't accommodate her, there was always the river, which would gladly swallow an old woman. Of course, there was the getting her to the river if for some reason she couldn't get there herself, but she had Milly for that. Twiss would just have to make sure she died first.

That was where Twiss's real fear came in, the kind that arrived in the late hours of the night disguised first as something else—a lamp shade, a shadow, a creaking floorboard—and burrowed in between what she wanted and what she could get. Instead of whispering, like every other decent, well-bred fear, this one yelled in her ear while she slept.

Fat chance of dying outside, Twiss! We have the pope to accommodate! Do you know what kind of God power it takes to organize a procession of that size? Through the streets of Vatican City. Those great cobbled messes! So you see, there is not much God power left for someone as unlovable as you.

All will leave you . . .

"Did you hear that?" Twiss would say to Milly after the voice had trailed off.

"What?" Milly would say groggily from her bed.

"The Scornful God voice."

"You were dreaming."

"Maybe I'm going crazy."

"You've always been crazy. Go back to sleep."

"You have to promise me something."

"I promise to wheel you onto the porch."

"Because I can't die inside this house," Twiss would say. "I can't die like *them*."

"Then I won't let you," Milly would say.

Twiss would think of her mother and her father. She'd think of the town fair and of Father Rice—of all the ways her Purple Prairie Tonic succeeded and all the ways it failed.

"The bathtub was *full* of weeds," she'd say to Milly, thinking of the green stains, which had faded but were still visible around the rim of the tub. "What was I thinking?"

"You were just being you," Milly would say and roll back onto her side.

19

Y ou are a wonderful young woman! Father Rice assured Twiss in his letter back to her the summer Bett came down from Deadwater. Twiss had waited for his fourth letter with the same impatience Bett had waited for the first one from her mother, Aunt Gertrude. In her letter,

Twiss had written to Father Rice about the goings-on in Spring Green and had asked him about the goings-on in Illinois, as well as asking a series of questions about the state of her soul. Not going to church regularly after the Mrs. Bettle/organ/"Don't any of you care that you're going to hell?" debacle had made her less certain of her convictions, her nonbelief in belief. She'd written, among other things,

> *Dear Father Rice,*
> *I'm afraid I might be going to Hell, after all. A life of adventure, I think, may cost too much.*
> *What do you think?*
>
> > *Sincerely, Twiss*
>
> *P.S. Have you ever known anyone named Carlos Vidales of Rosarie?*
> *P.P.S. How is Beardsley?*

> *Dear Twiss,*
> *I can assure you that God looks gently on you—you are not, as your fears have it, going to Hell for your girlish (boyish?) misdeeds. Although it's extremely unpriestly of me, I should tell you I don't believe in hell; I suppose it shouldn't be capitalized then, should it? I believe that people have goodness in them and badness, too, and*

that in our lifetimes we usually display and witness both.

I apologize if my first letter had an ill effect on you; perhaps my cautioning planted seeds of fear? What I really want to say is this: You have always been so full of questions and passion and bravery, you simply can't expect your life to turn out like everyone else's in Spring Green. Even my life has taken a different course, and I didn't have nearly as much zest for the world as you do.

I'd like to tell you a story I haven't told anyone—take from it what you will.

When I was a boy, my mother said my favorite thing to play with was a plain gray stone. She said she took it from the garden one day and gave it to me, so that I might stop pulling on the hem of her dress and urging her to pick me up. She was busy, as country women often are. I remember taking that stone into my hands as if it were an extension of my mother and so would somehow keep me safe.

I grew up with that stone. I honored it. I even etched my initials into its hard skin. For years, I carried it in my pocket—to and from my father's untimely funeral, my brother's, and finally my poor mother's. Over time, the weight of the stone wore my shirt pockets thin. I remember the first time I felt for the stone and found it was not there: I was wandering along the country road by Lilly chapel. When my fingers met with fabric, I knew I'd lost the stone, but also that I'd lost something less explicable, too. Although I'd known it intellectually for quite a while, I understood then—I felt it then for the first time in that empty pocket —that there was no one left in the world who loved me.

It was a feeling I never quite recovered from. I walked inside Lilly chapel to sit down and I never really got up again; that is, until now. Fear kept me indoors for most of my life. The possibility of love is what finally brought me out. For myself? Another? I'm not certain, even now.

I found my stone the morning I decided to leave the church and Spring Green, you see, when I was cutting the weeds back by the road. I don't know what it meant or means, but I have enjoyed the not knowing even if it has translated to some loss— heavy at times, I admit—along the way.

From your very own, Father Rice

P.S. Yes, I knew a man named Carlos, once. Why do you ask?

P.P.S. Thank you for asking after Beardsley. You would like him. Beardsley's been out west—before his mother became ill and he came back to Illinois to care for her (and before the accident at the mill). He rode horses in the Great Wild West Rodeo in Cheyenne, Wyoming. He's also been to the Continental Divide!

After Twiss finished reading Father Rice's letter at the mailbox, she walked back down the driveway with the rest of the mail tucked under her arm and Father Rice's letter tucked into the pocket of her coveralls. Although his stone story seemed sad to her upon the first reading and maybe a little miraculous, too, for now Twiss focused on the fact that he'd told it to her and no one else rather than on its meaning. She also focused on the *You are not going to hell* part. And the *You are a wonderful young woman!* part. It was nice to be called wonderful by an adult instead of awful, terrible, deficient, sadistic, selfish, greedy—yikes! that list was getting long. Twiss's favorite of the unfavorites was contrary (just for the sake of it!).

She kicked at the gravel in front of her, smiling at the reddish dust that clung to her shoes and coveralls, at the anthills between her feet and the slivery spiderwebs in the switchgrass on either side of the driveway. She'd been so distracted with Bett in the house and her father in the barn and Father Rice in one-third of a room in Illinois that she'd missed the slow accumulation of summer this year; she hadn't noticed the leafy stalks of rhubarb or the toothy cotton plants that had sprouted up in the alfalfa fields on the other side of the road. Or the bright orange tiger lilies, which grew everywhere in the country despite their being unwild.

The beginning of August was Twiss's favorite part of the summer; the world seemed the most alive and full to her then—*the most everything.* Even the earth smelled earthier somehow. Twiss loved the days just before the world started to turn inward again, to shrivel and brown. In the past, she'd take long walks around the property, memorizing the overgrown look of the land and the garden, the grass and the trees, the black upturns of field soil, so that in winter she'd have the promise of summer inside of her, the melting, the growth.

Twiss flipped through the stack of mail beneath her arm. When she noticed the brown letter addressed to her cousin, she gave up memorizing the look of twisting vines. The envelope, which Bett had waited for all summer, was worn badly at the top as if it had been opened and closed many times before the final sealing; it said Deadwater without saying it at all.

Twiss ran into the house.

"Bett!" she called. "Your letter finally came!"

Bett was scrubbing down the linoleum in the kitchen, which Twiss's mother had asked her to do (forgetting about Bett's new nails—but Bett said, *It's all right,* when Twiss's mother remembered on her way out the door). She and Milly went to the general store to see if they could extend their credit line with another basket of Milly's sugar cookies until next week when their father received his paycheck from the dairy, which was even smaller than when he'd worked at the golf course and which Twiss's mother had trouble making work.

When Twiss gave Bett the letter, Bett said, "It's from Deadwater."

"That's good, right?" Twiss said.

Bett got up off her hands and knees. "If it were still June or July maybe. I've written my parents a letter every week since I've been here. This is the first one I've gotten back. The postman must feel sorry for me."

Bett took the letter upstairs with her and didn't come back down.

Twiss finished scrubbing the linoleum and then waxed it, too, because the silence in the house felt the same as it did the night she returned from the golf course, when she'd tossed her pillow at Milly and Milly had tossed it back and Twiss had fallen asleep thinking about the lonely look of the flag pin in the seventeenth hole. After Twiss was done with the kitchen floor, she moved on to the floor in the living room. The letter from Deadwater was a strong reminder that in a month Bett was going to go back there, a truth Twiss couldn't scrub or wax away. In a fit of sadness and something else she couldn't quite identify, she took Bett's hip boots from the closet and hid them deep in the cellar where light didn't reach. She couldn't imagine spending almost a whole year without Bett. She just couldn't.

The morning dragged on and on, with Twiss watching the cuckoo clock and waiting for Bett to spring forth. She didn't want to go up there without being invited, but at noon, after attempting to write a letter to Father Rice—*Dear Father Rice, Why did you tell* me *that story and no one else? What is a Continental Divide?*—she went up to her bedroom anyway.

"It's me," she said to Bett, pressing her face against the door. "Can I come in?"

"All right," Bett said.

When Twiss walked into the room, she found Bett sitting on her bed instead of on the SS *Forest.* "I feel braver over here," Bett said.

Twiss sat down beside her cousin. When she saw the wet spots on her pine needle pillow and on Bett's cheeks, she said, "What's wrong?"

Bett touched the worn part of the letter. "Why did your mom marry your dad?"

"I'm not really sure," Twiss said. "She says for love, but she never says anything else."

"Didn't your dad used to be an amazing golfer?"

"He still is," Twiss said.

Bett smiled faintly. "My dad can catch a trout with his bare hands."

Twiss looked toward the window and the barn, her father. Ever since he took her to the course after it had closed, she'd lost the feeling of him watching over her and Milly, which made her wonder if he'd been watching over them at all.

Bett let go of the letter. "My mom says she married my dad because he fried his own eggs in the morning. She says she's divorcing him for the same reason."

"Your mom and dad are getting a divorce?" Twiss said.

"I knew it since she sent me down here. I just didn't know it officially."

All at once, Bett pulled Twiss to her. "I'm going to be all alone."

Although Twiss had seen Milly and her mother cry plenty of times, and although she'd cried a few times herself, seeing tears roll down Bett's cheeks frightened her.

"No, you're not," she said to Bett.

Twiss stroked her cousin's hair as softly as her calloused fingers could. Bett's skin smelled of slightly soured milk and starch, which might have been off-putting to other people but wasn't to Twiss. With her cheek, Twiss grazed her cousin's shoulder and neck and the little blue vein that pulsed between them.

"Everything's going to be all right," she said as gently as she could.

Bett pulled back from Twiss a little. She looked at her a long while before she traced the freckles along the bridge of Twiss's nose with her index finger.

"You've got the Big Dipper on your face."

"I do?" Twiss said.

"I almost believe you," Bett said, her hands on her stomach. Quickly, before Twiss even knew what was happening, she pressed her lips against Twiss's which were chapped and a little bit sunburned.

The two girls kept their eyes open and on each other; it was then that Twiss noticed the tiny dashes of green in her cousin's brown eyes, which reminded her of crocuses peeking out from the earth uncertainly in April, the first evidence of spring. *You are someone worth looking at,* Twiss thought. She didn't realize she was being kissed until the kiss was over.

"If you were a boy," Bett said, "I'd marry you right now."

Twiss touched her lips with the tips of her fingers, wondering about the tingling sensation at the corners of her mouth, the leaping of her heart against her ribs.

Bett drew her fingers to her lips too. "Promise me you won't tell anyone about my parents. You're the only one I can stand knowing the truth."

After that, the two of them went back downstairs as if nothing had happened.

Twiss wasn't sure what *had* happened, only that she felt strangely happy, floaty even, when earlier she'd felt grumpy. Milly and her mother came back from town, and Bett helped them prepare a meatless lunch—*Thank the Lord!* she said in a voice as happy as anyone else's.

Twiss went out to the barn to ask her father for advice about her tonic. The fact of Bett's lips pressed against her own made Twiss forget about what Bett had told her, the same way she'd forgotten about Father Rice and his stone.

Selfish, she'd later think of her response and wish she'd done more to assure Bett that everything really was going to be all right. Maybe then it would have been.

As it was, Twiss skipped all the way to the barn. Dr. Greene and Mrs. Collier, both long without a spouse (although for not much longer as fate would have it), were supposed to be bringing over a bag of medicinal roots as well as a few cases of Mrs. Collier's Mason jars that afternoon. Mrs. Collier said she had better things to do than make jam now that Dr. Greene had taught her how to drive. She'd taught him how to knit.

"You have to be careful," Dr. Greene had said when Twiss told him she'd been thinking about using rhubarb leaves. "You don't want to accidentally poison the entire town."

"I guess not," Twiss had said.

Mr. Stewart, Milly's science teacher, had also offered advice. He'd brought over a glass beaker and a pair of safety glasses from the laboratory at school, as well as a sheet of paper filled up with equations.

"Maybe you should show that to Milly," Twiss had said. "She got an F because she wouldn't dissect a sheep's eye. I'd get an F even though I would."

"It was a brain," Mr. Stewart said.

"See?" Twiss said.

Mr. Stewart folded his equations and put them back into the pocket of his pants. "Your sister may be the only one who doesn't think I'm irrelevant."

"Milly doesn't think anyone's irrelevant," Twiss said.

Twiss knocked on the barn door.

"Dad?" she said, just as her father came to it with Rust-O-Lonia in his hand. His arms were covered with sand and sweat. A wood chip was stuck to his cheek.

"Bett says I have to put something secret in my tonic," Twiss told him, which Bett had told

243

her when she'd passed by the bathroom and saw Twiss dumping baking soda into the tub— *People won't want to pay for what they can mix up themselves. You've got to give them the impression of exclusivity, like, "If you don't buy this, you won't have a shot at happiness."*

"I'm making something too," Twiss's father said.

Now was the time to ask what he'd been doing in the barn, but Twiss couldn't. "Bett said people like secrets even though they say they don't," she said instead.

"How old is your cousin?"

"Eighteen," Twiss said.

"I'd have thought she was older than that," her father said.

"Why?" Twiss said.

"For everything she understands."

"Like what?" Twiss said, thinking *Bett's mine!*

"She's a really good listener," her father said.

"I haven't noticed," Twiss said, thinking *You're mine!*

Twiss was about to tell her father that Bett had broken whatever confidence they had and told her and Milly the story of Jester almost drowning in the river, when it occurred to Twiss that that might have been his aim. But why?

"When it's finished," her father said, looking at Rust-O-Lonia and then over his shoulder at whatever he was making in the barn, "everything will be wonderful again."

Even though Twiss could have pushed past him and discovered what was going to make everything wonderful again, she didn't want to have to take what wasn't hers; she wanted to be invited in. That her father had invited Bett into the barn made Twiss wild with jealousy, although she was confused about who she was jealous of.

"Bett has a bald spot on the back of her head," she told her father.

"Is that so?" her father said.

"She has lice, too. When I changed her sheets, I saw them jumping all over her bed."

"It can't be as bad as that," her father said.

"Her toenails curl under they're so long."

"We should write to the *Guinness Book of World Records*."

"They break off," Twiss said. "I doubt they'd get here in time."

Her father put down Rust-O-Lonia. "You're greener than the greenest green."

"Bett thinks green is just a color," Twiss said.

"In Deadwater, it probably is," her father said.

Before Twiss could open her mouth again, her father latched on to her arms and spun her around like he used to when she was a little girl. "Who's my little champion!"

"Put me down!" Twiss said, although she clung to his back the way she'd seen Milly cling to

Asa's in the meadow. "I feel sick! I might throw up on your shoe!"

Her father set her on the ground, but not immediately. He spun her around one more time. While he spun her, he sang, "There's nothing as wonderful as spinning my daughter around on a summer afternoon" to the tune of "Paper Moon."

"Those aren't the real words," Twiss said.

"They're the only words I can think of right now," her father said.

Which made Twiss forgive him for the milk pail and for Jester—whatever he'd meant by telling that story. "I was just kidding about Bett and the bald spot and stuff," she said. "She just got a pedicure. It's supposed to be French."

"Your mother must be jealous," her father said. "When I met her, she used to have perfect little pink seashell toenails."

"Now she has wolf feet," Twiss said. "Every night, she tears up her sheets."

"You're terrible," her father said.

He reached into the back pocket of his trousers and handed Twiss a note to give to her mother. This time, the note was folded several times and taped securely shut. It was written on light yellow writing paper instead of on a scoring card.

"Don't read this one," he said to Twiss very seriously.

"What does it say?" Twiss said.

"It's a secret," her father said.

"Then why don't you give it to her yourself?"

"Just promise me you won't open it," her father said.

"I promise," Twiss said.

"Double promise," her father said.

"I promise."

Twiss set off toward the pond to look for her secret ingredient, but she stopped when she got to the place where the reeds came up to her waist, and the barn and house were shielded from her view. She'd never read her mother's or father's notes without Milly standing beside her to translate their words into words that were more hopeful, but Milly was busy standing in the kitchen drafting plans for her cake for the town fair. She'd said she wanted to win the twenty-five-dollar prize to help bring Father Rice back, but tractor sketches were strewn all over the kitchen table, along with bowls of bright green frosting and a miniature steering wheel she'd fashioned from a rope of black licorice.

Plus, Milly's face couldn't hold a lie, even for twenty-five dollars.

Earlier, she'd gone out to measure the backseat of the car.

"Don't forget to account for potholes," Twiss had said as a joke.

"You're right," Milly had said thankfully.

Mrs. Bettle had brought over a twenty-pound

sack of flour for Milly to experiment with once she'd learned of the contest. Mrs. Collier had brought the leftover sugar she used to use for canning. The crowning offer was a small bottle of liquor from Mr. Stewart, who claimed he'd fallen in love with a woman once over a forkful of Grand Marnier–infused frosting.

"Estelle," he said. "That was her name."

"What does it taste like?" Twiss said.

"Oranges," Mr. Stewart said.

"What happened?" Milly said.

"She didn't like fossils as much as she thought she did," Mr. Stewart said.

"Mrs. Bettle's not married," Twiss said to Mr. Stewart. "I bet if you drank the bottle instead of putting it in a cake, you'd fall in love with her, too. She looks like an ottoman, but you don't seem concerned with the more superficial qualities of women."

"Twiss," Milly said.

"Milly," Twiss said.

"She's right," Mr. Stewart said. "I'm too sentimental for my own good."

With her father's note in her hand, Twiss sat in the reeds. She snapped one of them off and positioned it between her thumbs. She used to be able to play the entire national anthem on a single reed, but today the reed broke after only a few notes, although *Oh, say can you see . . .* was just enough to attract Kingsley, the grandfather of all the snapping turtles that lived in the pond. Twiss jumped up and away. She didn't toy with Kingsley the way she did with the other turtles; unlike his female counterparts, Kingsley lunged for whole limbs, vital organs. He smirked the way Twiss imagined real kings did when they sentenced someone to death.

Why had her father given her a note that didn't look anything like the others? When had he gone into the house to get the yellow paper? The tape? The nerve? Twiss thought about what she could do, what she *should* do, which led her to another thought, and then another. No teacher had ever believed her when she claimed that the dog ate her homework, and she was certain her father wouldn't believe it if she told him Kingsley ate his note, either. But Twiss offered it to Kingsley anyway, who snapped the words up quickly, but with no more interest than he paid a golf ball or a tin can. Then he dragged himself back to the pond.

Maisie . . .
Margaret . . .
I love you . . .
I hate you . . .

What would her father have written? What came between love and hate, Maisie and Margaret? Twiss went back to the house to draft a new note. Since her father hadn't written the note on old scoring paper, the message may have been more positive than the other ones. She didn't know why, now, after so many notes, this one felt so crucial to the future of their family. Lately, her mother was less mournful when she gazed at the barn, as if, like Aunt Gertrude, she'd begun to figure out how to live without Twiss's father. *Dear Maisie,* she wrote, forming the letters in the slanty way her father formed his, *I miss your perfect little pink seashell toenails. Will you go to the fair with me? Love, Joe.*

After she perfected his handwriting, Twiss folded the note the way her father had and taped it closed. Then she went to the garden where Bett and her mother were pulling up carrots and potatoes and placing them in their aprons.

"Dad said to give you this," she said.

"What is it?" her mother said.

"How am I supposed to know?" Twiss said. "It's taped shut."

She pulled a carrot from the earth and threw it in the grass before she stomped back into the house. But from the kitchen window she watched her mother turn away from Bett to read the note. Her mother held on to the note with one hand until she saw how securely it was taped. When she let go of the end of her apron so she could use her other hand to open it, the carrots and potatoes she'd gathered fell to the ground.

"Are you all right?" Twiss heard Bett say.

"Clumsy is all," her mother said.

Bett went back to pulling up carrots, Twiss blushed at the thought of her cousin's lips on her own, and her mother opened the note. After her mother finished reading it, she folded it back up and tucked it into the pocket of her dress.

She knows it's not from him, Twiss thought. *She'll give me a turn with every belt in the house.*

But just before her mother went back to the carrots and the potatoes, back to whatever she and Bett were talking about before Twiss had interrupted them, her mother looked down at her soil-black feet and wiggled her toes.

That afternoon, Twiss's mother and Bett sat on the porch together with glasses of iced tea, looking at a book about French impressionists. ("I love the way he captures light," her mother said, to which Bett said, "Was the world a better place back then?" to which her mother said, "The world was always a better place back then.")

"Even the lily pads look hopeful," Bett said.

"Serene, I think," her mother said.

"Is there a difference?" Bett said.

Her mother placed her hand on Bett's.

"My God," she said. "I'm going to be sad to see you go at the end of the month."

Bett didn't say anything—she just kept staring at the lily pads, the yellows and greens and blues. Usually, she would have said something about lily pads in Deadwater, maybe how they ate frogs and insects that hopped onto them.

This time, she stayed silent.

"I can't wait to go up there," Twiss said, not understanding that the home Bett had left wouldn't be the home she returned to. "I'm going to canoe until my arms are like paddles."

"I'll have a different kind of countdown going then," her mother said.

"We don't canoe for fun," Bett said.

I'm sorry, Twiss mouthed to Bett, but Bett ignored her.

"What if I don't come back?" Twiss said to her mother.

"Just make sure to send my real daughter back," her mother said. She turned to the next page in the book. "Isn't it interesting how they bundle their haystacks in Europe?"

Twiss got up from her chair.

"I hate the impressionists!" she said, dragging Milly off the porch. "Moan-nay. Man-nay. Fan-nay. They make me want to draw pictures of the guillotine."

"What are we doing?" Milly said, hopping on one foot until she'd pulled her muck boot onto the other and then hopping on that foot until both feet were clad in rubber.

"Finding a secret," Twiss said.

She dragged Milly along through the back-yard, past the site of their unfinished tree house, until they were in the woods and Milly didn't need to be dragged anymore.

"I need to finish designing my cake," Milly said, but she kept walking anyway.

"You'll win whatever you make," Twiss said.

"This one has to be special," Milly said.

Twiss thought of the tractor drawings, of Asa and Milly pressed together in the meadow, of Bett's parents, and she stopped walking. "You have to promise me something as my sister."

"What?" Milly said, running into her back.

"That you won't leave until I'm old enough to leave, too."

"I thought you were going to pitch a tent in my backyard," Milly said.

"What if you don't have a backyard?" Twiss said.

"Then we'll have to put you up in the trees," Milly said.

"With a hatch, so I can see the stars?"

"Aren't we supposed to be finding a secret ingredient for your tonic?" Milly said.

"I did something," Twiss said, turning around. "I don't know if it's good or bad."

She told Milly about her father's note and about giving it to Kingsley, and then about her forgery and their mother's response to it. Twiss was expecting Milly to say that she'd have to apologize and bear whatever punishment their parents bestowed on her.

"That was one of the nicest things you've ever done," Milly said. "Dishonest, but nice."

253

"I did it for him," Twiss said.

Milly picked a wood chip out of Twiss's hair. "You're allowed to love her, too."

The two of them didn't find a secret ingredient for Twiss's tonic that day, even though they walked all the way to the river and back up through the fields and the woods. Somewhere along the way, Twiss had stopped worrying about the secret ingredient for her tonic and started to think about what might come of her note, her mother's wiggling toes, the belief in love.

20

Although Milly and Twiss spent most Augusts in Spring Green sitting on the porch with cold washcloths wrapped around their necks to keep off the heat, this year they spent the month getting ready for the fair. In an unusual show of generosity, their mother gave them fewer chores to complete and more time to tinker with their cake and tonic recipes. She'd even offered input, as did Mrs. Bettle, Mrs. Collier, Dr. Greene, and Mr. Stewart. In four weeks, the house accommodated as much traffic as it usually did in a year.

On the night before the fair, Mrs. Bettle decided Henry should run through a final dress rehearsal of "Ave Maria" in front of a crowd, since he was used to just performing for her. She'd brought along a cuttlebone in case he needed to be coaxed.

"I understand completely," Dr. Greene and the others said.

Bett had gone for a walk because she said she needed to be alone—since her mother's letter had arrived, she needed to be alone a lot. Twiss's father was in the barn.

Henry turned out to be quite a showman. When he finished singing, he bowed. Mrs. Bettle had sewn a tiny top hat for him.

"Oh, Henry!" she said. "You've made me so proud!"

"You've made me so loud," Henry said.

After the performance, Milly sliced up the last of her experimental cakes, a round vanilla cake she thought she might use to make the wheels of tractor, but decided against when she figured out how to make more realistic wheels by using a Bundt pan.

"Where's the real one?" Mrs. Collier said.

"I want it to be a surprise," Milly said.

"We're under strict orders not to go down to the cellar," their mother said. "But I don't need to see it to know she'll win. She's made eight cakes to get to this one. No one else will have worked that hard or gone through that much flour."

"*Seven,*" Milly said.

"I'm sure it will be wonderful," Mr. Stewart said.

"Father Rice will certainly be pleased," Dr. Greene said. "All this for him."

"Has anyone heard from him?" Mrs. Bettle said.

"I have!" Twiss said proudly. "We write letters to each other."

After the last piece of cake was eaten and everyone left, Milly went back to the cellar to examine her cake. Twiss stayed on the ground floor with her mother, who was cleaning up in the kitchen, humming "Ave Maria" as she wiped up the counters.

"He was surprisingly good," she said. "For a parrot."

"Parrots are smart," Twiss said. "Or didn't you know?"

Her mother stopped wiping off the counters in order to wipe off her hands. "I would be sad if you ran away, by the way," she said to Twiss. "Who would I have to scold?"

"I guess Milly would have to take up the slack," Twiss said.

"That might be asking too much of her," her mother said.

She handed Twiss a note to give to her father, which made Twiss think *It's about time!,* since she'd delivered her forged note nearly a month before. This one was written on pink paper with yellow roses hand-stenciled in the corners. Her mother opened up one of the cupboards and took down a piece of cake she'd hidden between a bag of rice and a box of cornmeal. "He always liked vanilla," she said and went back to the counters.

"Vanilla makes me want to throw up," Twiss said, but she took the note and the piece of cake out the front door. Although she had no intention of offering this note to Kingsley (her mother's looping handwriting was impossible to duplicate) or reading it, she was tempted by the words *For Joe,* which graced the front of it prettily.

No, no, no, she told herself. *I will not be a glutton for punishment.*

To distract herself, Twiss thought about Henry's stupid little top hat and then Mrs. Bettle's rear end. She thought of her tonic, which was sitting up in the bathtub, still foaming like the mouth of a rabid animal from all the baking soda she'd added. She'd put most of it in the Mason jars, and, as the name promised, it was purplish even if it wasn't all the other things she was planning on promising people. When thinking about her tonic didn't work, Twiss did the only thing she could think of to prevent herself from opening her mother's note; she set the note and the piece of cake on the water pump platform and climbed up into the nearest lilac bush to create a distraction: the barn window.

Should she look or shouldn't she? She was looking already.

The barn was dark except for the yellow light in the hayloft, which illuminated the loft and the dusty space directly below it. Twiss dropped the sprig of lilac she'd plucked from the branch when she saw the troughs of sand where the troughs of water used to be. The wall between the troughs, which had never been used to water horses or cattle as they were intended, had been knocked down and the equipment pushed into a corner and covered with a green tarp, on top of which sat a milk bucket and a triangular flag. On the opposite side of the barn, four evenly spaced moguls made of sand occupied the space where the extra bags of feed for the chicken used to be.

Twiss knew what her father had built. She'd watched him play the eighteenth hole countless times in the years he'd worked at the Spring Green course, as well as the last time he'd played it, when his ball landed in a fairway divot and Persy landed in the stream.

Her father walked into the light and out again.

"Dad!" she said, even though a pane of glass and a shadow were between them.

She'd never loved him or believed in him as much as she did just then—he was going to be the golf pro again! He hadn't given up on himself or on them. Maybe he was close to rebecoming what he'd been and recovering what he'd lost; maybe that was the reason Twiss hadn't felt him watching over her or Milly lately.

"Dad!" she said again. "I'm coming!"

Twiss was on her way down the lilac bush and was ready to burst or plow or smash through the barn door and jump straight into her father's arms like she did when she was a little girl, when she looked at the window again and saw Bett.

She and Twiss's father were standing between the second and third of her father's handmade moguls, looking toward the troughs of sand. Her father had his hand on Bett's shoulders, as if he were squaring her for a shot. Bett's cheeks were flushed, and the top button of her dress, the light green one Twiss's mother had given her, was undone.

"*Dad?*" Twiss said.

And then, beginning to lose her hold, "*Bett?*"

Twiss fell the rest of the way out of the lilac bush, and though the branches scraped her skin and she hit the ground hard, she hurried to the barn door, which she ripped open.

"Dad!" she yelled, and he turned.

Her father looked surprised and a little bit scared, which told Twiss she was right to have interrupted.

Bett dropped the golf club on the dirt. When she bent to pick it up, the little blue vein pulsed on her forehead.

"Twiss," she said in the same voice she'd said, *You've got the Big Dipper on your face.*

Twiss realized then that a new kind of love—different from the sisterly or fatherly kind or even the motherly kind—was what she'd felt when Bett's lips were pressed against hers the morning Aunt Gertrude's letter arrived. She knew because she was jealous of her father.

"Why didn't you tell me what you were working on?" Twiss said to him.

Her father's face said *I'm sorry.*

"He couldn't," Bett said, coming toward her. "We—"

Twiss backed away from the barn. She started running because the rush of her feelings frightened her and she didn't know how to untangle them. On her way to the driveway, she passed the water pump, the piece of vanilla cake, and the pretty pink note.

Dear Joe,
I would be honored to go to the fair with you.
Love, Maisie

21

Milly went into her father's old room, the prebarn, postmatrimonial spartan square. All that was left was a mattress with a head-shaped stain, a creaky box spring, and a skyscraper of dust sprouting ambitiously from each corner. After their parents died, they'd set the buck's head on their father's mattress—temporarily, they agreed—and shut the door.

Three years later, when they reopened it, the mattress was stained yellow and the skin and fur on the buck's head had peeled back, revealing the bones that had held it together in life and now in death, white and brittle as chalk. A pair of sensible sisters would have taken the buck out to the woods and let the animals take what they would and let the elements take care of the rest. Milly and Twiss hauled it up to the attic.

Twiss had wanted to send the buck's head to Bett, and Milly had had to work hard to convince her to leave Bett alone.

"Can't we at least send her its eyes?" Twiss had said. "We don't even have to write a return address on the envelope. The eyes speak for themselves."

Milly had put a mental hand on her hip

because, even then, she was tired of lifting up her real one. "How would you like to receive a pair of wolf eyes in the mail?"

"I'd like it just fine," Twiss had said.

"Go ahead then," Milly had said, but Twiss never did.

Milly went back into their mother's room to retrieve the bird book, which Twiss was outraged Milly had kept all of these years. Twiss was always threatening to burn it, but she said the act of burning it would lend it more credence than it deserved—which was really just Twiss's way of saying, *You deserve more than a lousy book about birds. We both do.*

Milly took the bird book up to the attic, although she had to rest on each step before she climbed the next one, her hip was so sore. If she'd purchased a more reasonable walker, she might have actually used it up where it was dark and no one would see her.

"What's the difference if people see you?" she could hear Twiss saying.

That was another interesting aspect of living with the same person for all your life; after fifty or sixty years, you didn't even have to be in the same room to have a conversation anymore. "I'm allowed to have a pinch of vanity, aren't I?" Milly said.

"You don't measure vanity like salt," Twiss said.

Milly turned on the light with one hand and clung to the banister with the other. She hadn't been up in the attic since she'd had to show a repairman where the roof was leaking. That day, she'd stopped at the top of the stairs and pointed at the bucket full of brownish water overflowing onto the floorboards in the corner.

"The water will keep finding its way in," he'd said. "I've seen it in these old houses before. At first, you'll use up all your pots and pans trying to contain it. You'll develop a system. The frying pan for the little leak, the saucepan for the medium one, and the Crock-Pot for the big one. You'll get to thinking your system's working fine. Well, even. Then one day you'll wake up and your bed will be floating."

Although the repairman's story didn't frighten Milly into going down to the bank and applying for a home repair loan, it did remind her of the story Bett had told about the flood before Deadwater was called Deadwater. She'd always liked the part about the jar of beef jerky getting caught in the gutter. Milly had never wanted to go there, in part because she didn't think she'd be able to survive what Father Stone would have called the ungodliness of such a place—if he didn't like leeches, he certainly wouldn't have liked murderous birds—but also because she was afraid of just how different it would be than Bett had described. People might not have had to canoe to get where they wanted to go. They might not have been hopeless and then what had happened would start to seem the way it had seemed to Twiss all along: unfair.

Milly sat on the nearest box that would support her weight. The box was full of her mother's old magazines, which were covered with green fuzz now. Apparently, it had been easier to carry them up two flights of stairs than to carry them to the trash on level ground.

"I might look at them again," Milly remembered telling Twiss. And she remembered thinking that she genuinely would, perhaps on a slow afternoon when the weather wasn't cooperating or if she wanted to get a new idea for a blanket or a scarf, although there was a limit on how many scarves a person could make in his or her lifetime.

"Just like I might finish my model airplane," Twiss had said.

"I'm still keeping them," Milly had said. "I don't think our mother would appreciate us throwing them out. Where do you think she got the idea for lamb *au lait* with root vegetables?"

"A French insane asylum?"

"Here," Milly had said, holding up one of the magazines, which was an admitted stretch since no recipe to her knowledge had ever called for lamb with milk, but she felt her mother deserved credit for all that she'd tried to hold together in the midst of everything falling apart.

"It was her own fault," Twiss had said.

Milly looked around the attic, at the boxes and chests and the half-finished projects scattered across the floor as if a storm had blown them there. The air up here seemed different than it did on the floor below; it smelled of toadstool and must, and it was sweet and acrid from years of being shut up without the sift of free-flowing air. Milly shifted her weight from one buttock to the other and in the middle of this maneuver (because at her age it really was a maneuver) she saw the case of leftover Purple Prairie Tonic, which was still contained by Mrs. Collier's Mason jars but was no longer evocative of anything in bloom. The jars were sitting on the floor below the boarded-up window as if the tiny slant of light might revive them; beyond the window the birds—finches, bluebirds, and a single upland plover—were chirping.

"I know you don't really think that," Milly said.

The sight of the Mason jars led her back to the town fair.

She could see Twiss rearranging her jars of Purple Prairie Tonic from a simple line into a pyramid, trying to sell them with a manic energy and an equally manic twinkle in her eye. She could see her mother and father strolling along in the late light, untwining their fingers, it seemed, just so they could entwine them again. And she could see Bett.

But of everything she saw, the motion of the Ferris wheel was the only thing Milly felt, the sailing up and the sailing back down.

22

The morning of the town fair, Milly fluttered around her cake, making last-minute adjustments to the decorations—tractor axles and gearshifts weren't as easy to render out of flour and butter as she'd thought they were going to be. The axles were nearly impossible to make symmetrical, and the gearshift wouldn't stay in the neutral position. Everyone else was working his or her hardest to distract Milly from completing this fine-tuning part of the process. Her mother was helping Mrs. Bettle subdue Henry ("It isn't fair! I don't want to go to the fair! I want a chocolate bar!" he kept saying, to which her mother said, "I hear you, honey; I'd like a chocolate bar too"), Bett was helping help Mrs. Bettle, and her father, by some odd miracle, had finally come out of the barn.

"What can I carry?" he said, and was handed Henry's cage and told to take it to the car, as if he'd merely been on vacation and had returned restored and a little bit brown.

The only person absent from the morning's bustle of events was Twiss, whom everyone assumed was out finding the ingredient that would make people want to buy her wellness tonic if the promise of happiness wasn't enough of a pull to give up a nickel. Twiss must have come to bed late the night before because neither Milly nor Bett had woken up, and she must have gotten up early because they didn't see her in the morning, either. She'd made her bed, which was unusual, but sometimes Twiss forgot that she was supposed to be rebelling.

"Your sister's determination is truly remarkable," Dr. Greene said to Milly. "I'm thinking of giving her my medicine bag. I'm too old to practice anymore. My hands shake too much. Besides, I think she has what it takes to be a doctor."

"A woman doctor?" Mrs. Collier said.

Dr. Greene put his hand on her shoulder and smiled at Mrs. Collier in a knowing way. "It's no different than a male knitter."

"Where is the infamous child anyway?" Mrs. Collier said.

"She's fourteen," Milly said.

"Anyone younger than I am is a child to me, dear," Mrs. Collier said.

Milly would have been more concerned about Twiss's whereabouts if her father were still out in the barn, but the problem of Twiss's forged note seemed to have resolved itself during the month of August without any intervention necessary on either of their parts. Besides, Milly was so busy thinking about the best way, given that Mrs. Bettle and Henry were squeezing in with them, to transport her cake from the house to the fair without damaging it that she didn't question either where Twiss was or how the problem had been resolved.

Even in their family, once every great while things just seemed to work out.

"This is the best-looking cake I've ever seen," Mr. Stewart said to Milly. "That's the luckiest young man in the world you've got there. I hope he knows that."

"It's for Father Rice," Milly said.

"After you, Asa was my best student," Mr. Stewart said.

"What are you two talking about?" Mrs. Bettle said, walking over. She was wearing a red polka-dot dress and a matching hat, which, along with the circles of strawberry-colored rouge on her cheeks and the frilly lace bows fixed to the tips of her shoes, made her look a little like a cupcake. "As you know, I don't like secrets. Now fess up."

Please don't tell her, Milly thought. *She'll tell Henry, and Henry will tell everyone at the fair.*

Mr. Stewart smiled. "We're talking about

the compounds in sugar. It's a water-soluble crystalline carbohydrate. There are three classifications: monosaccharides, disaccharides, and trisaccharides. What do you think about the saccharide family?"

"The only ride I care about is the one Henry and I are getting into town this morning," Mrs. Bettle said. "Parrots don't like jostling."

"What can I do to help?" Mr. Stewart said.

"You could escort me to the car," Mrs. Bettle said. "It would be just like me to trip over a pair of muck boots and ruin Henry's big day. He's been practicing for weeks, haven't you, my little sugar beet? Poor thing. See his eyes? I've seen dead people who look more alive."

He's a parrot, Twiss would have said, if she were there.

"Cucumbers work for that," Milly said because she wasn't.

"Henry hates cucumbers," Mrs. Bettle said. "But I'd take a slice or two. If Henry doesn't sleep, I don't sleep either. We've suffered a bout of insomnia recently. I do all right, but Henry says the most appalling things after a night of no sleep."

Milly cut the ends off a cucumber and handed them to Mrs. Bettle, who tucked them into her purse. "I hope you're planning to drive, Margaret," she said on her way out the front door. "We're going over the bridge, after all."

In the living room, Bett was fixing her hair in the mirror beside the bookshelf. She'd already put one of Milly's butterfly combs in and was wrestling with the other one in hopes of mashing down a cowlick that made a patch of her hair stand up like a weed.

"I'll never get used to this," she said out loud, but to herself.

"To what?" Milly said.

"Everything it takes to be marryable on this side of the Mississippi."

Milly took the comb out of Bett's hands and placed it in her cousin's hair. "Don't let Mrs. Collier hear you. She thinks everyone younger than her is a child."

"She should stick to thinking about jam," Bett said.

After Milly had adjusted the comb, she stepped back to have a look at the overall effect of her placement and to see if the two butterflies and their wings lined up. After negotiating the axles and the gearshift, her sense of symmetry had improved.

"I think Dr. Greene loves her," she said.

Bett looked toward the kitchen, where Milly's mother and father were standing. Milly's father had a pencil in his left hand and her mother had her back pressed against the molding. From the living room, it looked like they were either about to kiss or about to measure each other's heights. Both of them were smiling.

"You're the worst kind of optimist," Bett said, as if something about the view caused her sadness. She took the butterfly clips out of her hair and gave them back to Milly. "You always believe in love."

When Twiss didn't pile into Dr. Greene's car or their own with everyone else, it was decided that their little motorcade would have to leave her behind. Mrs. Collier honked the horn several times in a row; ever since she'd learned how to drive, she didn't like standing still for too long. She and Dr. Greene were talking about taking a trip out west, where Mrs. Collier would have miles of open road to roar the engine across. Dr. Greene thought that seeing the cutout of the Grand Canyon might be inspiring to his new interest in female handiwork. Mr. Stewart had expressed interest in such a trip—for the geology.

Milly's mother offered the driver's seat to Milly's father, but he said he'd been looking forward to riding, if that was all right with her.

Looking forward? Milly thought.

"You rest," her mother said. "I'll drive."

Although Milly was enjoying her parents' seemingly genuine affection for each other, a smidge of Twiss's pessimism seeped in. *What did you do with my real parents? The ones who hate each other? The ones who write "No, I will not!"* The people in the front seat seemed like

271

imposters, only they were of an unusual sort: They were impossibly friendly, impossibly nice. Could Twiss's note, her scrawling "perfect little pink seashell toenails," really have been that transformative? This morning, Milly had walked into the bathroom to brush her teeth and saw her mother sitting on the edge of the bathtub, trimming her toenails and sanding down her calluses with a pumice stone.

"We can't leave Twiss behind," she said.

"We can't wait for her either," Mrs. Bettle said. She was sitting beside Milly in the place where Twiss usually sat. Since Mrs. Bettle was larger than Twiss, Milly was forced to ride with her cake on her lap and Bett was forced to squeeze in next to Henry in the very back. Bett was afraid that Henry would defecate on her new crystal shoes and so placed them beneath a pile of wrinkled golf shirts and a pair of golf trousers.

"It's timeliness that's next to godliness," Mrs. Bettle said. "Not that your sister is known for her cleanliness, either. Her fingernails are filthy."

"That's because she worked so hard digging up things for her tonic," Milly said.

"This is no doubt another one of her schemes," Milly's mother said. "To hold us up long enough for all of us to miss the fair."

"That does sound like our Button," Milly's father said.

"That's what Rollie calls her," Milly said.

272

"It's decided then," her mother said.

On their way out of the driveway and down the country road, Milly scanned the meadow and the pond, the woods and the water pump beside the barn. She knew that Twiss was all right in the physical sense—her sister always managed to get herself out of whatever trouble she'd managed to get herself into—but that something else was wrong. Twiss would never have abandoned her tonic and the town fair otherwise; she'd already predicted how many of the jars she would sell and what portion of a train ticket that would buy for Father Rice, and for the first time in her life, she had learned how to navigate fractions—*The lowest common denominator of five-sixths, one-fourth,* she'd said, *is twelve!*—as if in her head a light had gone off.

As suddenly as Twiss had mastered basic math and her parents had returned to communicating the way that normal parents did, Milly's cake and the cuff links she'd been dreaming about buying suddenly didn't seem as important as they had all along. What would anything really be without Twiss to pitch a tent in her backyard? Or in a spare bedroom with a view of the stars? The worst kind of trouble for Twiss to get into was the kind she couldn't easily get out of: the mental kind.

All Milly really knew was that something was askew, like the weather vane pointing north when it should have been pointing south, and that Mrs. Bettle took up too much room. When they went over the first of the bumps on the bridge over the Wisconsin River, Milly wasn't holding on to the cake as tightly as she'd planned and it tipped this way and that, its oversized tractor wheels and perfectly aligned axles mashing against the side door of the car.

"My cake!" she said, when what she meant was *Where are you?*

Milly didn't survey the damage her cake had incurred until they arrived at the fair because at that point in the day so little could be done to mend it. The judging had been scheduled as the first event of the fair in order to prevent the late morning and afternoon sun from liquefying the cakes into slicks of buttercream and slides of chocolate. Milly had brought along a sculpting spatula, but had left everything else behind.

"It's not so bad," Mrs. Bettle said.

Milly placed the cake on the hood of the car and everyone gathered around it, assuring her that the dented folds of black frosting on the wheels were hardly noticeable and wouldn't affect her chances of winning the prize.

In a strange kind of unison, they said, "The hubcaps are still intact."

"Nobody cares about hubcaps," Milly said, staring at the John Deere lettering and beneath it the PROPERTY OF THE SPRING GREEN

GOLF COURSE lettering, which she'd designed to look like a stamp but which had been badly mauled. "It looks like it's been in an accident."

"What do you think, Joe?" her mother said.

"Accidents aren't always what they seem," her father said.

Twiss would have told her the full truth—*It looks like it ran sideways into a cow!*

Bett held her index finger just above the top of the cake, as if she were going to take a swipe of the black frosting, but ended up putting her hand on Milly's shoulder instead.

"It's more genuine now," she said.

"Yes," someone said. "They're flawed by their nature."

"I've never seen one without a scratch."

"If you don't count the red Farmall."

"I don't."

"We won't!"

The judges weren't as interested in genuine replicas of farm equipment as everyone thought they'd be. Sitting on the panel were three of the top members of the Sewing Society, who were wearing their yellow hats, which were only remarkable because of the impression of exclusivity that they gave off, something like a No Trespassing sign fixed to a barbed-wire fence. Between tipping their hats to dab at their foreheads with matching yellow handkerchiefs, the three women waved away blackflies, which had been flying over from the livestock ring.

The prize went to a woman who'd made a crumble-top brown sugar apple pie that looked more like a pile of horse manure than a delectable dessert. When the judges handed her the over-sized check, the woman displayed it long enough for the man from the *Gazette* to take a photo-graph and then handed it right back.

"For the Society," she said, looking at Milly's mother. "Not every one of us here's a thief. Some of us think about the greater good of the town."

"What's she talking about?" Milly's father said.

Her mother took his hand. "Just something you missed while you were in the barn."

A pie isn't the same thing as a cake, Milly thought. *What have you done with my mother?*

Although she didn't win the cash prize, the panel decided Milly shouldn't walk away without winning something, so she won the prize for the most unique cake. One of the judges walked over to the livestock arena and came back with an ancient, downtrodden-looking goat with a long white beard and white, foamy cataracts in both of his eyes.

"Here," she said and handed Milly the lead rope. "We were going to sell him to the slaughter-house, but, congratulations, he's yours now."

Normally, Milly's mother would have stepped in, but today her mother just smiled girlishly. She said, "I don't know how we'll ever get him into the car," when she usually would have said something like, "That's all the snubbing you're capable of?"

"What am I supposed to do with him?" Milly said.

"Whatever you want," the panel reiterated. "He's yours now."

Milly never expected those three words—*He's yours now*—to be the words she'd remember all of her life.

Bett started laughing a deep guttural laugh, a man's laugh. "I'm sorry," she said, when people turned their attention away from Milly and the goat to her. "I can't help it. It's just so obviously wrong. Milly won a goat. A *goat*."

"And a fine goat he is," Dr. Greene said.

"A real blue ribbon winner," Mrs. Collier echoed.

"What do people want with a giant check, anyway?" Mr. Stewart said.

"When they can have parrots and goats," Mrs. Bettle said.

"He's not so bad," Milly's father said, clucking his tongue.

"A farm can always use a goat," her mother said.

"You've all got a lot of nerve!" Milly said, raising her voice for the first time in her life. She yanked the lead rope harder than she intended to, which made both the goat and the thick white hairs on the back of his neck stand at attention.

"I had plans for that money," she said and started off in the opposite direction of the crowd. "Plans!"

Without any further yanking, the goat trotted along beside Milly as if she'd been his owner all along. She and the goat didn't stop walking until they got to the edge of the fairground, where the waist-high weeds met up with the ones that had been mowed down to her ankles and she saw Twiss, who was dragging a case of tonic through the field on a creaky metal dolly. When Twiss waved, Milly let go of the lead rope, but the goat didn't leave her side.

"Top of the morning!" Twiss said, as if she'd merely overslept and missed nothing more than breakfast. She was wearing a dress a handful of sizes too large for her with sunbursts of yellow lace embroidered from the hem to the neckline. Her cheeks were as pink as calamine.

"What's with the goat?" she said.

"What's with the dress?" Milly said. *Where were you?*

"Isn't it amazing?" Twiss said. "It's like happiness can be sewn."

She parked the dolly of tonic beside the goat. Where she'd come from and where she'd been, Milly didn't know. All Milly knew was that when Twiss opened her arms to give her a hug, her anger—visions of someone besides Asa wearing the tractor cuff links, or worse, someone besides her giving them to Asa—came bubbling up.

"You ruined everything!" she said to Twiss. "I would've been paying more attention if you hadn't run off like you always do when you want attention!"

Before she knew what she was doing, Milly had pushed her sister down to the ground, an action that, along with her parents' imposters' posturing, brought to mind a game called Opposites Day, which she and Twiss used to play.

The only person who seemed exactly like herself today was Bett—on the ride into town, Henry had avoided the used golf shirts and, instead, had defecated on the sleeve of her dress, and in retaliation, when Mrs. Bettle wasn't looking, she'd plucked out one of his bright green feathers.

"What did you do that for?" Twiss said, brushing the dirt off her knees, which she'd skinned in the process of falling down. Tiny trickles of blood flowed down her legs.

"Everything," Milly said, taking up the lead rope again.

The fair went on with Milly and the goat lingering at the sidelines, watching the gravel parking lot so that she would be the first to see when Mr. Peterson and Asa arrived. Although the cake was ruined and she hadn't won first prize, she was ready to tell Asa the whole of her feelings for him, to collapse in his arms.

"Take me away from here," she imagined saying to him. Never mind that people only talked with that kind of false earnestness in the movies. Never mind.

"Where would you like to go?" she imagined him saying back.

"Nowhere. Anywhere."

"How about the boat launch?"

"That sounds nice," Milly would say.

It would be the great romantic moment of her life; they wouldn't need cakes or cuff links or a pair of crystal shoes. At the boat launch, he'd park the car and run around to her side to open the door so that he could help her down. The two would walk to the end of the boat launch, with the sandstone cliffs looming above them and the water flowing below them.

"Glaciers came through here," Asa might say.

"I know," Milly might say back. "About twenty thousand years ago."

"Right, and the sandstone's even older than that."

"Five hundred million years or so," Milly would say and smile. She'd just happen to have Mr. Stewart's fossil in her pocket, which she'd pull out to illustrate what the words *five hundred million years* couldn't illustrate. "Did you know that fish can drown?"

Asa would pull out the little purple flower Bett said he had in his front pocket the other day when he walked into the bridal shop and look at Milly for a long moment before he took her in his arms, and even though Twiss would have thrown up or climbed into a tree, Milly would yield to the weight of his body and the downy hairs at the back of his neck.

But Mr. Peterson's shiny black car never arrived.

Milly stood in the same place for as long as she could, but eventually the goat got hungry and she was forced away from the weeds, which the goat had rejected for nourishment in favor of the scent of melted butter that was infusing the air. Milly walked past the drops of Twiss's dried blood, back into the crowd.

She was careful to avoid Twiss, who was standing in front of her stall of purple tonic, belting out false promises of all the ailments it would take care of and waving a miniature American flag stapled to a stick. Milly lingered behind Twiss's stand, petting the goat and letting him lick the palm of her hand.

"Step right up!" she heard Twiss say. "Tell me what you're suffering from. Whether it's a goiter or your gallbladder, the key to happiness is only a nickel away!"

A small crowd had gathered around her, although Milly didn't see anyone pulling nickels, lint covered or otherwise, out of their pockets.

"Only yesterday," Twiss said, "I had the ache of a lifetime. But as you can see, after drinking my tonic, I am well as well can be. Have you ever seen such rosy cheeks, such a healthy youthful glow?"

"No, I haven't," someone said. "But you're young, and I'm old."

"No matter," Twiss said. "Purple Prairie Tonic is one hundred percent guaranteed. You'll look and feel better or I'll put your nickel back in your pocket. That's a promise."

"Aren't you that dairyman's girl?"

"Wasn't he a golfer?"

"Aren't you the troublemaker who sprays everyone's daughters with hoses?"

"I used to be," Twiss said, curtsying, although she was careful to cover the scrapes on her knees with the hem of her dress. "But I drank Purple Prairie Tonic, and now I'm as ladylike as any other proper Spring Green girl."

Then came the *oohing* and the *aahing,* and the jingle of one nickel and then another clinking against the empty Mason jar on the table.

"It's a miracle!" someone said.

"How did you do it?" another said.

"Well, I have to admit," Twiss said, taking the first of many successive bows, "it was truly difficult to squeeze happiness into a jar."

When Twiss became too busy handing out jars

of her tonic to notice her sister passing by the front of her stand, Milly skirted the crowd with the goat in tow to get closer to the roasted corn; although a goat was the last thing she wanted to be responsible for, it didn't occur to her that she could let go of the rope at any time.

After the first wave of happiness purchasers had come and gone, Milly looked back at Twiss's stand and at Twiss, who was arranging what was left of the tonic into the shape of a pyramid, carefully balancing glass upon glass and then gauging the speed of the wind with her finger, the force it would take for the whole thing to fall.

"Egyptians drank this tonic in the times of AD and BC and CCD," she said to a new group of onlookers, the scrapes on her knees concealed beneath her dress. "How do you think they had enough strength to build the pyramids? How else would they have ascended into heaven? With Purple Prairie Tonic in their stomachs, they didn't have to wait for the Lord to accept them. They walked all the way up by themselves."

By noon, all of the bottles of tonic were gone.

Milly bought an ear of roasted corn for the goat and one for herself. The two found a place tucked away beneath the wooden bleachers.

"I guess you should have a name," Milly said to the goat, to distract herself from the fact that she was behaving eerily like Twiss in that she was sulking.

When he'd finished his ear of corn, Milly gave him hers. She'd never named a goat before, and her track record for naming things wasn't exactly spectacular; although Hammer really was a hammer, utility wasn't the point of a nickname. Affection was. Milly thought of mixing up the letters in Asa's name, but his name was a palindrome.

Twiss would have been able to think of a name without even seeing the goat, just as she could make fun of someone without seeing his or her face, which brought to Milly's mind the vision of Twiss yelping from a tree the day that Milly made owl cookies, and she and Asa walked through the meadow together. The vision clicked.

The goat would be therein and forever called Hoo-Hoo.

"You're lucky," Milly said, when he *maaed*. "I could have just called you Goat."

Milly and Hoo-Hoo ended up staying under the wooden bleachers all day long, gladly and gratefully missing whatever was going on outside and above them (she'd heard the roar of an engine: the propellers of a biplane, a crop duster?). She'd thought of walking home, but home, even though she knew the route, seemed unreachable now.

When the first signs of night came, and the first stars peeped through the high feathery clouds fanning out across the sky, she and

Hoo-Hoo came out from under the bleachers to stretch a little and to walk around. Even though Milly hadn't slept, it felt like she had. The back of her dress was soiled and her hair had come unpinned.

"How do you like that?" she said to Hoo-Hoo, who *maaed*.

Although Milly could have made amends with Twiss or gone to the square dance to look for her parents or seen the last of Henry's "Ave Maria" performances, miniature top hat and all, Milly paid two nickels, one for herself and one for Hoo-Hoo, to the man who ran the Ferris wheel and who didn't like the idea of a goat counting as a person, but submitted when Milly smiled at him. She and Hoo-Hoo climbed into the red bucket seat, just as the Ferris wheel lights came on. When the man in coveralls started the ride, he waved at Milly and told her to hold on. Milly tied Hoo-Hoo's lead rope around her waist so that if he fell she would fall, too.

The two of them went up, up, up to a place in the sky where Milly could see the whole of the town fair as well as the town. Milly saw the crowd of people flocking to Twiss's empty stand and Mrs. Bettle reaching into Henry's cage. She saw Dr. Greene and Mrs. Collier walking along, and Mr. Stewart trailing behind like their child. She saw other people's parents, but not her own.

It wasn't until Milly saw Bett, standing by herself in her blue dress and even bluer-looking shoes, which were sparkling in the early evening light, holding what looked like a stone in her hand, that Milly questioned her eyes. From this vantage point, it looked like Bett was standing beside the river, an impossibility made possible by height.

Just after the Ferris wheel reached its pinnacle, there was a great downward jolt, and the stone in her cousin's hand changed into what it really was: a golf ball, which cast a glow white and peculiar against the blue of her shoes and dress, the blue of the evening light. Only then did Milly see what Twiss would have seen if she wasn't busy defending her jars of happiness: that everything below her and Hoo-Hoo was too good to be true and, like the Ferris wheel, would eventually have to come down.

23

Bury that bird already!" said the Scornful God voice, whose timbre had begun to sound remarkably similar to her mother's and was just as grating on Twiss's nerves as it was sixty years ago. "Have you gone mad, child?"

"I'm not a child," Twiss said, although she wondered if such a statement could ever really be true. She'd grown in age, yes, and in body, surely, but inside, Twiss felt the same way she had when she was a girl, only she could no longer take off running in any direction, which made her feel freedomless—the worst kind of *less*.

Twiss put the goldfinch back into her front pocket and buttoned the pocket shut. Before she heard the Scornful God voice, the mother voice, she'd planned on walking to the gladiola bed in the backyard. Now she stayed by the water pump out of spite.

"What does the bird have to do with it?" said the voice. "It's me you're mad at. You never did like me much. You think I'm a Parisian snob."

"You're not Parisian," Twiss said. "You're dead."

"You only liked me when I left you alone."

"You might try doing that now," Twiss said.

"You're the one who keeps dredging me up."

There was a pause in the conversation.

"What are you waiting for?" the voice said. "He's dead, Theresa Wis. We all are."

So many years had passed since someone had called her by her full name that it took Twiss a moment to remember that the name belonged to her: Theresa, after the nurse's dead mother, and Wis, because the first thing Twiss tried to do as a newborn baby just out of the womb was eat a clump of black Wisconsin dirt, which her father,

when he'd finally come to the hospital from wherever he really was, had placed in her tiny hand.

"I don't know anymore," Twiss said to her
mother.

She began to walk away from the water pump
hoping for a reason to turn around again,
although she couldn't pinpoint what that reason
might be, or should be, only that hearing her real
name had done something to her equilibrium.

"Wait a minute," her mother said. "I have
something to ask you."

"What?" Twiss said, wondering if this would
be the moment her mother finally made sense of
history for her: the sharp decline of their family,
the giving in and the giving up.

"When you come will you bring along some
of that dark chocolate I used to like? They only
have milk chocolate here. I always wince when I
bite into it. Wincing, in my understanding, isn't
supposed to occur in the afterlife."

"I'll pack up the Eiffel Tower, too," Twiss said.

"No need," her mother said. "We've got one
just like it."

Twiss continued walking so as to escape her
nonexistent yet persistent mother. Even when
she reached the front door of the barn, she could
still hear her mother talking about the price of
binoculars in heaven, as well as the price of *pain
au chocolat.*

"The currency's doled out the same way as it

was in life," she said. "I suppose Father Stone wasn't that far off the mark. He joined us a few years ago, in case you didn't know. The last member of the Sewing Society, too. Up here, she looks just like a goat."

Twiss opened the barn door and quickly sealed herself inside. Although she'd destroyed all other evidence of the rectangular space ever being occupied by her father's miniature back nine, there was still a fine layer of sand on top of the dirt floor, which Twiss had swept out of the barn countless times and which had come back over the threshold in dune force just as often. Even though the barn no longer belonged to her father, and the sand had been reduced to a blend of finely divided rock and benign mineral particles, each day that she entered the barn through the utility door, and just before she began to launch balls out of it toward the chicken coop and the pond, she picked up the broom and swept. Twiss had always been a literalist of the most basic sort; if you could see it, then it was probably still there.

The image of Bett and her father was in the sand, in the wood, in the little square window, which she'd caulked shut after her father's funeral. The image was burned to the inside of her eyelids, so that even now when she closed her eyes, she saw the two of them standing between the seventeenth and the eighteenth hole, beneath a single dim yellow bulb.

24

After she saw her father and Bett together in the barn sharing what should have belonged to her, the night before the town fair, Twiss started running. When she reached the end of the driveway, she saw that she had three choices: to go left, right, or home. Up the hill was Father Stone and down the driveway was home. Twiss went left, all the way down Fox Hollow Road, across the river, past the golf course, and into town. The farther away from the barn that she got, the stronger her legs felt and the stronger, too, her resolve to keep going.

All together, she ran five and a half miles before she got to the brown house with the dark green shutters—the ones with the pinecone cut-outs—at the end of Forestry Lane and stopped. Only when she arrived did she realize where she'd been running to all along.

On either side of the stone walkway was a row of red pine saplings, which shook in the breeze as if they were cold. The street was aptly named; the saplings were the only real trees on the whole lane. The rest, mostly old-growth maples and oaks, had been cut down during the last century to build the town of Spring Green.

As if they'd been worried and waiting for her, just after Twiss stepped up onto the porch but before she'd had a chance to catch her breath or to steady herself enough to extend her index finger to ring the bell, Rollie and his wife came to the front door. Twiss was bent over the porch banister, holding the muscle stitch that had formed in her side.

"Good Lord, child," Rollie's wife, Adele, said. "Are you hurt?"

"Are those tears or sweat?" Rollie said, hurrying to her as if she might collapse.

But before Twiss could say she didn't know, Adele reached for Twiss's hand and pulled her gently inside the entranceway and into the dining room. She and Rollie had been getting ready to eat supper together. Placed on a yellow gingham tablecloth with an oak tree embroidered in the center of it were two green bowls and two glasses of cold milk. The house smelled of chicken and celery and freshly baked bread.

"You must be starved," Adele said and sat Twiss down in her spot.

Twiss wasn't hungry, but the sight of the food on the table, as well as the house itself, comforted her as it always had when she visited as a girl. On several occasions, Rollie and Adele had invited her over for supper after school (unlike her father, Rollie saved his money, which meant there was enough of everything for Adele to make supper and dessert each night of the week). Twiss had never been farther into the house than the dining room or the kitchen, but she was so fond of its appearance that she'd nicknamed it the Tree House because it was brown and green, and because all over the house were bowls filled with pinecones and fall leaves and placards that said things like TREES, TREES! WONDERFUL TREES! or HOME IS WHERE A TREE IS! THEY TOO HAVE HEARTS! in different shades of green.

The irony of Rollie spending nearly every day of his life keeping grass trimmed to a quarter-inch height on a treeless golf course had never occurred to her until now.

"What happened?" Rollie said, examining Twiss from across the table. "Your eyes are all red and swollen. Your arms and legs are cut up."

"Let her eat," Adele said, drawing her finger to her lips like Twiss's mother sometimes did. Adele ladled out a bowl's worth of chicken noodle soup and cut off a thick piece of bread from the loaf and buttered it. Then she went into the kitchen and came back with a bowl of raspberries and a yellow sponge cake.

"I had a feeling someone was coming," she said. "I never make sponge cake."

"I *love* your sponge cake," Rollie said.

"I know you do, dear," Adele said, placing her hand on his shoulder. "It's just that we usually have tea and fruit in the summer. Whatever doesn't make the kitchen hot."

After supper, Adele took Twiss to the bathroom upstairs so she could wash up. At home, Twiss would have protested, but here, on this night, she didn't. The scratches on her arms and legs from the lilac bush were bright red and throbbing as if she'd been stung. Adele laid out two pink towels for Twiss and a matching pink robe.

"I know pink's not your favorite color," Adele said. "I would have come up with something else if I'd known you were coming."

Twiss ran her fingers along the satin piping around the collar. No one had ever laid out towels and a robe for her before. The only reason anyone had ever taken notice when she went into the bathroom was that she took longer than everybody else, and there was only one bathtub in the house. *You're slower than the slowest slow,* her mother would say. After Twiss had taken a bath, her mother would get on her hands and knees and scrub the tub out before she'd get in. She said that if she didn't clean it beforehand it would be like taking a bath in the pond.

"I don't hate pink as much as everyone thinks," Twiss said to Adele.

After Adele filled the bath with cool water, she tucked a strand of loose hair behind Twiss's ear. "I'll be right downstairs. We both will. If you need anything."

From inside the bathroom, as Twiss peeled her sweat-soaked clothes off onto the floor and stepped into the tub, she could hear Adele and Rollie talking at the top of the stairs.

"Don't you think it's a bit unusual for a girl to run five miles at night all by herself? I have a mind to go over there and sort this out while she's in the bath."

"You'll do no such sorting."

"If he struck her, I'll wallop him out of Spring Green."

"You're too old for fistfights."

"Well, *something* must have happened."

"She'll tell us if she wants us to know."

"They don't deserve her."

"She's Button," Adele said. "I know."

Taking a bath in Rollie and Adele's house after seeing her father and Bett in the barn and running the five and a half miles into town (she didn't want to correct Rollie, but the last half mile had been the hardest both because her cramp had gotten worse and because she'd been able to see Rollie's house by then) should have felt more unsettling than it did. The fact was that she'd finally gotten exactly what she'd always wanted: to see what it would be like to have different parents, a different family, and a different, barnless home.

Twiss dipped below the surface of the water, pretending the bathtub was the river and the foam created from the lavender bar of soap Adele had placed on the edge of the tub brown river foam. She kept her eyes closed and pictured what she always pictured when she was looking for reassurance: the river family in their watery river home.

We shall have chicken noodle soup for dinner! she thought. *Oh, yes! We shall! We shall—*

And tomorrow we shall search for a new front door . . .

If Twiss lets us.

Me? Twiss thought, and she discovered beneath the cool, clean water at the bottom of an even cleaner bathtub what she'd always known. There were no river people living cheerfully at the bottom of the river, eating trout sandwiches and *shalling* each other every two seconds.

The police had found the bodies, white and bloated, tangled in a beaver dam a mile from where they had gone under. In the space of a few afternoon minutes, an entire family had died. A little girl, with thick brown braids down to her waist, whom she had known.

The entire town had turned out for the funeral. Before and after the service, they lingered around the font, signing the cross on their bodies with holy water and then re-signing it, all the while waiting for an assurance, based on the details, that this couldn't happen to them. Milly and Twiss and their mother and father had lingered, too, and for too long. The sight of the white and yellow field daisies blanketing the little girl's coffin had worked its way into Twiss's memory. That had been the girl with the braids' name—Daisy.

Twiss opened her eyes under the water and saw the procession to the cemetery, the groups of men in black suits carrying the coffins as if they were carrying the whole river, the whole town. And then she saw her father, walking in front of her, just out of reach.

Twiss burst up from beneath the clear, cool bathwater.

"Help!" she gurgled. "I don't want to drown!"

Adele hadn't gone downstairs like she'd said she was going to. Instead, she'd taken one of the wooden chairs from the dining room table and set it down next to the bathroom door as if she'd expected such an outcome out of an activity as tame as an evening soak.

"I'm here," Adele said, opening the door.

"What is it?" Rollie called.

"She's had a scare, that's all," Adele called back.

Adele was a short and round woman, almost exactly Mrs. Bettle's size, though Twiss wouldn't have used the word "ottoman" to describe her. Adele didn't look strong, but she lifted Twiss out of the tub and swaddled her with the pink towels as if she weighed no more than a wet leaf. "You're safe now," she said, stroking Twiss's cheeks.

Adele instructed Rollie to get one of her nightgowns from their bedroom, which he handed through the door with his eyes closed.

"I see nothing," he said, squinching up his eyes further. "Nothing at all."

After Adele adjusted the nightgown to fit Twiss better, she led Twiss into the small square bedroom situated beside their own. The paper on the walls depicted row after row of tiny yellow ducks. It wasn't until Adele dabbed salve on her arms and legs and drew the covers up to her chin and Rollie kissed her forehead and the two of the stood at the door that Twiss realized the room had been meant for a child.

"Do you think I could have a piece of paper and a pencil?" Twiss said.

"Of course," Adele said, hurrying out of the room and hurrying back into it with the requested materials. "Sometimes it helps me to write out my thoughts, too."

"Thank you," Twiss said.

"You don't need to thank us, Button," Rollie said.

Adele took his hand. "Having you here makes home feel more like home."

The next morning, after Adele had made Twiss tree-shaped pancakes drizzled with syrup and gave her a dress to go home in—*I've got two leftover from when I was young,* she said. *One has lace on it and one doesn't*—Rollie drove

Twiss across the river and back out to the country. When they got there, though, everyone was already gone.

"Where do you suppose they're at?" Rollie said.

"The fair," Twiss said, relieved to see the empty driveway. Although she'd been gone only a single night and a small part of a day, the house and the barn looked different to her now, as if overnight either her vision had sharpened or she'd grown up.

"It looks like it's been beaten up."

"What does?" Rollie said.

"The barn," Twiss said. "The house."

"The house needs a new roof," Rollie said. "If that's what you mean."

"I guess that's what I mean," she said, even though what she really meant was *It looks like it might tip over.* From the driveway, Twiss saw Kingsley dragging himself around the perimeter of the pond. When she felt an urge to kick a tin can in his path to see if he would eat it or not, she knew she hadn't grown up that much.

"Should we pack up your tonic?" Rollie said. "It's already nine o'clock."

On the way from his house to hers, Twiss had told Rollie about her tonic, as well as its primary and secondary purposes: to raise money and to bring happiness to all of the unhappy people in Spring Green, or at least those who went to the fair.

"The money's for Father Rice," Twiss said.

"And you're sure he wants to come home?"

"I can't think why he wouldn't," Twiss said.

Rollie helped Twiss load the tonic into the back of the car. Though he'd offered to carry the tonic to her stand, when they got to the fair, Twiss said she wanted to carry it herself.

"I think I've got a dolly in here," Rollie said. "I don't want you pulling a muscle."

The two of them got out of the car and stood at the back of it for a few minutes, each of them picking at their fingernails, the dust on the hood of the car, their clothes.

Rollie deserved to know what had made her run—Twiss knew that. But she also knew she couldn't say what she felt about Bett or the strangeness of Bett and her father playing golf in the barn. In the light of day, Twiss didn't know what she'd really seen anyway.

"Adele wanted me to tell you you're welcome at the house any time," Rollie said. "I haven't seen her this happy since I came home with the pine saplings last spring."

"Tell her I promise to stop by," Twiss said.

"She bought those towels years ago. Last night was the first they've been used."

"They were really soft," Twiss said.

"She liked you using them," Rollie said. "I did too."

Twiss thought of the wallpaper in the room Adele had led her to last night and wrapped her arms around Rollie's waist. She squeezed him the way she used to squeeze her father whenever he'd gotten a hole in one.

"If I hadn't been born already," she said to Rollie, "I'd have liked to be your child."

Rollie reached into his pocket and pulled out a gleaming quarter, which he placed in Twiss's palm. "Go on now, Button. Sell your tonic. Make us proud."

Twiss walked through the secondary parking lot, for those who came late or who were hauling trailers behind their tractors, and the primary parking lot, before Rollie got back in his car and drove home. Instead of following the dirt footpath to the official fair entrance, Twiss pushed the dolly through an unmowed field so she wouldn't have to stop and explain herself to someone like the Beetle or Mrs. Collier.

When she saw Milly at the edge of the field standing in the grass with a knobby old goat, her legs carried her to her sister, the one person who could understand what couldn't be understood. Milly had earned an A in philosophy.

"Top of the morning!" Twiss said when she got close.

I'm so glad to see you, she thought, but ended up with, "What's with the goat?"

"What's with the dress?" Milly said.

Twiss ran her fingers over one of the lace sunbursts. She'd chosen it over the nonlace

300

dress to please Adele, who like every other childless woman in Spring Green had probably always wanted to dress a little girl. The other dress was more utilitarian; it was made of dark blue crepe and looked like something one might wear to a secretarial interview.

"Isn't it amazing?" Twiss said. "It's like happiness can be sewn."

Milly didn't say anything more about the dress. She didn't say anything at all. In one strangely graceful motion, she dropped the goat's lead rope, leaped forward like a deer over a fence, and pushed Twiss down hard to the ground.

"You ruined everything," she said and picked up the lead rope again.

Twiss was so surprised at finding herself twice now on the ground that she didn't attempt to run after Milly or even wipe the dirt off the lilac bush scrapes that had reopened on her knees. She stayed still, watching the drops of blood emerge from beneath her skin and gather together like an army, until the drops became trickles and gravity pulled them over her shins, down to her ankles, all the way to her toes.

When the blood dried, Twiss got up to join the rest of the fairgoers and to set up her tonic stand. In the afternoon, after the frantic sales and the even more frantic returns when her tonic failed to miraculously heal all ailments, Twiss walked around the fair looking for Milly, who had pushed her down, true, but who would also pick her back up.

Twiss looked in all of the places she thought Milly might have been—Milly had always enjoyed the craft section of the fair, where women sold linens and blankets embellished with butterflies and ivy, tiny purple crocuses, tiny everything. When she came to a stand where a woman was selling pink and blue layettes to expecting women wealthy enough not to have to sew their own, she stopped walking.

"Have you seen my sister?" she said to the woman, wondering how babies could be that small. The knit baby socks looked like they wouldn't even fit on her pinky toes.

"What does she look like?" the woman said.

"Long blond hair," Twiss said. "Eyes green as leaves."

"I saw a girl with red hair and a blue dress," the woman said. "She kept touching the pink clothes. I had to ask her to move along since she didn't have any money."

"That's Bett," Twiss said, with the same confusion of feelings she'd felt the night before rising from somewhere deep inside her. "She's got weak lungs. She's probably going to die."

Before the woman could say anything, Twiss continued searching for Milly. When she passed the stand where the woman with tea leaves had read Milly's future last year, she paused. This year, a man selling tarnished doorknobs occupied the stand.

"How else are you going to open a door?" he said as if Twiss had asked him a question.

Twiss continued on through the fair, nearly knocking over an old woman and a child, past Mrs. Bettle's stand, where Henry was singing "Ave Maria" to a crowd that kept saying, "What happened to the man who put nails through his tongue?"

"He's a parrot!" Mrs. Bettle kept saying. "He's singing the Lord's song!"

When Twiss reached the end of the fairgrounds and the haphazardly mowed field on the opposite end of the parking lot, she didn't find Milly, the comfort she was looking for.

She found her mother and her father.

Her mother was in the process of climbing down from a bright yellow biplane and her father was smiling just as brightly at her from the ground below. The pilot had given her mother a pair of aviation goggles to wear, which made her look like an insect.

"Twiss," her father said when he saw her, but Twiss didn't respond.

Her father was holding a burlap sack of kidney beans. "Your mother guessed the right amount exactly! One thousand three hundred and ninety-eight. She won a free ride."

"You wouldn't believe how beautiful it was!" her mother said, taking off the goggles and kissing her father several times on the cheek. "Oh, Twiss, you would have loved it. I kept thinking about you while I was up there. You should take a ride and see for yourself."

All at once, Twiss's father picked her mother up and spun her around and around the way he used to spin Twiss. When he finally set her down again, he smiled at her and kissed her forehead. The two looked like they did in a photograph that had been taken of them once, only there was no watermelon seed.

"This has been such a wonderful day," her father said to her mother, drawing her to him. "And you are such a wonderful woman to have forgiven me. And it only took you a month. You're a saint, Maisie. You really are. I didn't think you'd be able to do it."

"Forgiven?" her mother said.

"I found a doctor," her father said. "I talked to Bett last night. She's agreed to go."

"She's been to the doctor," her mother said, a trace of worry spreading across her face.

"He doesn't do that kind of procedure," her father said. "He doesn't believe in it."

Her mother pushed back from her father's embrace.

Her father turned to Twiss. "Didn't you give her my note?"

Twiss's eyes grew wide and her skin paled. She had been wrong—whatever this was, the sting was worse than the belt. She looked at her father, who looked at her the way he did the night he drove them onto the golf course illegally, when it no longer mattered if Rollie had altered the sand moguls or not. It was a look that hit Twiss squarely in her heart. She thought of the chill blue silk against her skin, of Lewis and Clark, warm summer days just like this one. She thought of how her father had taught her to swim and how she'd pretended to drown so that Bett would save her. And she thought of Kingsley, the turtle, who had snapped up a letter whose words, even unread, changed all their lives.

Bett's pregnant. I'm responsible.

25

Isn't this inconvenient? Milly thought from her box-chair in the attic, although inconvenient wasn't the right word for what she was: stuck— in the past, in the present, on a cardboard box designed to hold book weight, not human weight with all of its unruly waves of flesh, its sprawl of limbs and tendons. If only she'd taken Twiss's suggestion of each wearing plastic whistles around their necks, Milly could have whistled for help.

"This is what you made me leave the barn for?" Twiss would have said.

Twiss had gone out for ice cream one day and had come back with two old-fashioned butterscotch sundaes and two bright orange whistles that said home of the kickin' orange dream cone and were as blinding as the saloon signs at night.

Sometime in their sixties, the world had reached the Age of Neon.

"What happened to handing out a spoon?" Milly had said.

"Don't say it," Twiss had said. "I'll throw up all over you."

"We're old."

"You're right. We should just curl up and die."

"Why is it always youth or death with you?" Milly said, although she knew what her sister meant—age had become something you had to constantly think about and plan against, as if age were a storm and the still-working parts of her body shutters.

At this point in her life, Milly supposed there should be no more attic trips for her. Perhaps no more trips in general. Climbing stairs, as well as climbing in and out of the car, was getting to be too defeating. Lately, when she and Twiss went on their Sunday drives, Milly would stay in the car while Twiss walked down to the river or up a hill or across a narrow footbridge with weeds sprouting up between the woods slats. Milly had stopped wanting to get out to see again what she'd seen the previous Sunday and the Sunday before that.

She felt a little like the red crop trucks they saw when they were out on their drives, the ones hauling loads of hay or wheat or corn, sputtering along the roads like invalids, waiting to get to wherever their drivers were steering them and be unburdened until the next farm acre was picked clean by a group of school-age kids calculating what new thing they could buy with their paychecks—kids who were overjoyed by the extraordinary price of farm machinery that might have done their jobs for them if not for the fact of the drought, which yielded stunted crops that weren't worth what they used to be worth.

Cynicism. There. Bett would have been proud.

When the time came, Twiss might have to wheel her onto the porch. Forget the Age of Neon or the Age of Scorn; the Age of Exhaustion ruled now. How could Milly be expected to traipse across fields and up hills and down to rivers, past broken-down houses that used to be fine once upon a time, when a freshly white-washed porch and honeysuckle twirling up the railings were all most people could hope for?

How could she be expected to possess the desire when she lacked the simple ability to hoist herself up from a moldy box in the attic?

What was she doing up there anyway?

Oh yes, the bird book, which was also old and yellowed and brittle at the spine. The best Milly could do was set the book on the musty floorboards and wait for her legs to come back to life again or for Twiss to come back inside, which Twiss wouldn't do until the last possible moment because she said she couldn't breathe with plaster and horsehair surrounding her on all sides. Milly looked at the book and at the darkened attic, which was the only place besides the river that still had water left in it. When she saw a box with Bett's name scrawled across its side in red marker, she thought *I'd have won this consequence,* remembering the time Bett dared Twiss to stand a full minute in the attic and say the words "Bloody Mary" three times.

"Bloody Mary," Milly said now, knowing that it was a game, but also knowing that she wouldn't say it three times in a row. She'd lived this long without seeing the bloodied head of a woman popping out of the woodwork. Why did she need to see one now?

"At least I would have won the attic part," she said, as if Bett were hovering over her bed again, trying to force her to do whatever would appall her sensibilities the most.

The summer Bett stayed with them, Bett taped the IOU to Milly's headboard, obscuring the fleur-de-lis carved into the wood, so that Milly never forgot what she owed.

"Take it down already," Twiss said at the end of the summer.

"But I signed my name," Milly said.

"It was a stupid game," Twiss said. "One you didn't even want to play."

Was that all? Milly thought.

Playing Truth or Consequences with Bett had seemed like playing life or death. Other girls their age painted their nails or wrote the last names of the boys they wanted to marry in their diaries. Other girls spent long summer nights projecting if the boy of their dreams would get down on one knee or on two. They spent hours teasing out the details of their future proposals. Would he promise a country home on a pleasant hill overlooking the river? Or would it be a modern-looking house in town? Would he slide the ring on her finger for her or allow his sweetheart to do it herself? While other girls planned their future weddings down to the kinds of cakes they thought they might like to serve, Bett had Twiss running around without her underwear on, hanging from trees in the moonlight, invoking spirits who took joy in menacing young girls. She had Milly giving up her secrets only so she could make fun of them.

After Bett had learned of Asa's difficulties with speech, she'd started calling him the Mongoloid Boy. One of the things Milly always regretted was that she'd never said anything more than *He's not a mongoloid!* on Asa's behalf because she didn't want to have to explain what he was to her. Even Twiss lacked the courage or the drive to really go against Bett until Bett gave her good reason at the end of the summer. And then all she could do was ball up the IOU and throw it out the window.

All she could say was, "It's over now."

26

Their mother drove herself home from the fair, shut herself in her bedroom, and wedged a chair beneath the doorknob. She wouldn't let their father see her even when he pounded ferociously on the door.

"Margaret!" he yelled over and over again, clawing the wood with his fingernails.

What had always struck Milly was that her father didn't come to her mother's door with professions of love or even a real apology. He came to it as if their marriage depended not on those things but on an act of aggression, submission.

Please open this door.

For three days, Milly's mother didn't say a word to him or to anyone, nor did she leave her bedroom, even for a trip to the bathroom.

"She didn't mean anything to me," her father kept saying from his place on the hallway floor. Although Milly had brought up a tray of food for him, he, too, wouldn't eat or drink anything. He wouldn't move from his position on the floor.

"Why are you making him food?" Twiss said.

"He still needs to eat," Milly said.

Twiss had taken the first of Milly's trays, and like the IOU, had thrown it out the window, so that the only ones enjoying a meal were the rabbits that lived under the porch. Kingsley had dragged himself over from the pond, too, which would have usually drawn Twiss to him. "He doesn't deserve to eat after what he's done," Twiss said.

"He'll starve," Milly said.

"He doesn't even deserve that," Twiss said.

The second tray Milly took her father after Twiss stormed out of the house with Hammer. On Twiss's way out, Bett cornered her against the coatrack in the front hallway.

"I can't bear you not talking to me, Twiss."

Twiss raised Hammer up in the air, as if she might strike their cousin. "Let me go."

"I need you," Bett said, crying. "You promised

me. You promised not to leave me all alone."

Slowly, Twiss lowered Hammer to her side. With a look of pain and sadness and anger—a kind of vulnerability Milly never saw again—Twiss said, "Why did it have to be him?"

"You're the only one who loves me," Bett said, crying harder.

"I can't," Twiss said. She bit down hard on her lip and walked out the front door.

"For God's sake, Margaret!" their father yelled upstairs. "She has a mole on the back of her leg. A hair grows out of it. A wretched black hair."

When that didn't elicit a response from Milly's mother, he added, "She doesn't even know what a green is."

Milly ran up the stairs. "*Shhh,* Dad. Bett's right downstairs."

"I don't care," her father said, raising his voice. "She swings a club like a mule!"

Milly knew her father was capable of cruelty, she just didn't know he was capable of cruelty of this caliber. If he'd known anything about women, he'd have known that denouncing one of them wouldn't bring you closer to the other. After all, her mother would have said if she were speaking, *I'm the one who's had to suffer for a bogey!*

"*You'd* forgive me," her father said.

"Dad," Milly began.

"Well, wouldn't you?"

When Milly didn't immediately say yes, he added, "Don't you?"

Milly stood there, wishing she were in the barn and Twiss were in the hallway because her father wouldn't have asked this question of Twiss, and even if he did, her answer wouldn't be as important to him as Milly's was. Goodness had never been expected of Twiss the way it was expected of Milly. Twiss was allowed her tantrums and rages and hammering sessions in the barn—she'd always been allowed to have a reaction that was less than graceful. And because she was closer to their father than Milly was, she could say, "I'll never forgive him!" loud enough for her father to hear because, despite a bout of nail-sharp anger, even Twiss knew that over time she'd think of all the Sundays he took her golfing and called her his little champion and she'd do just what she said she wouldn't, what she said she couldn't: She'd forgive him. Maybe not for everything, but for enough.

"Why did you do it?" Milly said to her father. "We could forgive all of the others, but not Bett."

Her father leaned against her mother's bedroom door, as if he'd accepted that it wouldn't be opening any time soon. "She was the only one who didn't know who I used to be. When she came into the barn, she looked exactly the way I felt. Ordinary."

Her father slumped down even farther. "I don't

know what's wrong with me. My mother said I was born selfish. I used to make her and the others call me Champion. Once, I told her she was a bad mother because she wouldn't use the rag money to buy me a pair of golf shoes. I hated her for being poor. I hated myself."

"We all loved you whether or not you could play golf," Milly said.

Her father covered his face. "I don't. Golf was the only way in."

On the fourth day, Milly's mother dragged the chair away from the door. She called for Milly, who'd been shuttling from room to room opening windows and lodging kitchen utensils in the tracks of the ones that had a tendency to fall down. The day was hotter than the one before. Even though the walls, along with every-thing else, were sweating, her mother had taken the extra wool blankets from the closet and draped them over herself on the bed. Her father was still camped out on the hallway floor.

"I want you to write a letter to my sister," her mother said before Milly could set down the carafe of water she was holding. That morning's *Gazette* had stressed the importance of hydration; water, the writer said, was the only element essential to human life, which made Milly want to write a strongly worded letter to the editor: *You've obviously never been in love.*

"Aunt Gertrude?" Milly said.

Her mother had drawn the shades, which gave the effect of twilight even though just beyond the windows the sun was shining brightly without a single discouraging cloud in the sky. The bedroom smelled of sweat and urine.

Milly moved to open a window. "What should I say?"

"I don't want fresh air!" her mother snapped.

And then in a softer tone, "You're good at finding *les mots judicieux*."

"*Judicieux?*" Milly said.

"Words that cover up how you really feel," her mother said.

Milly sat on the edge of the bed as if anchored by a thread. Although her mother hadn't escaped the sphere of Twiss's wrath—*If she'd been a better wife, maybe this wouldn't have happened*—she'd escaped Milly's. Milly had always been able to see through her mother's hard edges, the repetition of certain phrases year after year, to the core of her desires. She could see that like most people in the world, her mother just wanted to be loved.

Whenever her mother had been particularly unhappy in the past, she'd tell the story of how she and her aunt had given up their inheritances and married for love.

"We weren't given what we were promised," she'd say.

"What were you promised?" Milly would say.

"I don't remember anymore."

"I could help you," Milly said once, when she was a little girl.

She'd explained about the game she and Twiss played whenever they lost track of their thoughts. One of them would say a word and the other would have to say everything they associated with that word until they remembered what they'd been thinking about.

"It's not that kind of forgetting," her mother had said.

"Dad," Milly had said anyway.

"That's your word," she'd added, when her mother didn't say anything. "You're supposed to think of another one that goes with it."

Her mother had looked up from the wash bucket. "Regret."

This was years before Milly's father sequestered himself in the barn, when he still played golf like a pro. Still, it was this moment that Milly remembered more than others: her mother bent over the kitchen floor on her hands and knees, with a cloth in one hand and a scouring pad in the other, the end of her braid trailing in the wash bucket. Before she'd said her word, she'd looked at Milly with a softness she rarely allowed anyone to see.

"My sister's smarter than I am," her mother said now, knowing every sad detail about Milly's father and Bett. She tucked a wool blanket beneath her chin. "She always was."

"Didn't you earn all A's in high school?" Milly said, even though she knew what her mother meant. Although Milly was the one who earned perfect grades term after term, Twiss was the one with all of the creativity and the daring. Milly may have known how to balance both ends of Mr. Stewart's chemistry equations without making a mistake, but Twiss was the one who possessed the heart to be a real scientist.

"Gertie finally left him," Milly's mother said, picking at the wool. "Bett's father."

"Where did she go?" Milly said.

"Home," her mother said after a while. "I had a letter from Butterfield just before all this happened. To think I spent hours trying to come up with the right way to tell Bett, to spare her grief, *damage*, while she and your father were doing what they were doing in the barn. Some things just make you want to curl up and die, don't they?"

Milly thought of the man from Bett's story, who'd collapsed while trying to cross the bog and ended up decomposing in a closet, while Bird Daddy lived happily in his place.

"My father went to get Gertie," her mother added. "All she had to do was write a letter. It's been eighteen years—you'd think it would have taken more than that."

"Do you want me to write a letter to him too?" Milly said.

"I'm too old to go home now," her mother said. She looked toward the windows as if she could see past the thick shades all the way to Butterfield. "He had big hopes for us."

Her mother turned on her side. "I guess we all did."

Milly went downstairs to find the address book and the roll of stamps. Was this an occasion for the good stationery or for a note card or a piece of scrap paper? Milly saw the appropriateness of all three.

Even though her mother had barricaded herself in her room and her father had glued himself to the foot of her door, and neither of them would eat a scrap of food, it didn't yet occur to Milly that everything wouldn't eventually be all right again. She thought of what Father Rice had once said about miracles, but parents resuming the role of being parents didn't seem like the same thing as a chicken laying an egg twice in one day.

What happens tomorrow?

The moment Milly sat down at the kitchen table, Bett wandered into the room. Not only had Twiss disowned her, their father and mother wouldn't acknowledge the fact of her physical presence in the house either. Overnight, Bett's status had changed from beloved to despised.

She looked stricken, as if she might collapse. No longer was she wearing the blue dress Mr. Peterson had bought her; she was wearing one of her own dresses, which had disintegrated in the wash bucket, but which she'd mended solidly enough to put on. The gray material was not fine, or flattering against her skin.

Her fingernails were jagged from biting them. Her feet were bare.

"Please let me sit here," she said to Milly.

Milly didn't want to be mean to Bett, but she didn't want to be nice to her either. Though what happened wasn't Bett's fault—*because* it wasn't Bett's fault—she was the easiest one to blame. She thought of every mean thing Bett had ever said to her, as well as every mean thing she had done, to fuel an emotion that was unnatural to her.

"Do what you want," she said to Bett.

The two of them sat in silence for over an hour, Milly writing words on the back of her chore list and scratching them out, and Bett looking out the window as if the view might harm her. In the distance, and although it wasn't Sunday, church bells chimed.

"Since I got here I knew home wasn't going to be home anymore," Bett said abruptly, as though Milly had asked her to justify herself, and maybe she had by being silent. "I shouldn't have gone near the barn, but I couldn't stay away from it. He told me things about you all, as a family, what everything had been like before. I told him things too."

Milly put down her pen. "You knew your parents were getting divorced?"

Bett looked as fragile as she had the day she arrived, despite having a clean bill of health instead of a pair of weak lungs and boots with cardboard soles.

"Yes," she said. "That's why my mother sent me down here."

Milly thought of the ground bees and how miraculous it really was that not a single one of them had stung her cousin even though she'd thrust her hands straight into their home.

Once Bett started to cry, Milly couldn't hold on to her anger anymore. She reached into her dress pocket and handed Bett a handkerchief with her initials embroidered at the corner.

"I wasn't born in a canoe," Bett said, her eyes regaining the puffiness they'd finally lost. "I'll probably have to give birth in one, though."

Milly thought of the baby growing in her cousin's stomach. Just before her mother had shut herself in her bedroom, she'd said, *I may as well be dead if that baby breathes life.*

"Maybe it won't be as bad as a canoe," Milly said.

"I keep trying to think like you," Bett said, rubbing her stomach as if the baby were whimpering in its watery world instead of Bett in the dry, late summer one. "You're the only one who's ever brushed out my hair. Why were so nice to me when I was so mean to you?"

"You're my cousin," Milly said. "Besides, that's what people are supposed to do."

Bett smiled a little. "You would have made it in Deadwater."

"Thanks," Milly said. "I still don't think I want to go there."

From the folds of her dress, Bett pulled out a pair of knitted pink infant socks and set them on the table. "A woman at the fair gave them to me."

"How did she know?" Milly said.

"I guess it showed on my face."

Just then, someone knocked on the screen door, and Milly stood up to answer it. Mrs. Bettle had a way of dropping by at the worst possible moments. She'd probably want to talk about Henry and the fair, how ungrateful people in Spring Green were. *What kind of miracle were they looking for? They booed him. Henry has hurt feelings, you know.* Or it might be Dr. Greene and Mrs. Collier, stopping by to see if anyone wanted to take a drive with them and have a sew.

"I've already picked out names," Bett said.

Before Milly stepped onto the front porch to send the visitor away—no disturbances, her father had warned from his place in the hallway—she turned back to Bett.

"What are they?" she said.

Bett looked up from the pair of tiny pink socks. "There's really only one.

"Arabella," she said, touching her pale cheek. "Bella, for short."

Asa had come to talk to Milly's father but settled on a walk when Milly told him that her father wasn't feeling well and couldn't come down. The two moved up through the meadow, around to the pond, and back down to the vegetable garden again, which because of the differences in heat today, felt like entering and exiting three separate ecosystems. Hot, hotter, and hottest. Asa wiped the sweat off his forehead with the back of his hand, but instead of wiping his hand on his shirt like he usually did when he was mowing, he let his hand air-dry as if there was a sudden disjoint between his instincts and the weather.

Walking the property with Asa felt like swimming with a life preserver. As if for the last four days Milly had held her breath to stay afloat, she exhaled all that was stale and inhaled the fresher, less complicated scent of meadow flowers and soil.

I missed you, she thought, but said, "I'm sorry I don't have cookies for you today."

She was remembering the days earlier in the

summer when what kind of cookie would win Asa's heart had occupied her mind each time it rained and how complicated the process of elimination had seemed. "I would have made some if I'd known you were coming."

She latched on to the leaf of a tomato plant, remembering also when the fruit was still hard and green and full of potential. Now most of the tomatoes had turned red or orange and had either been pecked to pulp by the birds or had burst under the sharp glare of the sun.

"I don't even have lemonade," Milly said.

"Actually, I have something for you," Asa said.

He reached into the leather saddlebag he'd slung across his shoulder and knelt in the garden, even though he was wearing good trousers and a good shirt. He'd fixed his hair differently too. Instead of mowing, he looked like he was about to go to church.

"It belonged to my great-grandmother Kathryn," he said.

Milly opened the box Asa placed in her hand. Inside was a silver ring filigreed with vines and dotted with tiny diamonds. There it was—everything she hadn't written in a diary this summer, but everything she'd wanted anyway. The silver shone in the light like a lure.

"It's beautiful," she said to Asa.

"Since you brought me the owl cookies I haven't been able to mow a straight line," Asa said. "I was supposed to ask your father first, but I couldn't wait any longer. I thought I'd see you at the fair, but my father asked me to go with him to Illinois for the weekend. He had business there. I heard you won a goat, though."

"Hoo-Hoo," Milly said. "He's harassing the chickens right now."

Asa looked toward the woods and smiled. "I'm sure they're excited to have someone besides your sister doing that for a change. How is Twiss?"

The moment Asa mentioned Twiss, Milly's sense of her future with him, her entitlement to it, blew away from her like wind.

Promise that you won't leave until I'm old enough to leave too.

Twiss was only fourteen years old, and her mother and her father were in the middle of a war that couldn't possibly have a winner: Her mother was intent on not letting her father into her bedroom, and her father was intent on not leaving the floor in front of her door.

Margaret, Margaret, said her father. *Open this door.*

He used to call us his darlings, said her mother.

I hate you both! said Twiss, who'd never been skilled at being a peacekeeper. Even now, Milly heard the crash of Hammer in the barn.

"What did you say?" Milly asked Asa, thinking that leaving any of them behind would be like leaving people in the middle of a fire.

"I guess I asked if you would marry me," Asa said, blushing.

Milly imagined the baby struggling in her dark womb water, kicking her tiny feet, trying her best to stay afloat. If fish could drown in floods, then couldn't babies drown inside of unloved mothers, cousins cast aside?

Bett had once asked Milly what it felt like to almost die the day the three of them went to the river to swim out to their sandbar and bathe in the afternoon sun. The day when halfway to the sandbar, Milly felt a tug on her leg and was pulled down.

Consequence, she'd said that night, because she couldn't explain the feeling of water forcing its way inside of her. She figured that any consequence Bett could dream up for her would be better than being filled up with the equivalent of all that was dark and frightening in the world, all that was the opposite of the self she knew, of goodness and light.

After Bett and Twiss had laid her out on the sand and the water had come out of her lungs, and they'd informed her that she was not in fact dead, Bett had wiped the blood off Milly's legs and smoothed the hair away from her face.

"You owe me your life, you know."

Milly thought of Bett's blue dress and the SS *Forest* and the spotless film of Bett's lungs draped over a lightbulb like a lamp shade in the kitchen. She thought of how fond Mr. Peterson was of her cousin and how he'd lost a child of his own. A daughter with hair as red as apples.

Milly imagined Bett standing on a pedestal in the bridal shop, turning round and round to admire her new crystal shoes in the mirrors: a kind of life she'd never known before, and after all that had happened, would likely never know again.

Then she imagined Asa walking into the shop with grass stuck to his hair and clothes, looking up at Bett for a moment, more than a moment, and smiling.

Milly handed the box back to him. "I can't accept this."

"Why not?" he said, pressing his lips against her ankle as if she were merely teasing him.

"Because—," Milly said, closing her eyes.

"Because why?" Asa said, growing serious. Instead of kissing her ankle, he latched on to the hem of her dress as if he knew she was about to run away.

Milly visualized a pair of tiny pink feet and a tiny yet buoyant pink heart, which gave her the strength to say what, without them, she never could have said.

"Because—," she said, opening her eyes.

My darling. My darling. My darling.
See through me—
Run after me—
Don't let me go.

"I don't love you."

27

When Milly rang the cowbell for supper, Twiss was surprised by the sound of the bell and also by her enormous thirst, which had grown and grown and grown as if she'd been stuffing cotton balls into her mouth, like hours, one after another. Had an entire day already passed? Only a day? The clocks on the wall told you one thing. The clocks in your mind told you another. Twiss circled the barn until she was back at the place she'd started. The goldfinch was still in her pocket, as was her trail of footprints in the layer of sand.

Her mother was right. The goldfinch and the woman who'd run over it this morning had merely ignited her anger; her mother's age-old blindness had made it flare. For a woman who claimed she'd lost all of her hope the day Twiss was born, her mother seemed to have plenty of it left on the day she took a ride in the biplane while Twiss's father waved her on. If it had been Twiss, she'd have questioned her father's sudden reattachment to her.

She'd have said, "You can't just decide when you want to love me and when you don't. What have you done, Joseph?"

Because her father was never that happy without achieving a hole in one or buying a new silk shirt or receiving a compliment from the wealthiest member of the course, who'd offered to set up a life insurance plan but like his swing didn't follow through. Her father was never that happy when left entirely on his own, with no one to give him the validation he required to keep drawing in breath and letting it out again.

In a way, Bett was like all of the other luxuries her father brought home for himself over the years. There were the golf accoutrements and the marbled steaks, and there was Bett, who, like all the other trinkets, their family couldn't afford to keep but couldn't afford to get rid of, either. Despite what her father had done, Twiss missed those holes in ones. She missed the gleam of her father's teeth when he realized what he'd achieved.

"I'm counting holes in ones," he'd say. *I'm counting what I'm worth.*

On good days, Twiss would be able to think of her father without thinking about his hands on the light green dress, the sheer material that graced Bett's shoulders.

I miss you, she'd say to herself, because unlike her mother, her father never visited her out of kindness or scorn. He never said anything about a heavenly golf course or an even more heavenly pro shop, which left his legs wobbly whenever he entered it.

He never said anything at all.

I miss you, too, she'd say to herself on the bad days.

Twiss took a last look around the barn before she turned off the utility light and left it for the lilac bushes beyond and the scrap of shade their twist of branches offered in the early evening light. There were still a few good sprigs left, which Twiss clipped for Milly, who said the tiny flowers brought good fortune.

"At least the white ones do," Milly had said. "I don't know about the purple ones."

"So luck then?" Twiss had said.

"No, good fortune."

"What's the difference?"

"Chance versus fate."

"You mean *choices* versus *decisions*."

"They're pretty," Milly had said, sighing deeply. "I guess that's all I mean."

Twiss had never quite been able to leave Milly—and what she'd sacrificed—alone. After a lifetime together, she still didn't understand why her sister had declined Asa's proposal and sent Bett out to the garden in her place. Or maybe Twiss understood why, but couldn't forgive Milly for offering her future to Bett or forgive Bett for accepting it with only a trace of shame.

For Milly,
Because.

The day the bird book arrived, Twiss stood at the end of the driveway for over an hour, deciding whether or not to destroy the package or take it in to Milly. The return address made her want to set it on fire or hack at it with a knife—*Mrs. Asa Peterson,* penned so proudly in black fountain ink. *Here is your life—was your life.*

It was easy to hate Bett on Milly's behalf, to make up words Bett didn't actually write on the pale blue paper, but it was harder to justify hating her on her own behalf. No future had been taken from Twiss and no package had arrived in its place.

Except that it had.

All the nights they'd sat on each other's beds, and all the secrets they'd shared, added up to something between friendship and love. Twiss never forgot the feeling of Bett's lips pressed against her own, the lone kiss of her life, how she'd expected to feel nothing and felt every-thing. Unlike Milly, Bett wasn't beautiful, nor was she graceful or even particularly smart, but when she was in a room Twiss had wanted to be in that room too.

After all, Bett had *grrr.*

Father Rice was the only one who ever knew

Twiss's true feelings. On the night Twiss slept at Rollie and Adele's house, she'd written him a letter.

Dear Father Rice,

I wanted to tell you that you were wrong about me—I'm not brave at all. I ran away from someone when I should have stood still.

I love her, my cousin.

Please tell me what I should do.

Please tell me something.

Please come home.

Twiss

In the end, Twiss took Bett's package in to Milly because Bett had held Twiss's face in her hands that day on the bed and said, "If you were a boy, I'd marry you."

I'd have married you, too, Twiss had often thought.

Asa didn't escape Twiss's disappointment either. He was a coward in the garden that day, which made Twiss wonder how worthy of Milly he really was.

"I don't believe you," Twiss would have said, if she'd been him. "You didn't make anyone else a tractor cake. You didn't make anyone else owl cookies either."

If she'd wanted to get married like Milly, she

would have shoved that ring onto her fattest finger so it wouldn't come off unless someone either cut it or wrestled it off her. She'd have made Asa drive her to the golf course right then so that Father Stone could marry them, and the golf pro and his silver flask of whiskey could witness the union. Hang Bett. She'd have done something on her own behalf. She'd have looked after her interests better.

Milly was different. Up in the attic were boxes full of drawings of her future family from when they were young. There was rambunctious Jacob, and there was lovely, if a little different, Molly Blue. In most of the pictures, there was also a husband, tall and pencil-line thin, standing proudly beside his children even though he never had a name.

Milly's children were growing toadstools, while Bett's children were growing children of their own. That Bett and Asa lived less than five miles away, on Mr. Peterson's old farmstead by the river, had never stopped bothering Twiss. She still wouldn't drive that way into town.

"You don't have to do this on my behalf," Milly had said once, when they were out on a Sunday drive. Sometimes, the two of them would travel down to Cave of the Mounds or the state park for the afternoon. Either attraction required crossing the river.

They'd just turned onto the county bridge,

which still didn't have guardrails despite how many people had driven off it over the years, sometimes on purpose and sometimes by accident. Most were pulled up too late or not at all.

Milly gripped the door handle like she always did when they went over the river. "Half a century is an awfully long time to spite someone."

"Spite is too gentle a word for why I drive the other way," Twiss said to Milly, when what she meant was *You can't always explain why you love the people you love.*

28

All in the same year, after Bett had married Asa and given birth to her first child, both of Twiss's parents died. Her mother went first, technically by way of a fever although Milly believed by a broken heart, which Twiss believed was the same as surrender. Her father followed less than three months later. He'd lost his equilibrium by then and would roam the house in search of whichever of their mother's possessions he could get his hands on.

One night, he drank a bottle of their mother's perfume, a wedding gift she'd made last almost twenty years, fell down the stairs, and broke his neck. The undertaker said he'd never worked on a dead man who smelled as good.

"It's French," Twiss had said, of the perfume. "Millot's Crêpe de Chine."

She'd tried it on in the moments after her mother died, dabbing her wrists the way her mother used to. To Twiss, the scent (the bottle promised Italian bergamot, neroli, basil, Egyptian jasmine, and fresh aldehydes) was as complicated as her mother; the list of ingredients individualized what otherwise blended together. She didn't know why she'd put it on when she could have been doing more useful things. Her mother was still on the bed, with one arm dangling off where she'd tried to reach out to Twiss and Twiss had moved away from her.

"Just because you're sick doesn't mean you get to love me," Twiss had said.

She'd turned toward the window, toward the view of the garden and the barn, the folds of green fanning out and away from the house. She thought of her father, who was still sitting outside the door, foolishly hoping that the old adage *too little, too late* didn't apply to him, believing that it shouldn't. She thought about how she'd chosen him year after year, confusing intentions with outcomes, enthusiasm with self-interest. Her last conversation with her mother gripped her like a root, still, all because she couldn't have it with her father.

"Did I ever tell you I baked a heart-shaped loaf of bread?" her mother said.

"I hate bread," Twiss said. "I hate hearts even more."

Twiss had always believed that on her mother's deathbed, her true feelings for her mother would finally show themselves, as if for the whole of her life they'd simply been obscured by a sheet, albeit a black one. She'd counted on the words "I love you" rolling off her tongue as easily as the words "I hate you" did. She wasn't prepared for the smell of urine and sweat—the giving up or the giving in, which made her want to slap her mother's face.

Wake up! she wanted to say. *We've all lost something.*

"Do you remember that program I used to listen to?" her mother said. "*A Day in the Life of* . . . It always bothered me that they never did one on a housewife."

"People don't want to hear about that," Twiss said. "They want to hear about driving tundra buggies over crevasses in the Arctic Circle. They want to hear about watching the northern lights with polar bears."

"I knew you remembered that day!" her mother said.

"I'm not an idiot," Twiss said.

"I rode in that airplane," her mother said. "They could have done a *Day in the Life of* . . .

335

about that. That's not particularly ordinary."

"Well, it isn't extraordinary," Twiss said.

"How would you know?" her mother said. "You haven't flown over your life."

Her mother looked up at the ceiling, as if it were a window. "It didn't look how I thought it would. It looked so much better."

Her mother said the pilot of the biplane had gotten them into the air, bounding skyward, before she had a chance to change her mind out loud, which she'd planned on doing despite winning the kidney bean contest and Twiss's father waving her on.

"Unhappiness on the ground is one thing," she said to Twiss. "You can close a door on it. You can draw a shade. I was afraid of what might happen in the air."

What her mother said she remembered most vividly was the moment the river came into view and how the higher they climbed, the more it looked like a sheet of blue ice. From the air, she said, she couldn't believe that anyone had ever drowned at the current's hand. She said she couldn't believe the river had swallowed so many people's futures and spit out alternate ones in the space of a few minutes on peaceful Sunday afternoons.

"I have a theory about why your father can't play golf," she said.

"He hurt his hip," Twiss said.

336

"He has a conscience."

After that, the plane bounced over cool drifts into steadier air. When the pilot steered away from the river, the site of the Accident, her mother saw the old forestry road leading into Spring Green, which skirted the golf course and the town.

"Before you and Milly were born," her mother said, "a couple about our age stopped in to get directions one day. They were up from Madison, out on a Sunday drive, and had gotten turned around on the country roads. Your father wanted to be helpful. While I fixed lemonade, he drew a detailed map. He told them that once they got across the river, they'd be able to smell freshly cut grass. They'd be able to see perfectly aligned moguls."

"So?" Twiss said.

"He drew a map of the golf course," her mother said.

Twiss glanced at the bedroom door.

"The course looked more perfect from the air than it does from the ground," her mother said. "Golf balls dotted the green like pearls. I was sorry for your father."

When the pilot asked where she lived, Twiss's mother told him. Before he turned back for the field beside the town fair, the pilot flew her over their home: the house, the pond, the meadow, and the barn, the sight of which her mother said reminded her of the little matchstick houses she used to build when she was a girl. She said they were always flawless until she left them outside overnight and rain began to fall.

Just before the plane tilted up and away from the house, and the engines roared, she saw the garden and the clothesline, the bird feeder, which she'd filled with the last of her sugar cubes and a cup of warm water, and her floral aprons swaying in the breeze.

"I was sorry for me, too," she said. "Neither of us was given what we were promised."

Twiss opened the drapes as well as the windows, inhaling the fresh air until she could breathe without smelling urine. A hummingbird was perched on the sill.

"Shut those, will you?" her mother said. "I'm cold."

She unfolded the last of the wool blankets in the house and struggled to place it over her chest. When Twiss didn't move, her mother said, "I feel like I'm a million years old."

"Only fossils are that old," Twiss said, watching the hummingbird watch her.

"Then that's what I am," her mother said.

"You're demented," Twiss said.

"We're so much more alike than you think."

Twiss stared out the window, trying to gauge whether or not she would be badly hurt if she jumped onto the ground. When, after estimating the drop-off, she wasn't willing to risk a broken leg or a broken arm, she pushed the window as far up as it would go and the hummingbird flew away.

"I've always known you couldn't belong to anyone but me," her mother said. "In the hospital, you latched on to your father's fingers and wouldn't let go, as if you knew something about him you couldn't have known. You wouldn't even let me nurse you unless he was there. I thought you'd starve for all the golf lessons he gave that summer."

Twiss turned so that she faced her mother, who'd taken up the ends of the wool blanket and was rocking it back and forth in her arms as if an infant were swaddled inside.

May you sleep well tonight, Miss Theresa Wis.

Mama loves you ever so much and sends sweetest dreams to you.

"I'd rather die than be like you," Twiss said, thinking *I love you.*

Her mother looked up from the blanket and smiled. "I love you, too, Twiss."

A moment later, she was dead, and Twiss was putting on her perfume, dabbing at first, and then slathering. The only ingredients she could pick out were the bergamot and the basil, the overwhelming and the everyday.

29

Somewhere between youth and old age, it occurred to Twiss that loving someone and forgiving them were two very different things. She forgave her mother for their similarities, which she understood had caused most of their differences. She forgave her mother for that peculiar downsloping smile they shared, the ability to pick and nitpick, and for the blindness that had prevented her from going out to the barn before what was going on in the barn came to her, but Twiss loved her father too much to know how to either condemn or forgive him. All she'd ever been able to do was run away from him.

Whenever Twiss was in doubt of her love, she went back to the accident, and the days just after the fisherman pulled her father from the Wisconsin River and onto dry land again, before the event had taken on the weight of a proper noun. When she needed it most, Twiss found assurance in the details that her father had shared with her mother and Milly and her from his hospital bed, as well as the details he'd shared with just her after Milly and her mother had gone down to the cafeteria.

Twiss remembered being glad they were gone. She remembered nestling closer to her father on the metal hospital bed, smiling because she didn't have to share him with anyone else.

"What happened after the car landed in the water?" she said.

"Have you ever skated on ice that was too thin?" her father said.

"I only skate on that kind of ice," Twiss said.

Her father stroked the ends of her sticky hair. "I forgot who I was talking to."

Her father said that for a moment, the car had balanced on top of it before the tension broke and it plunged beneath the surface into dark water.

"It's strange," he said. "The feeling you have just before the bottom drops out on you."

"Like being scared?" Twiss said.

"Like being able to have everything you've always wanted at the same time."

When the car began to sink, her father's instinct was to stay still.

"Why?" Twiss asked.

"You can't explain instincts," her father said.

The car sank farther and farther down until the light dwindled then vanished altogether. The windows, which her father had rolled down at the golf course on account of the heat and the black vinyl seats, allowed the cold water to flood in and the river debris to flow freely through the car.

"I saw something when I was down there," her father said. "A family."

"The family who drowned?" Twiss said.

"No," her father said. "Your mother and Milly and you."

"What were we doing?" Twiss said.

"Living without me," her father said.

"Did we say anything to you?" Twiss said.

"Your mother smiled. She took the sundaes from the passenger seat and said, 'We've been waiting a very long time for you to come home.'"

After her father's funeral, which wasn't as crowded as they'd expected (none of their father's old golfing acquaintances showed up), Twiss went to the golf course and Milly went back to the house to serve the finger-sized ham sandwiches that Mrs. Bettle had brought over—apparently multibite foods weren't appropriate for a funeral—and to field questions lingering on people's minds and comments lingering on their tongues.

"He fell down the stairs?"

"Only a few months after your mother passed on?"

"What terrible luck."

"You poor, poor girls. Who will take care of you now?"

Before the funeral, one of the women from the Sewing Society had brought over a dense fruitcake, which Twiss had launched into the woods like a baseball after the woman had started back down the driveway toward her home.

"I don't even know who some of these people are," Twiss had said.

Mrs. Collier and Dr. Greene had offered to take Milly and Twiss in; on their last driving excursion, they had eloped. Mr. Stewart had offered to help, too, although he said it probably wouldn't look right to have two young girls living with him, a bachelor, in town.

"We can take care of ourselves," Twiss had said.

Which was only partially true. While they could physically take care of themselves— they'd been doing that for a long time now— they needed to accept Mr. Peterson's offer to pay the mortgage and the taxes on the house to make the statement fully true.

"I always admired your father," he'd said, handing over the first of the crisp white checks that would arrive on the last day of each month until the house was officially theirs. Both Twiss and Milly hated those checks, their consolation prize.

"His mistake shouldn't be your consequence," Mr. Peterson said.

Was it?

Wasn't it?

Their hearts had broken so long ago now that

the injuries done to them felt like an old scar on most days, in that no matter how much time had passed or how much a scar faded, and even though it may have no longer hurt the way it once did, the disrupted layers of skin on the surface never quite regained their former levels of functioning.

Twiss had fallen down many more times in her life than Milly had, but it was Milly's skin that was delicate as paper and was so easily marred. Even then, Twiss knew she'd stay with her sister in Wisconsin despite wanting to see Machu Picchu and the Continental Divide. She'd grow up with Milly and grow old with her, and then one day, if time had any kindness, she'd die with her. Leaving Milly alone would've been like leaving an injured bird in the middle of a road.

The day of her father's funeral, Twiss went to the golf course. She walked along the stream, half expecting her father to jump out from behind the brush at the stream's edge and declare all that had happened to be a joke.

And then, like in the old days, "Let's you and me play a round of golf, champ."

Except that he didn't jump out of his coffin, that great mahogany and silver contraption that Mr. Peterson had arranged for him to spend his eternal life in. He didn't shrug off the fancy three-piece Italian suit that Mr. Sprye donated to the cause, because he said the suit had brought him bad luck and luck was of no consequence to a dead man; since purchasing it, Mr. Sprye had fallen off his tractor, burned his hand on the stove, and narrowly survived an infection that had threatened to take his left foot. He wore his old, dirt-stained coveralls to the funeral, his old forlorn expression from when he didn't have anything to harvest.

That day, he gave a speech about men who try to take what doesn't belong to them and held out his blistered hand as evidence.

"I don't know why the Lord forgives only some of us," he said. "Why others are bound to their misdeeds as plants are bound to the earth."

"Finally," Father Stone said, "somebody has been reading their Bible!"

Twiss kept walking along the stream until she found Persy, mangled but shining brightly beneath the cool, clear water. The lovely persimmon wood had buckled inward on the side it had landed on and outward on the side that was facing up.

"There was a tornado," she said, gently lifting Persy out of the water.

And in a way, there was, although the last time the four of them—Milly, Twiss, their mother, and their father—had gone out to the storm cellar, Milly was fourteen and Twiss was twelve. Their mother had a keen sense for when and where tornadoes would touch down, and although she couldn't stop them, she would herd her family into the storm cellar like cattle into a barn. While the three of them huddled together on the wooden bench below ground, Twiss's father would be standing on the top stair reluctant to come down.

"Once upon a time!" her mother would yell up to him.

"It's just a little wind, Maisie!" he would yell down. "Girls, you're going to be all right."

The day that a tornado actually touched down in their own little purple meadow, Twiss's father ran down the stairs before her mother had a chance to pick up the book of fairy tales or even clutch it to her chest. The doors rattled and the oil lamp swayed and her father held the three of them with one arm and cradled the book with the other. Even after the tornado whirled back up into the clouds and on to another humble plot of land, he read—all the way through—until he got to the words, "And they lived happily ever after."

For weeks after the storm, he stayed home instead of going to the golf course. When Twiss's mother asked him why, he said, "I thought I was going to lose you."

And then one Sunday, just as the purple meadow flowers had grown back and the soil had settled back into the earth, her father, too, had settled back into his afternoon routine.

"I thought I might go hit a few balls today," he said. "Just a round, maybe two."

"I've got you now," Twiss said, cradling Persy in her arms the afternoon of the funeral.

She didn't walk by the maintenance shed that day or by the clubhouse or even by the pro shop on her way home. She didn't pretend that the sand moguls along the way were mountains that needed to be climbed in order to be crossed.

When she got home, she took Persy to the barn and performed a kind of surgery, a twisting of metal and reforging of shape, until he was as restored as he'd ever be. The evening had arrived and the mourners had left. Twiss dropped a golf ball onto the ground and stood at the threshold of the barn, squaring her shoulders in the fading light.

Milly had come out onto the porch and was calling for Twiss to come inside.

"Everyone's gone," her sister said. "Even Mrs. Bettle. Parrots get lonely, you know."

For all that had happened since the postman dropped Bett at the end of the driveway and all that had happened since their cousin had left their house for the first and the last time, Twiss believed that when she swung Persy the ball would soar clear across the meadow and even more clearly over the pond, and reach the pine trees behind the house.

It would be the shot of her lifetime.

But when the ball hit the roof of the henhouse instead of the trunk of a tree, when it bounced down the shingles with the vigor of a tennis ball, managing to heroically defy the laws of physics in order to break one of the square windows below, Twiss was relieved rather than disappointed because her lack of skill made her feel exactly like herself again.

She ran to retrieve the ball, leaping over every unmowed blade of grass in her way and trampling down every other mowed one. Just before she opened the door to the coop and bent down to step inside the stooped half-house, she looked back at Milly, who was waving to her from the porch steps with one hand and taking off her apron with the other.

"Come inside!" Milly called.

Amid the wild cluck of first-generation Raouls, of pale underfeathers floating up to the ceiling like ashes and falling back down to the ground like snow, Twiss waved back at her sister, smiling the only smile she knew how to smile, lifting her legs the only way she knew how to lift them, one after another. She thought about her mother and her father, the *I love you's* and *I don'ts.* The *I will's* and *I will not's.* She thought about Bett and her Deadwater stories, the tiny flash of green in her brown eyes.

Out of everyone, Milly was the only one who'd

ever played a miserable round of golf on her behalf or told her she was worth a million pine needle pillows or spooned her when she was cold. She was the only one who scooped her up when she tumbled to the ground all those years ago, and she was the only one who saw Twiss fly to the moon.

"I'll be right in," Twiss called back, and thought *We don't need anyone but us.*

30

L ife and death—what paltry words, what tarnished bookends, what unjust summation for drawing in a breath one moment and failing to release it the next.

At the first feeling of feeling, Milly got up from her box-chair, from the damp and the dust that shrouded history the way history shrouded life. She took a last look around the attic before she descended the stairs. She gave a little good-bye, a good night, to all of the treasures from her youth—her drawings, Twiss's notebooks, the model airplane that had come together piecemeal and had come apart in the same way — which were just that: treasures at the bottom of an ancient sea at the top of a clapboard house.

Don't stay up too long reading your cowboy books, Jacob!

Don't forget to say your prayers, Molly Blue!

I won't.

We won't.

If you have a bad dream, you can sleep in my bedroom.

Then I hope I have a bad dream.

Ten bad dreams.

Good night, Mother (in unison)!

It was a foolish and destructive game, Milly knew, but she played it anyway, out of happiness and sadness, the long hours of the afternoon. Her imagination was limited to her recollections of her own mother pulling the covers up to their chins and pulling them down over their feet, so that the western bandit who lived in the closet and the snake that lived beneath Milly's bed would have no milky young flesh to latch on to.

"Good night, children," her mother would say after a story.

"But I'm not tired!" Twiss would say, indignantly throwing off her covers.

"Be patient, my whirligig," her mother would say, gently pulling them back up to Twiss's chin. "One day, you'll be tired. You both will be."

Milly stepped down each of the attic stairs with the same gracelessness with which she'd climbed them, clinging to the wooden banister with one hand and feeling her way through the dark and onto the second-floor landing with the other.

Good night, children, she thought as she shut the door.

The moment their mother pulled their own door shut, Twiss would throw her covers off again. "I don't care what she says! I'm still not tired yet!"

And then to Milly, "Are you?"

"I haven't had a good night's sleep since you were born," Milly would say.

Twiss would jump off her bed and onto Milly's.

She'd say, "You can sleep when you're dead!"

While she was still relatively mobile, Milly went down to the cellar in search of supper. She didn't feel like eating toast and butter tonight or a hard-boiled egg, but she didn't know if she wanted to eat what had been preserved in the cellar years ago now either.

Amid the neat rows of Mason jars were pickled eggs and pickled beets and tomato sauce, whose age the *Guinness Book of World Records* would have been eager to document. In her youth, preservation had been securely linked to boiling and cooling the common Mason jar. Now most people bought whatever they craved at the grocery store, walking away with enough plastic to strangle an entire family of geese, of uncertain but curious goslings.

What an interesting, if deadly, concept: If one felt like coconut cream cake or hot dogs by the dozen, all one had to do was walk through the fluorescent aisles and place the items in one's cart. You could even buy day-old bread at a discount. Croutons in a box.

The cellar was a bit different from that. The pickled cauliflower on the top shelf looked so much like miniature brains that Milly gasped when she turned on the light. No cauliflower definitely, she decided, but the beets were OK. And the pickles. Some time ago, she'd gone on a canning spree, apparently. An entire shelf was devoted to the frog-skinned spears.

It was just like her to have dug up a garden's worth of cucumbers and spent a day with her hands soaked in brine. Milly wasn't a particularly good cook, nor was she particularly bad. The recipes she executed well were simple enough that her mind could be elsewhere while her body stirred or chopped or simmered or baked.

The only complicated recipe she ever got right was a triple-chocolate, triple-sugar soufflé, and then only for a few fleeting minutes before the whole thing deflated.

"I want you to do something for me," she'd said to Bett, moments after leaving Asa alone and on his knees in the garden.

Bett was so cheered by the prospect of being asked for a favor that she got up from her chair immediately. "Of course!" she said to Milly more eagerly than she'd said anything the entire summer. "Whatever you'd like."

"Promise?" Milly said.

"Cross my heart," Bett said.

"I just refused Asa's offer of marriage," Milly said.

Bett dropped the tiny knit sock on the floor.

"The reason doesn't matter," Milly said. "It's done now."

"I don't understand," Bett whispered. She was pale now, but the blue vein on her neck pulsed, betraying her quickening heartbeat.

"You don't have to," Milly said. "You have that luxury."

She turned away, so Bett wouldn't see the tears forming in the corners of her eyes or her effort to delay her sobs by placing a hand across her pale throat. In a softer voice, she said, "Please just go out to the garden and take care of him. Please just—"

Milly squeezed her voice box and then released it.

"I don't have it in me to ask you again."

"But he's yours," Bett said.

"No," Milly said, the taste of salt, of loss, on her lips. "He's yours now."

That day, Milly stood by the open window watching beneath the cover of the curtain as her cousin walked out to the garden. When she saw Asa get up off of his knees and brush the dirt from his trousers and Bett put her hand on his shoulder, Milly's legs buckled and she fell to the floor.

Twiss would have run out and pushed her way between the two of them. She would have said *I take it all back!* But Milly stayed on the floor in the heart of the kitchen, listening to the murmurs of Bett and Asa in the garden, and the shouts of her mother and father upstairs, and the pounds of Twiss and Hammer in the barn. She stayed because she couldn't leave and because she couldn't go, and even though there was no real hope left, she reached for the tiny pink sock beneath the kitchen table and that's what she hoped for.

When the cuckoo clock struck nine and the mosquitoes and moths were on the downside of flinging themselves against the screened door and the birds had stopped chirping and the sunlight had turned to moonlight, starlight, Milly got up from the floor and did the only thing she could think to do. She turned on the lights, opened one of the cupboards, and brought down a bar of baking chocolate and a sack of sugar, which she dipped her fingers into.

The taste of the fine crystal granules, the sparkle of them in the light, would always, did always, the whole of her life, remind her of the words she'd said to Asa in place of the ones she'd wanted to say to him.

I love you, she thought then, and every time thereafter that sugar was on her tongue.

She didn't want to know the significant details of Asa and Bett's courtship—the moment Asa realized he could be happy, or at least not miserable, with someone other than her. She wondered, though, about the small ones; had the ring fit onto Bett's finger or did it have to be adjusted? Did Asa's heart thump when he was with Bett? Did hers? Did she wear that blue dress, those crystal shoes? Did she spin round and round with Mr. Peterson's approval? Did she think of them as often as they thought of her?

As for the child growing inside of Bett, Milly didn't know; people didn't speak of such things, although they may have whispered. But not for long since Asa was Mr. Peterson's boy—his having so much money would have made the whole thing matter less.

Did Asa know? Did he care?

Milly had lived most of her life not knowing the answer to that.

Bulked together, her questions made her wonder how deep her and Asa's love could have been for either of them to give the other one up, but she guessed that if attachments could be formed in an afternoon, then detachments could also be formed in that frame of time.

Often, when Avery was running by on Saturday morning, Milly would feel an overwhelming urge to follow her, although she couldn't explain why. There was something about the silhouette of Avery against the rolling green hills and the curve of the blue sky, Avery's flaxen ponytail swaying in time with her legs and her legs propelling her toward the wide-open road ahead that made Milly want to run after her, to say *Take me with you.*

She saw Asa once, in the general store, after all of his children were grown and a few of his grandchildren, too. He was buying a package of framing nails and a tin of black licorice.

"Say hello to Bett for me," the clerk said. "I miss her stories."

"She's visiting her mother in Butterfield," Asa said.

Milly was already behind Asa in line when she realized it was him. Although his hair had grayed and his shoulders had stooped, and time had played out in all the usual ways with the rest of him, the hairs on the back of his neck were still fine. They were still blond.

He still tripped over his words, too, which made Milly ache. She was praying that the clerk wouldn't say hello to her until he was gone.

"I'm glad you're here, Milly," the clerk said. "Your soaps are in. The women from the Sewing Society have been eying them all day. I had to swat one of their hands for you. One of them said she'd been to Provence. They won't let my wife become a member. They say we live too far in the country. I saved a soap for her, if that's OK. My wife, I mean. Jinny."

"Of course," Milly said, and started for the door.

"What's wrong?" the clerk said. "Aren't you feeling well?"

"I'm a little dizzy," Milly said.

"I'll walk you out," the clerk said.

Asa turned around and met her eyes. "I'll walk her."

The two of them walked together only a hundred yards that day, out the front door of the general store and across the street to the car, where Milly had left Twiss reading the *Farmers' Almanac* and drinking a cream soda. That walk was the happiest of Milly's life. She and Asa didn't say anything to each other until they got to the car, which Twiss had abandoned momentarily for the hardware store. The almanac lay open on the passenger seat, and the empty bottle of soda lay on the floor.

Milly and Asa walked along the sidewalk as if they had always done so; their pace was slower since they were old now, but it was still synchronized the way it was when they'd walked through the meadow. This time, there were no black rat snakes, no reasons to jump onto Asa's back or for Asa to hold her.

The whole time, Milly could see the car, the end point.

There would be iced tea later, a quiet evening on the porch with Twiss. Perhaps talk of the new construction on the south side of town. The townspeople had voted for a town pool and a concession stand, where children could buy hot dogs and lollipops and bags of popcorn the size of drums. That was the only way that children would enter into the conversation, and Twiss would be careful to emphasize their greediness, their bratty tongues. She'd predict a pool bottom full of lollipops and old Band-Aids, fungus between fat toes.

Stop, Milly would want to say, but she wouldn't because her sister would only be trying to protect her from the vision of little girls in pink ruffled bathing suits and boys in blue swim trunks, their mothers scooping them up for supper, wondering if a bath would quell the scent of chlorine in their hair, if soap bubbles would be enough of a draw.

Stop.

And Asa did.

Just before Milly got into the car and Twiss returned with a new hammer and drove home the long way, past the house with grass for a roof and, now, the roots of an oak tree and a family of goats, past the fields of corn and wheat, soybeans in the odd years and potatoes in the even ones, Asa squeezed her hand as tenderly as he'd pressed his lips against her ankle in the garden all of those years ago.

"It was good to see you," he said. "You're as lovely as I remember."

"Yes," was all Milly could make her mouth say before Asa let go of her hand.

The next afternoon, when Twiss went out to the mailbox, she found a brown paper bag with Milly's name on it and brought it inside.

"It's about time you had a secret admirer," she said. "Aren't you going to open it?"

"I'll open it later," Milly said, meaning *when you're gone.*

After Twiss went out the barn, Milly went up to their bedroom with the brown paper bag. She looked out the window before she turned it upside down and the bars of lavender soap shaped like seashells and the card shaped like a rectangle came tumbling out. Asa's name graced the front of the card. A note graced the back.

I know why you did it, Milly. Bella swings a golf club just like him.

Milly sat a long time on her old twin mattress, staring at the fleur-de-lis carved into the headboard, at the life that didn't belong to her and the life that did, before she placed the soaps beneath the velvet tray in her jewelry box and closed it. She never washed her hands with a single one of the seashell-shaped soaps, although from time to time, when Twiss had gone for a walk or to the barn, she'd open her jewelry box and examine her only secret.

La joie de vivre. The scent of lavender. Forgiveness. Age-old love.

31

M illy gathered the pickles and the beets in her arms. She turned off the light in the cellar and went upstairs to start supper. Although there was nothing particular to celebrate on this day, on the one before, and probably on the one after, once she'd made the egg salad and opened the jar of beets, Milly decided a tray of biscuits wouldn't be too much trouble, and then it was back down to the cellar for jam. The day had been taken up by exhaustion, the dread and the fear of it, but as the sun slipped toward the horizon and night began to fall over the hills like a blue curtain, Milly began to feel less ready to fall into eternal sleep.

She looked in the cupboards to see what else could be made into a meal. There were two cans of chicken soup, which she heated on the stove.

In the refrigerator, she found a container of cottage cheese and a bag of carrots, which she peeled and trimmed the way her mother used to. She hauled out the sugar, boiled it with tea bags and water, and then iced the whole thing down. When she finally stopped herself, the kitchen table looked like a haphazard version of Thanksgiving. Even with the windows open and the fans running and the sun setting, the heat in the kitchen was intolerable.

Milly's urges to cook tended to come at inopportune times; either it was too hot or too cold or no one was hungry and the whole thing went to waste. That had been the way with countless meals, including the wedding cake she'd made for Bett and Asa.

The cake, a simple buttercream creation with yellow rosettes, had incurred wrath from both her mother and father.

"You're determined to ruin your life just like your father's ruined mine," her mother had said. "It's not as nice as Twiss thinks to wind up old and alone."

Her father had grabbed her leg as she walked by him in the hallway.

"You had choices," he said. "How could you give that up?"

"The same way you gave up golf," Milly said.

"I didn't give up golf," her father said. "It was taken from me."

Twiss was the one Milly couldn't tolerate criticism from.

"I'll take you there," Twiss said, and took the car keys off the hook in the kitchen. She didn't have a license, but as with the tractor, their father had taught her how to drive the car in the meadow when she was twelve. In case of an emergency, he'd said when their mother protested.

Milly and Twiss drove the long way to the country church, up Fox Hollow Road to Coon Rock, down through the apple orchards and the hayfields, past the alfalfa field that Tom Sprye had not yet relinquished, to the dirt parking lot behind the church, where the Sewing Society ladies were standing, fanning themselves with their yellow hats, ready to pounce.

The outside of the church was decorated with garlands made of ivy and white calla lilies that shone like diamonds in the light.

"I don't think I can go in," Milly said.

"I don't think I can go in either," Twiss said.

The two of them sat in the car, staring at the church.

"You can stop it," Milly's mother had told her, but she couldn't.

"Take me away from here," she said to Twiss.

"Where do you want to go?" Twiss said.

"Nowhere. Anywhere."

"I know where," Twiss said.

She backed the truck out of the parking lot and

headed for the old boat launch. They drove along County C Road, past the golf course and the ice-cream stand, to the boat launch, which was empty except for a fisherman and a bucket of fish.

Twiss parked the truck and got out.

"What's biting today?" she asked the old man, whom neither Milly nor Twiss recognized as Father Rice until they looked at him more closely.

"Rainbows," he said, as if he'd never left Spring Green. The limp side of his trousers was the only evidence that everything wasn't exactly as it had always been.

"Aren't you girls supposed to be at a wedding?" he said.

Milly stepped down from the truck with the cake. "It's over."

"That looks delicious," Father Rice said, eyeing the yellow rosettes of frosting longingly. "I haven't had a piece of cake since the last wedding I presided over, when I was still—well—anyway . . . I never could figure out how to work the oven for anything fancier than a potato beside that potatoes were all that was usually edible in the donation box."

"Why didn't you write me back?" Twiss said.

Father Rice cast out a line and wedged the pole between two wood slats in the dock. "I didn't know if I could come back here," he said. "To this valley. This river. These people. Until Mr.

Peterson showed up at my door with his son."

"Oh," Twiss said, obviously disappointed—a notebook's worth of questions sat on her night table at home and she'd only managed to ask the first, least important one.

When will everything be all right again? was the last question in her notebook—unwittingly, Twiss had left no room for an answer.

"I didn't know if I could be again who I was," Father Rice said.

Milly set the cake on the dock and, even though he hadn't asked for one, cut a piece for Father Rice. It seemed right for someone to eat the cake.

"Mr. Peterson lost a wife and a child and he's still managing to get along," Father Rice said, swiping at one of the yellow rosettes on the slice that had been cut for him. "I figured my losses were something I should be able to recover from."

"I waited for your letter," Twiss said.

"I hung yours up on the wall in my room," Father Rice said. "I'd look at them and wonder if it was possible to go home after everything I'd done. They were my bible. My cross to kneel before and pray on. Yours was the only smiling face in the room."

"I waited for your answer," Twiss said.

Father Rice took two of the fish he'd caught out of the bucket beside his one working leg and strung them together with fishing line before he handed them to Twiss.

"It's a trade," he said. "But I'll admit, it's not a fair one."

And then, sighing deeply, "Sometimes there isn't a clear answer, Twiss. That's the trouble with being a priest. You have to pick what you think is right."

"What do you think is right, then?" Twiss said.

Father Rice smiled. "I don't know. That's why I'm just an old man with one leg now."

Milly was kneeling at the end of the dock, with the cake by her feet. While she rinsed her hands in the water, she thought of the letter she'd written to Bett's mother, on the good stationery after all, and the game Twiss and Bett used to make her play before they fell asleep.

"Truth?" Bett would say. "Or consequence?"

Milly had never been able to see how one could go without the other.

The letter, which at one time was over three pages, ended up being only two lines, penned in her careful script.

Bett's getting married. What a blessing!

The last line had been what had saved Milly from the first. It was the way she had to see things. After all, who was to say that she and Asa would have been happy? She'd never spent more than an hour with him at one time. She'd never even seen his feet bare.

Milly's parents had known each other much longer and much more intimately than that, and they were sitting on either side of a door, as if they'd forgotten how to open it.

Still. There was the sight of Asa on the tractor, the fine golden hairs that graced the back of his neck, and the shape he made against the bright blue sky. *Still.*

Milly lifted the cake from the dock and set it on the water. She watched it float for a second or two before the current pulled it beneath the surface and carried it downstream, down to whatever was lost.

On the way home, in the hayfields between the river and the house, a starling flew into the windshield. After Twiss had swaddled it with fabric from her coveralls, Milly held it on her lap, stroking its nape and crying, lightly at first and then harder and harder.

Twiss put her hand on Milly's knee and kept it there the rest of the way back.

It'll be all right, her hand seemed to say. *We'll be all right.*

Over the years, they'd rescued hawks and owls and wild geese, catbirds, wrens, and herons. But no bird had ever seemed quite as beautiful as that ordinary starling.

When they got home, Milly and Twiss took it into the bathroom and set it on a nest of towels. The starling lay unconscious, its black feathers pinned against its body. Milly and Twiss sat on the cool floor watching each other and the starling, as if one or the other might tell them what they should do next, what they could do next.

All day and into the night, they sat in the bathroom waiting for something they couldn't put a name to, while Asa and Bett said "I do," while they drove off in a direction of their choice, to a place of their choice, for better or worse, for life.

Eventually, Milly and Twiss fell asleep, Milly with her legs tucked neatly under the rest of her and Twiss with her legs sprawled out at dramatic angles across the bathroom floor.

The starling slept too.

After several hours of absolute stillness, a leg twitched and then a wing, and Milly and Twiss opened their eyes. *Rise up,* the wounded parts seemed to say to them.

Rise up and fly!

And just like that the starling was gone, out of the tub and out the front door.

32

Milly knew what people thought: that they were just the weird old sisters who rescued birds, just like the crossing guard was the man with no teeth and the house on Oak Street was haunted and the river bottom was home to people who were missing their limbs and their eyes. That was the way with small towns, and there was something comforting about that.

Milly set the table on the porch and rang the cowbell for supper.

A few minutes later, Twiss came walking across the field of prairie onions and bluestems, a bouquet of lilacs in her hands.

"What's all this?" she said, when she reached the porch.

"Supper," Milly said, smiling.

Twiss handed her the lilacs. "I'll get the vase."

"I'll get it," Milly said, noticing the goldfinch peeking out of her sister's front pocket, which Twiss had forgotten to bury in the gladiola bed.

After supper, Milly would urge Twiss into the bathtub like her mother used to do when Twiss was little and had wet her bed. Her mother would exchange the wet linens for dry ones while Twiss blew soap bubbles around the bathroom, pretending they were bullets and she was a cowboy. Wetting her bed was the one form of losing control Twiss had ever been sensitive about as a child, and their mother had gone to great lengths to spare her embarrassment.

While Twiss soaked this evening, Milly would take the goldfinch out back with all of the other birds that had been lost. She'd say a few words or she wouldn't; if not, the birds that weren't yet lost would gather in the branches of nearby trees and on the slanting eaves of the house and on the red sugar feeder meant for hummingbirds, but that also attracted every other kind of bird to its nectar, and do her trilling for her.

"Tell me about your day," she said to Twiss.

"Well," Twiss said. "Snapper ate another one of my balls, and the Raouls weren't too pleased to see me either. Mostly, I just wandered around, though."

Milly went inside to get the vase. She filled it with water and arranged the lilacs, which smelled more wonderful than any perfume she could have bought. From the screen door, she watched her sister take off her muck boots and set them on the stairs in the same impatient way she had all her life. Her hands were shaking again, but otherwise she seemed all right.

"What did you do today?" Twiss said.

"A little of this," Milly said. "A little of that."

Before the two sat down to supper, they sat

together first on the peeling brown porch steps, Milly with her feet placed firmly on the bottom step and Twiss with her feet splayed out on the crumble of loose dirt below it, a glass of iced tea between them. Beyond the porch and their feet were the rolling hills, the county and country, and the winding Wisconsin River, which gained and lost strength, narrowed and widened, rose and fell, all the way down to the Mississippi and the Gulf of Mexico, the confluence of river and ocean.

Twiss picked up the glass, drank the tea down halfway, and held the glass out to Milly. "I've been so thirsty today," she said, wiping the corners of her mouth with her sleeve and her forehead with the back of her hand.

Milly glanced at the sky, which, although it was still clear and high above them now, would eventually bring gray and rain because that was the nature of weather patterns.

The nature of nature.

"Me too," Milly said and took the glass from her sister.

ACKNOWLEDGMENTS

The Bird Sisters could not have been written without the support of my wonderful husband, Hans, and my lovely daughter, Ava; to them, I am eternally grateful for letting me sneak off at strange hours to write this novel and then listening to me fret about it for more months than any of us can (or wants to) count. My dear mother, father, stepmother, and four brothers have also supported me passionately along the way, even when the novel was still a distant dream of mine. To my dedicated teachers at Penn State and at the University of Massachusetts, I must say thank you, especially to Charlotte Holmes, who taught me how to write bravely and beautifully. Her writing was and continues to be a strong model for my own. Without her, I don't think this book would have become this book. There are others, of course, to thank. The incomparable Margot Livesey, Noy Holland, Sam Michel, and Tony Giardina. My best gal and talented writer and teacher, Dani Blackman, has put up with my writing and me for many years now; she's talked me down from more than one metaphorical ledge. Dani is magical, essential, and wise; I am truly blessed to know her. My gifted and incredibly kind agent, Michelle Brower, believed in *The Bird Sisters* from the very beginning and worked extremely hard to get the book into the right hands during a time when hands weren't flying up left and right for first fiction. Those hands ended up belonging to Kate Kennedy at Crown Publishers, who has been absolutely lovely to me, both as a friend and an editor. I envy myself for getting the chance to work with this savvy wonder woman! To the rest of the team at Crown, thank you with all my heart. From copyediting to design to publicity, I have been continually amazed by the attention devoted to this author and her bird sisters.

ABOUT THE AUTHOR

Rebecca Rasmussen's stories have appeared in *Triquarterly* and *Mid-American Review* magazines, and she has been a finalist in both Narrative magazine's 30 Below contest for writers under the age of thirty and in Glimmer Train's Family Matters contest. This is her first novel. She lives in St. Louis with her husband and daughter and teaches at Fontbonne University.

Visit her at www.thebirdsisters.com.

Center Point Publishing
600 Brooks Road ● PO Box 1
Thorndike ME 04986-0001 USA

(207) 568-3717

US & Canada:
1 800 929-9108
www.centerpointlargeprint.com